MY
HUSBAND'S
EX

BOOKS BY ROSIE WALKER

MY HUSBAND'S EX

ROSIE WALKER

bookouture

Published by Bookouture in 2024

An imprint of Storyfire Ltd.
Carmelite House
50 Victoria Embankment
London EC4Y 0DZ

www.bookouture.com

ISBN: 978-1-83618-154-5
eBook ISBN: 978-1-83790-943-8

To my dad, Alan.
Thank you for your belief, kindness and support.
I love you.

Better keep the devil at the door than have to turn him out of the house.

Scottish proverb

I stare out of the rain-streaked car window, trying to see the Scottish landscape as the car whips past rust-coloured heather and mud. It's a relief to be out of the city, even though the journey from Edinburgh has been such a nightmare. This part of the Highlands is beautiful, but there's something sinister about these craggy hills and rugged peaks. The pine forests seem to bristle with movement, like we're being watched as we drive by. Above us, the sky is heavy with rain, the day dark even though it's only late morning.

I reach across and lay a hand on Ted's arm. His knuckles are white on the steering wheel, and he leans forward to peer through the windscreen as the wipers swish back and forth at frantic speed. Our green air freshener swings from the rear-view mirror every time the car takes a bend.

At my touch, his frown deepens. He must be tired. He's been working hard in the run-up to Christmas and the journey has been long. I feel a pang of sympathy and squeeze his arm before letting my hand drop. I fiddle with the radio, scanning for channels until I finally hear a crackly Scottish accent:

'... Storm Callum changed direction... hitting the Highlands and northern Scotland later today bringing strong winds and heavy rain... weather warning...' The voice fades to static and Ted leans forward and turns the radio off.

'Everything is grey up here. Grey stone, grey people, and grey sky,' he mutters, reaching up to wipe at the foggy windscreen with his sleeve. 'At least it's not snow. Things get pretty wild out here when it snows. Ten-foot drifts, buried cars and the like. We could be stuck here past New Year.'

Ted can't bear the darkness and the cold. Just one of the reasons why he left this area as soon as he finished school, and only returns for weddings, funerals and holidays. His parents love living up here, though, and I've started to yearn for the open spaces and big skies of the countryside, even just for a few days. Not that I can see any sky today. Only dark clouds.

Today Ted's here for me. Because I asked. Because we need it. Not because he wants to be here, that's for sure. But I know he'll pull a smile onto his face when we arrive and celebrate with me and our daughters because he's a great dad.

'We'll be there soon,' I say without conviction, glancing at my watch. We've been on the road for almost three hours; a bumper-to-bumper crawl along the M9 motorway held us up as the heavy rain reduced visibility to almost nothing.

'I thought we'd pass a petrol station somewhere,' I say to Ted, glancing at the fuel gauge, where the little orange light blinks to tell us that we're nearly out. I don't mention the service station we drove past, where I urged Ted to stop and he refused, assuring me there'd be another further along the route.

He shrugs. 'That's the countryside for you. We're so used to the city now. Everything we need is usually just around the corner. It's not like that out here. It's harsh and remote, Sadie.'

'It's beautiful too,' I try.

He glances at me and raises an eyebrow before returning his gaze to the misty road ahead. 'When you can see it,' he says, a laugh in his voice.

'I'll text Matt and ask him to bring a container of unleaded for our return journey.' I open my phone contacts and click to Ted's brother, but there's no signal. I put my phone back in my pocket.

'How much longer?' asks Charley from the back, her voice a whine.

Out of the corner of my eye, I see Ted's shoulders tense. She's been asking that every five minutes since we turned off the motorway.

I pull a smile onto my face and turn around, the seat belt cutting into my shoulder. Tamara and Charley are curled up on the back seat, Charley pulling against her seat belt, which is covered in *Gabby's Dollhouse* stickers. Next to her, Tamara is fast asleep, her head lolling to the side and her hands neatly folded in her lap. I wonder once again how Ted and I produced such different children: Tamara is the only eight-year-old I know who makes her bed every morning and always uses a bookmark. Charley is her opposite: two years younger, and all chaos, all the time.

'Not long now,' I promise.

Charley presses her fingertip against the window, drawing a sad face in the condensation, her lip sticking out in protest. 'You said that *ages* ago,' she whines. 'I want to be there already. My legs hurt.' She kicks the back of Ted's seat.

He glances at her in the rear-view mirror and flicks the indicator, slowing the car to turn off the main road. 'Just a few miles, Charley,' he says.

As we turn, I see two dark-clad figures walking along the road ahead, barely visible in the dusky light. Hikers, I guess. Both are difficult to see in this gloom; they should be wearing high-visibility vests or something. They're hunched against the wind, hoods pulled up over their faces. That's not my choice of hobby, but to each their own. I'd rather be curled up in front of the fire with a glass of wine and a romance novel.

The car jostles along the narrow lane, flanked by pine trees on either side. I can't believe how dark it is, even though it's almost noon. It's like the sun barely rises this far north before it begins its descent back behind the horizon.

'It's at the end of this track,' Ted says to me, his eyes flicking to the GPS. The map is all green, showing no roads except the one we're on, and no houses. Just countryside for miles.

The place I booked is truly remote, an old hunting lodge in the middle of nowhere. Just us at the dead end of a track, miles from anywhere, surrounded by hills and sheep. The perfect place to gather together, to celebrate with family, and to fix what's broken between me and my husband.

Suddenly, the car emerges from the pine trees and ahead of us is a huge mountain range with snow-capped peaks. Tucked at the foot of the hills is a beautiful grey stone house with a slate roof, hugged by a deep, rushing river, its waters brown and icy with just-melted snow from up in the hills. There's nothing beyond this house, just hundreds of acres of wild land that belongs to the estate: the river, a woodland, and farmland for miles in every direction. Salmon, deer, Highland cattle, sheep. It's richness and desolation all at once.

The white-framed windows of the grand house glow with light. My heart soars. It looks so warm and inviting. So safe. There it is: our home for the next four nights: Red Hart Lodge. It's exactly what I wanted. Perfect for a cosy family Christmas.

Ted slows the car as we cross the narrow stone bridge, barely one car wide, below which the land drops away sharply. I lean my forehead against the cool window and peer down at the river rushing by below, its peat-stained water deep and threatening. I mustn't let the girls play near those steep banks. One false step and they'll be pulled under, dragged away.

Soon we stop on the gravel drive outside the front door, wake Tamara and step out into the cold. The girls run ahead of us up the path, giddy with the wind and rain. With their hoods up over their heads, they look like little sprites as they dart around, pushing each other in some invented game. Ahead of them looms the grey stone lodge, the hills, and the trees. A formidable backdrop. I wish I could take a photo, but my phone would be drenched in moments.

My skin prickles as I get the sense I'm being watched, and I scan my surroundings, peering into the shadows between the trees. There it is: from the shifting branches above our heads, roosting crows watch my every move. I stick out my tongue at the closest one perched on a low branch, its beady eye observing me, head tilted. With a smile, I look around to appreciate the icy weather and the space to breathe, even though the air chills my lungs. Even the brutal environment can't dampen my spirits: we're finally here.

Tamara and Charley rush in ahead of us and straight up the wide staircase, squabbling between them about who gets to choose their bedroom. There are five bedrooms, and only one of them has twin beds, so I let them run on ahead while Ted and I unload the car and stack our bags on the slate tiles just inside the door.

I know from the website that there are enough rooms upstairs to keep them busy for a little while: as well as all the bedrooms, there's also a library/study, a big bathroom with a claw-foot bath, and a staircase up to a locked attic that the current owners use for storage.

Finally, the car empty, I let myself look around the massive entrance hall. Wood panelling, deer antlers on the walls. Tartan carpet running up the stairs. It's just like the pictures I saw on the website: quaint, opulent and so peaceful. It'll be less peaceful tomorrow when my in-laws arrive, bearing presents and expecting a full dinner spread. I'm grateful my mum can make the journey too: she needs the company, even if she'd never admit it.

I sit on the old church pew by the door and unlace my hiking boots as Ted closes the door against the weather. He tugs across the heavy curtain to block the draught, and then joins me on the pew, wrapping an arm around my shoulders as we survey the huge pile of stuff to put away.

'We got here,' he says, letting out a heavy sigh.

I lean my head against him for a moment, savouring a moment of peace before the girls clatter down the stairs. He presses his cheek against my head, his beard prickling my scalp and his arm heavy around my shoulders. We're pulling together today. I hope it's a sign of good things to come. We need it.

'We found our bedroom!' Charley shouts.

'And a door to the attic,' Tamara adds, as she jumps off the last step.

Ted and I exchange an amused glance. She spent the first hour of the car journey from Edinburgh this morning rambling about old houses in the Scottish countryside and her sheer certainty that there would be a secret room, forgotten attic or boarded-up basement full of long-lost belongings just waiting for her to find. And – of course – a mystery for her to solve. She'll have poked every piece of wooden panelling that lines the walls, hoping that a spring will click and a secret compartment will slide open like she's in the *Secret Seven*.

'OK, take your bags upstairs and then we can have hot chocolate.' I point to Tamara's moon-and-stars patterned backpack and Charley's unicorns and rainbows.

'Tamara, you're the boss.' I ignore Charley's dramatic sigh. 'And you're in charge of unpacking. Pyjamas on beds, books out ready for reading before sleep. Toothbrushes and toothpaste by the sink in your bathroom. Charley, you help. Everything you need to be ready for Father Christmas's visit tomorrow, OK?'

Tamara nods enthusiastically – she loves a job and especially loves delegating. Charley nods too, with slightly less enthusiasm than her older sister. As they ascend the stairs I can already hear Tamara's muffled instructions to her little sister, like a high-pitched drill sergeant.

I collect our boots and line them up on the boot rack by the door. My socks leave damp footprints on the slate tiles. 'Hot chocolate for the girls, and wine for the grown-ups,' I say to Ted, who flashes me a grin.

I look up at him, into his crinkly blue eyes, and feel a rush of affection that he indulges me, that he came all the way up to this remote part of Scotland even though it's not special for him. Even though he hates the countryside, prefers the city. He doesn't even like Christmas that much. But he's here, for me. For us.

He wraps an arm around my shoulder and kisses my head. I feel small next to his six-foot frame, and snuggle into him, inhaling the smell of the outdoors from his jumper: wind, rain and winter air.

He leans down and picks up the box of wine bottles, which rattles as he lifts it to his chest. I gather a few bags of groceries and follow him through the long corridor towards the back of the house.

The kitchen is like stepping back in time: a warm Aga fills the room with a comforting fug of warmth, and there are marble countertops, a Belfast sink, a kitchen island and stools, and cute little period details on the walls – servants' bells and a weather-vane. I suppress a squeak of excitement. It's perfect.

I open the back door and a gust of cold air hits me in the face like a slap. The rear courtyard is square, with a barrel-vaulted archway leading to the front of the house. The main house curves around two sides of the courtyard, and the other two sides must be old stables and outbuildings. Above my head, a crow whirls and swoops, riding the wind high in the grey sky.

There's a rusty table and chairs in the corner nearest to the kitchen door; a suntrap in warmer months. But now, I shiver and close the door on the horrible weather, then I fill the kettle from the tap and place it on the Aga. Then I raid our grocery bags for hot chocolate powder and mince pies. I line up two mugs for the children and two wine glasses on the kitchen island, while Ted grabs a knife from the block and slides it along the packing tape on his box of wine.

I feel a little thrill of hope in my chest: everything is going to plan. Ted was quiet on the journey here, but his smiles and his affection indicate he's thawing. He's coming around to being here, I just know it. This was a good idea after all.

I'm searching drawers looking for a bottle opener when a bell shrills.

Ted and I pause, glancing at each other in puzzlement. Then it rings again and Ted points up into the corner of the kitchen, where there's an old-fashioned Bakelite doorbell, hammer still vibrating against the metal.

I close the drawer and head back to the front door, a frown on my face. We aren't expecting anyone until around ten or eleven p.m. when Ted's brother Matt is due to appear. The rest of the family arrive tomorrow for Christmas dinner: my mum and Ted's parents Patricia and Neil. A whole gathering of us, together under one roof. But that's tomorrow. Most of today – Christmas Eve – is supposed to be just the four of us, and an early night for the girls so Ted and I can talk, think, and be together to repair our marriage.

Perhaps it's just the owners, checking we have everything we need, I think to myself as I pull back the heavy curtain in front of the door and immediately feel the wall of cold air that's gathered behind it. But in their email they'd said they live miles away, and that they know people who rent this place want privacy, so they'd only visit in an emergency. Frowning, I slide back the bolt, turn the ancient mortise key and pull open the door.

A rush of rain blasts me in the face and I shiver, my shoulders hunching against the chill. I reach up and swipe my fringe out of my eyes.

Two figures stand on the doorstep, both wearing dark coats, their hoods pulled up to obscure their features. One tall, one small. I take a step back, my stomach churning.

We're so alone here, thirty miles from the nearest town. A significant drive to the nearest neighbour. No phone signal. There's Wi-Fi, but we haven't yet located the promised piece of laminated paper with the password on it.

Ted grew up in this area and told me what it's like: even though the rural residents are far-flung, everyone knows everyone's business. Even though we've seen no one since we turned off the A82, everyone knows we're here. And everyone knows we're alone. Defenceless. With two small children and a house full of Christmas presents. My babies are in this house. The intruders can have it all. As long as they don't hurt my children.

My hand clenches around the door handle, ready to push it closed if I need to. But a foot shoots out and steps across the threshold.

The tall one lowers their hood to reveal tousled hair in a pixie cut. She smiles, unveiling two dimples in her pale cheeks. The shorter one glances up, eyes barely visible below the hood.

It's two women. Well, one woman and a girl not much older than Tamara, their noses red and their mouths pinched against the cold. *Are they lost?*

The woman looks past me, over my shoulder and into the opulent entrance hall. Her smile grows wider, showing dazzling-white teeth in a neat row. The smile doesn't quite reach her eyes.

'Oh my God.' Ted's voice sounds from over my shoulder, and I turn to see he's right behind me, his face pale with shock. He raises a hand to his head and tugs at his hair.

He's what the woman is smiling at.

'Alice,' he croaks, almost to himself, his eyes wide.

Alice. The familiar name punches me in the chest. My mouth falls open and I turn back to the two figures in our doorway. My stomach contracts, but I don't have time to react.

'Hello, stranger,' she says to him, her voice gravelly.

Ted's ex-girlfriend steps into the house without looking at me, pushing me out of the way. She throws herself into my husband's arms.

2

Stunned, I stand for a moment, my hand still on the doorknob as their footsteps recede into the house, Alice chatting to Ted and the little girl following behind. I don't think Ted's said another word, Alice drawing his stunned figure along in her wake as she ploughs her way into our house.

I recognise her. She looks almost the same as she does in Ted's old photographs, the ones he keeps in their shiny orange Kodak envelopes in the back of his bottom desk drawer. From university, before he knew me. Even now, with cold-pinched skin and rain-slicked hair, her beauty is arresting. The kind of looks that make men offer to carry shopping bags and rush to hold open doors. But there's something uncanny about her, too; I saw a glassy cruelty in her eyes as they skimmed over me in their search for Ted.

A blast of wind and rain hits me in the face and I pull the heavy oak door closed reluctantly, as if by shutting it I'm accepting that they're here, that we've invited them in.

I clench my teeth and follow them into the living room, where Alice is standing at the window still wearing her muddy boots, looking out at the mist rolling down the side of the mountain in the distance. My eyes skim the room and the warm tones of the traditional furnishings: forest greens, deep reds, varnished woods. I take in the large wing-backed armchairs on either side of the fireplace, the sturdy oak coffee table and the two green velvet sofas. I shudder slightly as I catch sight of the deer antlers hanging over the fireplace. I'd much prefer to see the real thing, grazing on the hills. Alive.

Alice turns as I walk in and gives me a charming smile. 'I'm Alice. And this is Natasha,' she says, gesturing to where the girl is huddled by the radiator, her back against the metal and her arms wrapped around herself. Natasha hasn't taken off her coat, and I can see her shivering from here.

'You must be Sadie,' she says, stepping towards me. She reaches out a pale, thin hand to shake mine. No wedding ring, I notice.

I glance at Ted, still hovering by the door, his face frozen in confusion. He shakes his head slightly at me. In that way of people who've been married for a long time, I can tell what he's thinking just from the set of his jaw and the movement of his eyebrows. *I have no idea*, his expression says. *This wasn't me.*

'Yes. Ted's wife,' I say, hearing a territorial note in my voice. I'm not a jealous wife, usually. I'm comfortable in my own skin, confident that my husband is faithful. But something about this stunningly beautiful woman, her sharp teeth and her unsmiling eyes makes me want to step between her and my family. Ted has held that hand, the one she's offering to me just now. He's curled that hair around his fingers. He once memorised every contour, every pore and every detail of that face; knew it better than his own, once upon a time.

Am I that insecure? Whatever I'm feeling, I squash it down.

Alice's hand is icy cold and her fingers barely move to grip mine. She's frozen. Suddenly, whatever happened in her and Ted's past is irrelevant: here are two people who are – what?

Lost? And certainly cold in the Scottish wilderness on Christmas Eve.

I make eye contact with Alice and smile. 'It's nice to meet you. Both of you.'

Natasha turns and moves her mouth in an approximation of a smile. Her eyes squint, half-closed with the cold. Her mousy hair falls in damp tendrils on either side of her face, like a curtain protecting her from onlookers. She hunches her shoulders like she wishes she could disappear inside herself. I feel a pang of sympathy, remembering that feeling, being that age. No longer a little kid, but not yet a teenager either. The awkward in-between.

There's a short silence and my whole body itches with the need to fill it. I have so many questions. I'm a therapist; it's my job to study people, to ask questions, to investigate. I'm naturally curious. But there's a vibe from Ted, rolling off him in waves. *Mind your own business*, he's telegraphing at me, eyes wide and almost panicked.

'Get warm,' I say to them both. 'I'd just put the kettle on, so we'll make some hot drinks.' Whatever is going on, it can wait until they've warmed up. And the poor child is innocent of anything, just miserable and desperate for shelter, clearly.

Alice wraps her arms around herself and almost bounces with enthusiasm. 'Oh, yes, please.'

'Take your boots off and make yourselves comfortable,' I say, glancing again at their muddy boots on the thick carpet. I'll have to vacuum before we check out, I think, adding another item to my already overwhelming mental to-do list.

I give Ted a pointed look and he follows me into the kitchen, still shaking his head in confusion.

'I have no idea what they're doing here, Sadie,' Ted says as soon as we're alone. His eyebrows are cinched in the centre, two deep lines between them betraying his confusion. His sky-blue wool jumper perfectly matches his eyes, and there's a new sprinkling of white in his salt-and-pepper beard. His hair still stands up where he tugged at it earlier.

I'm suddenly filled with the need to run away, to lock the door, anything to keep Ted and me together alone. We have so much we need to fix, and we can't do it with all this chaos around us. We'd already come to the most remote spot in the Scottish Highlands for Christmas in an attempt to do that, but distraction has just followed us here.

I busy myself looking for a teapot and tea bags. Without turning from the cupboard, I ask the question that's been niggling since Ted realised who she was. 'Have you been in touch with her?' I keep my voice steady, and I make sure my diction is clear even though I'm facing away. I can't afford to let him pretend he doesn't hear me, as he sometimes does. I need him to answer me.

I know Alice was important to him, once. His last relationship was a nasty break-up, he'd told me when we first met. He didn't tell me much else, and I didn't pry. I liked to think I was secure enough to know that if he wanted to be with me, he would be. And if he didn't, he would leave and I would survive.

Now, Ted and I have been together for twelve years, married for ten. We've never had a moment when our marriage felt threatened by someone else, so the insecurity and fear I'm feeling right now is new.

Not to mention I'm twenty pounds heavier than I want to be, my neck skin crinkles when I turn my head a certain way, and I'm pretty sure my once-thick and unruly mane of hair is getting thinner as I approach the dreaded perimenopause. Meanwhile, Ted's still the same jeans size he was when we met, his deepening laughter lines make him more handsome, and his greying temples evoke George Clooney.

And in the next room sits Alice, waif-like and dimple-cheeked, who has probably never grimaced at her reflection in a magnifying mirror in her life.

It feels juvenile and I hate myself for asking if he's been in touch with his ex. But we're in a strange place in our marriage and our lives, and things feel particularly vulnerable.

Ted crosses the kitchen and rifles through the grocery bag. 'I haven't spoken to her since we split up. Fifteen years or something. How would she know I was here?' He finds the chocolate digestives and adds them to the tray, then makes a start on the hot chocolates, slopping cocoa powder across the marble countertop with a shaking hand. His movements are abrupt and careless, and I can tell he's genuinely disturbed by Alice's presence.

Relieved, I pour boiling water into the teapot and line up mugs on the tray. Part of me had feared that our recent issues had triggered a nostalgia for his carefree youth and he'd found Alice on Facebook or something. I get it, I do. Day-to-day marital conflicts and humdrum family life might pale in comparison to the technicolour memories of your first love. But he's standing here in the kitchen, by my side, just as baffled by their presence here as I am.

'Why us? Why now? You've been out of touch for years.'

Ted opens and closes his mouth. I know he's not a talker, and he's easily overwhelmed – but I can't stop talking.

I have a vague memory of Ted telling me that Alice grew up in this area, too. The pang I felt when he told me they lived close enough that they could pop around to each other's houses unannounced, like some people did as teenagers before mobile phones. Not me, but some.

'Why is she here, Ted? What does she want?' The questions come out of me in a rush, my voice getting louder with each one.

The kitchen door opens and Tamara and Charley burst in, Charley's hair bursting from her ponytail and her hoody half-hanging off one shoulder. Tamara looks neat and tidy as usual, in her specially-selected Christmas jumper featuring a penguin wearing a hat and scarf.

'Can we explore the house?' Tamara asks, her voice high

with excitement. 'It's so old. I bet there are secret compartments and hidden rooms everywhere.'

'Will Father Christmas still bring our presents if the storm comes?' There's a note of panic in Charley's voice.

Tamara rolls her eyes at her little sister but I flick her a look and nod indulgently, with a glow of excitement in my chest. Charley's my last baby and I want her to believe in magic for as long as possible. She's only six, and I'm hoping there are still a few years of belief before it's shattered by reality. 'I already told Father Christmas that we aren't at home and that he needs to reroute your presents. He's got special magic so his sleigh can get through any weather.' Her expression clears, replaced by joy and excitement. Then I turn to Tamara. 'Let's explore the house in a bit. I can't wait.'

Under my breath, I whisper to Ted: 'And why would Alice want to come here?'

He holds out both hands to me. 'Slow down. We don't know yet.' He shrugs and drops my hands, turning back to the drinks and assuming a calm tone in front of our daughters. 'We can ask, I guess.'

Charley grabs my hand and swings on me like a monkey on a vine. 'Can we have squirty cream?' she begs. I point her in Ted's direction, where he's stirring the hot chocolate powder into boiling water.

I find a milk jug and fill it, adding it to the tray. 'Yep. We can ask,' I say to Ted, marvelling at our ability to have two conversations at once and how normal that's become since the kids arrived.

Tamara glances at the mugs and then down the hallway towards the living room. 'Who's here?' she says, trepidation in her voice.

'Is it Grandma and Grandpa?' squeals Charley, jumping up and down. 'They're early! They have presents for us!'

'Here, take these.' I thrust a box of mince pies into Tamara's arms and guide her to the door. 'And shush,' I say to Charley, steering her by the shoulders after her sister. I pick up the tray and gesture for them to go ahead. 'No, it's one of Daddy's old friends. And her little girl. Well, a big girl compared to you.'

Tamara looks at me, her dark-brown eyes serious and sparking with interest. She stands up to her full four-foot-something height and reaches up a hand to smooth her already neat hair. I suppress a smile. Sometimes she makes a little gesture and it's like looking at a miniature version of Ted's mum. 'How old is the big girl?'

I shrug and signal for her to keep walking. 'I'm not sure. Let's ask them that, too.' I flash Ted an attempt at a supportive smile. He doesn't smile back, instead adopting the look of a condemned man walking to the gallows as he follows us into the living room.

Without her coat and curled up in the corner of the overstuffed green velvet sofa in the living room, Alice looks tiny and fragile, like she hasn't eaten properly in weeks. She's almost the same size as Natasha, who still huddles by the radiator wearing her coat.

'Ooh lovely,' says Alice. She sits forward and ruffles her hair; it spikes up into a perfect tousled pixie style, as if she's just walked out of a hair salon. 'And you must be Ted's daughters,' she says to the girls.

I raise an eyebrow. *Ted's* daughters. I refuse to let her ignore my existence, and clear my throat. 'This is Tamara and Charley. They're eight and six.' I slide the tray onto the coffee table and sit down in a wing-backed armchair next to the fireplace.

Charley climbs onto my lap, eyeing Natasha across the room. Tamara stays next to Ted, near the door. They'll be quiet for a few minutes, as they often are when faced with bigger kids. Stunned into silence, yet desperate to make friends.

'Natasha, want a hot chocolate?' Ted asks, stepping into the room and perching on the opposite end of the sofa as far away from Alice as he can get. His body language is so awkward, so stiff.

Natasha doesn't answer.

I glance at Alice, who gives me an apologetic smile. This one does reach her eyes. 'Sorry. She's had a tough time lately. I guess she doesn't feel like talking yet. I bet she'd love a hot chocolate, wouldn't you, Nat?'

The girl doesn't look up, but she nods and sidles around to sit next to Alice, a small smile on her lips and hands tucked up inside her sleeves.

When everyone has a warm drink, I lean forward in my armchair. 'Alice,' I say, careful to sound friendly but firm. 'We're expecting family very soon to celebrate Christmas, and I've got to ask...'

Ted freezes, his mug halfway to his lips. If he could disappear into the sofa, he would. He hates confrontation in any form, and I know that if either of us is going to face this head-on and work out why they're here, it has to be me.

I'm the pusher in our marriage, the one who makes things happen. I like to think of myself as one of those icebreaker ships, pushing through pack ice to create a safe waterway for my family to follow behind in their rowboats. It's not a role I particularly enjoy, but it's one I think is necessary in a family. Otherwise nothing would ever get done: no holidays booked, no mortgages renegotiated, no handyman to build shelves in that annoying cupboard. So I'm going to ask the questions.

'We're just wondering what's going on. I know you and Ted used to be friendly, but I just...' I pause, trying to work out how to phrase this without sounding rude. 'I know you're from around this area, and there seems to be some kind of mix-up; is it possible you're in the wrong place?'

Alice's eyes widen, and she looks even younger than usual

in her surprise. Her mouth opens and closes, and her eyes flick back and forth from me to Ted. 'I don't understand,' she says, her voice quivering. Her smooth, pale skin looks even paler in her confusion. 'I thought you...'

Her voice fades as she frowns and reaches into her back pocket. She pulls out a mobile phone, its screen cracked down the middle. She pokes at her phone with her unpainted fingertips – fingernails surprisingly ragged and bitten – then holds it out to me. 'Look.'

On the screen is a messaging app, a circle with Ted's face in the top corner and a message bubble from him below that. 'What...?' I say, my words fading as my eyes scan the cracked screen.

Hi Alice, the message reads. *My family will be staying at Red Hart Lodge over Christmas this year and if you're in the area...*

Alice's voice doesn't waver this time. 'Ted invited me, Sadie.'

3

Ted blinks at me, his mouth open and his brow furrowed. He looks shell-shocked, his jaw slack and skin grey. Suddenly, his recent frown lines make him look haggard, not handsome. 'Sadie, I didn't invite them. This is...' His voice fades and he shifts in his seat, his hand on his chest as if trying to calm his heart.

'I don't understand,' Alice says again, as I hand back the phone. There's a crinkle of confusion between her flawless eyebrows. 'The invitation is right there, on the screen.'

She's right, that's a message from Ted, inviting her and her daughter to spend Christmas with us and our family at Red Hart Lodge. His full name is there, and his profile picture is the one he's had for a couple of years: him kneeling on a Fife beach on a windswept autumn day, an arm around each of our children.

'Ted?' she asks him.

On the sofa next to Alice, Natasha sinks into herself further. 'This is so embarrassing,' she mumbles to herself. I feel a flash of sympathy for the girl. This must be excruciating.

Alice reaches over and squeezes Natasha's knee, with a

sympathetic smile on her face. Two spots of red appear high on her cheekbones.

Ted holds a hand out to Alice. 'Can I see the message, please?' To my relief, Ted's using his polite-yet-distant voice, the one he uses for chats with colleagues and acquaintances.

She hands her phone to him and he stares at it, his whole body frozen in place as he reads. He hands it back silently and gives her an apologetic smile as he shrugs one shoulder, seemingly baffled into silence.

He seems so shocked, but is something else going on? *Did he want them to come?* I want to believe that he was over Alice when we met, that he never wanted or needed to see her again. That he hasn't thought of her since long before he met me and we fell in love.

But everyone wonders about their ex, don't they? He told me once, after a few drinks, that he used to search for her online almost every day when they first broke up. In an incognito browser so no one would know. Facebook, Google, Twitter. He never had any hits. He said he wasn't looking for reconciliation. They were over, she'd made sure of that. He just... wanted to check she was OK. That she was happy.

At the time, I told myself that was fairly normal. Everyone wonders about their exes, especially if the break-up was messy. Surely it was a sign he was a good guy. That he cared, even though she broke his heart. But now I'm looking at it in a new light.

What if there's always been unfinished business there? What if he continued to search for her? And Ted's about to find out the answer he needed all those years ago, when he used to search for her. *What will that answer do to us?*

The last couple of months haven't been easy in our marriage. Is this the result? As soon as we hit a rocky patch, did his mind wander back to his ex? Maybe he searched for her again and this time he found her, one way or another.

I usher Charley from my knee and stand up. 'Ted,' I say, beckoning him as I turn to head out of the room. 'Girls, maybe you could show Natasha some of the decorations we brought. Let's make this room a bit festive when Dad and I come back.'

Alice watches us leave, a glint of something in her eye. Glee? Is she enjoying the chaos she's causing in our marriage? I give her a breezy smile on my way past, trying to show that nothing she can do will rock this boat. Even if I don't know that's true.

In the kitchen, Ted pulls a stool out from the island, scraping the legs on the floor. He gestures for me to sit and then he sits next to me and grabs my hand. Our knees brush together, and I resist the urge to move away from his touch. I don't know the truth yet. I need to listen.

'I didn't send that message, Sadie.' He maintains eye contact, his ice-blue eyes not wavering from mine. His voice is soft, pleading. Not defensive or brittle, as it might be if he was lying. 'Please believe me. I must have been hacked or... I don't know.' He squeezes my hand. 'Maybe she faked the message? Maybe it's not even from me, it's like a clone account or something. I know this is difficult to believe, but I'm as baffled as you are. Really.'

His eyes are filled with emotion as they search mine, and my stomach flips. He's still so handsome, so rugged-looking with his dark beard and crinkly eyes. It's easy to forget to really look at each other, when we're battling through every day: work, kids, dinner, baths, bed. But I don't want to forget to look at each other. I don't want to be in a place where I wonder if he's unhappy enough to contact his ex.

I want to believe him, I realise. He's my husband, and she's a stranger. A stranger who treated my husband so badly that he didn't want another relationship for years. I had to pick up the pieces of his broken heart and help him trust again. Ted's no stranger. I have known him for more than a decade and loved him for almost as long. He's the father of my children. He's stuck by me through the best and – more recently – the worst. Why would I take Alice's word over his? I can't. I won't.

His hold on my hand tightens even further and I wince. 'Ouch,' I whisper, flexing my fingers, and he immediately loosens his grip and pats my hand in apology.

I meet his eyes and give a slight nod. *I believe you*, I say with my eyes.

He visibly relaxes, his shoulders loosening. He takes a shaky breath. He raises my hand to his lips and kisses my knuckles, then he holds my fist against his cheek.

'So, what now?' he asks, dropping our hands and turning to place his elbows on the countertop, his hands in his hair.

'How did they get here?' I ask, unable to remember the crunch of tyres on the gravel drive or the sight of a parked car over a raincoat-clad shoulder when they appeared on our doorstep.

He shrugs. 'I don't know, but they were drenched and freezing. I don't think they came in a car.'

I glance out of the window at the grey sky. I can see the wind buffeting the trees and the sky is dark and menacing. Dead leaves swirl around the rear courtyard. The storm hasn't hit yet, but I can see the beginnings of it gathering on the horizon. 'The weather's getting worse, too. If they walked here, I don't think they can walk back.'

He sighs. 'We could give them a lift home. Wherever that is.' I can see the exhaustion in every muscle of his body. Not just emotional exhaustion from the stress of Alice's arrival, but he's already driven for hours today, through wind, fog and driving rain.

'Didn't you say her parents live around here?' I feel a bubble of hope that I might have found an escape from this strange situation. Maybe I could do it. I hate driving, but it'd get them out of the lodge and give us our Christmas Eve back. I need this day to move on. I need Alice to leave so Christmas can start. I feel like I've been waiting for them to leave since the moment they arrived.

I imagine the conversation in the car as I drive them away from the lodge. Just the three of us: me, Alice and Natasha. Would she continue her charm offensive without Ted's presence, all gentle smiles and soft tones? Or would she change without a man to witness her wiles? Perhaps we'd just sit in silence as I peer through the windscreen, trying not to drive us off the road and into a ditch.

'No fuel,' Ted reminds me. 'We can't drive them anywhere.' I remember the blinking light on the dashboard as we drove the last few miles this morning.

I close my eyes and drop my chin to my chest.

After a moment, he touches my hand, triumph in his eyes. 'We can ask Matt to give them a lift when he gets here.' He glances at his watch. 'He said he was arriving later, right?'

Yes. Matt texted that he had to finish work before driving up from Manchester in his BMW, no doubt breaking the speed limit at every opportunity. I nod in agreement, with a frisson of pleasure that Ted and I are united in this. Instead of pulling apart in a crisis, we're working together. A united front. After the last few months, it's a welcome change and I hope it signals a turning point in our relationship.

Bolstered by our conversation, Ted and I slide from our stools and into the hallway, where we can hear Charley chatting away to Alice through the half-closed door, a ramble I've heard many, many times, about *PAW Patrol* and why it's unfair that Ryder was the boy chosen to work with the PAW Patrol dogs when other kids might do a better job if they got the chance. I imagine Alice's blank-faced expression as she nods through it.

I pause, noticing Alice and Natasha's dirty boots just outside the living room, mud falling from their soles onto the slate tiles. 'You go ahead,' I say to Ted, as I bend to pick up the boots. Both pairs are scuffed and worn, although they're relatively good quality brands. Perhaps they're the kind of Scottish people who enjoy hiking. 'I'll just put these by the door.'

I set their boots on the rack and glance at the coats, noticing Alice's sodden jacket hanging on top of Ted's, rain dripping to the floor and getting Ted's coat wet too. I pick it up to move it to its own peg, when I see something shiny in the left pocket. I don't know why, but I reach inside and wrap my hand around something cold and hard, drawing my hand out with a gasp.

Alice is carrying a sharp knife with a black handle, its blade pointed and curved. At the hilt, where the hinged blade meets the handle, I see encrusted specks of dark red, like rust. *Or dried blood?* I suddenly feel sick.

'What the hell?' The knife is old, the handle scuffed and the blade cloudy with fingerprints. But the blade is sharp, with the tell-tale erosion of years of maintenance to keep it that way. It's a folding knife, so with shaking hands I fold the blade back into the handle so I can no longer see the dried blood. I slip it into my pocket, ready to confront Alice as soon as possible.

What is she up to? Why is she here? I think back to their two silhouetted figures, hoods pulled up over their heads as they stood on the step. Alice's foot shooting out to prevent me closing the door. My first instinct was that these strangers were here to rob us. Something about the furtiveness in their movements sent my instincts tingling that these two people signalled danger. Even though Ted once knew Alice – once *loved* Alice – that promise of danger could still be true.

This woman has a knife. And now she's in our house.

4

'And my brother should be here later this afternoon, so he'll be able to run you wherever you need to go,' I hear Ted saying to them both as I enter the room, Alice's knife in my pocket.

Alice looks frustrated, her arms folded across her narrow chest. *Good*, I think. She thought she could just stride in here and interrupt our celebrations, and she's seen very quickly that Ted and I are a team. That she can't disrupt this as easily as she expected. Whether the invitation message was faked, or she somehow believed it, she's probably feeling very awkward right now.

Ted crouches by the fireplace, lighting the fire. The flame catches quickly, the wind outside pulling air up the chimney and encouraging the fire to surge through the balled-up newspapers and deep into the well-constructed pile of sticks and coal.

He has put a playlist of cheesy Christmas songs on the little Bluetooth speaker, and Mariah Carey's *All I Want for Christmas Is You* fills the air. I hate that song. It's everywhere for weeks and Ted's heard my rant about it. In my mind, we'd decorate the tree to smooth-voiced crooners like Bing Crosby's

White Christmas, one of my favourites. I love the dreamy choral backing vocals and the cinematic strings.

But at least he's trying. He's not that into Christmas, and I know he's put that music on for me. He's trying to repair us, just like I am. Ted looks up at me as I cross the room, and he flashes me a smile. I smile back, trying to show I'm grateful. He didn't invite Alice here. This is happening to him as much as it's happening to me. It must be confusing and strange for him, too.

The girls love the more modern songs. In the far corner, Tamara and Charley happily kneel over a heap of red bead garlands, pulling them and laying them flat in an effort to untangle them.

'Feels very Christmassy in here,' I say, before mouthing a silent *thank you* to my husband. I widen my eyes at him, trying to signal that I found something, but he doesn't catch on, poking violently at the fire to send a wave of sparks up the chimney, and then straightening up to move the guard across the fireplace.

Next to Alice on the sofa, Natasha's curled up with her legs tucked under her, looking almost like she could fall asleep with boredom. I get the feeling that if she had a mobile phone, she'd have her face buried in it right now. I wonder why she doesn't. She looks about the age that kids get them nowadays. Now that she's taken off her coat, I notice that her jumper's hood has pink bunny ears; a strange cheerful contrast to her withdrawn demeanour.

I feel a small pang of guilt; no matter what Alice wants or why they're here, Natasha is a child, it's Christmas Eve, and she's clearly very unhappy. I look around the room, taking in the scene which is so far from what I imagined this afternoon to look like.

Alice looks up from the laminated sheet in her hand. She smiles and waves the shiny piece of paper. 'I found this on the sideboard. Your instructions for the rental. Use the fireguard, basement door sticks when it's raining, Wi-Fi password, watch out for angry deer...' She giggles.

Tamara and Charley look up from their decoration-untangling efforts.

'Deer? Like, Father Christmas's reindeer?' asks Charley, scrambling to her feet. She stands up on tiptoes to see the paper. 'Can I see?'

'No pictures. Just loads of boring rules.' Alice flips it around to show her and she quickly goes back to the bead detangling. 'We don't have reindeer in this part of Scotland, but we do have big stags. And they roar and grunt and shout at each other, especially in the dark in the winter. So if you hear anything weird at night outside your bedroom window, don't worry too much. It's just the deer playing with their friends.'

Tamara's eyes go wide and she shakes her head as if to rid herself of the image. My mouth forms a tight line. She's always been easily spooked, and I can imagine that stags are the kind of thing that might wake her in the small hours with a nightmare. Especially with all these mounted skulls and taxidermy animal heads on all the walls. *But Alice doesn't know Tamara's a nervous kid*, I think, trying to be charitable.

'Mummy, we're hungry,' Tamara says in a quiet voice, speaking for both her and Charley.

I look at my watch, glad of something to distract her. With a pang, I realise it's lunchtime. *Past* lunchtime. 'No wonder,' I say. 'Alice, Natasha, are you hungry?' Now that we know they're leaving later and Ted has passed on that message for both of us, I can dredge up some cheer and generosity for our unwelcome guests, even though I didn't bring enough food for them. I'll have to dip into supplies for tomorrow and Boxing Day.

Ted joins me in the kitchen, followed closely by Alice.

I suppress a groan that she's followed us in here.

'Wow, beautiful kitchen,' she says, running her fingertips along the smooth marble surfaces. 'Can I help at all?'

She climbs onto a stool and picks up the bottle opener, flipping it open and closed. She looks slightly awkward, like she wants something to do with her hands.

I shake my head quickly. I don't want her help. Let her feel awkward. I grab a large wooden chopping board from a drawer and peer into the fridge.

Ted smiles, his eyes flicking from me to Alice. 'Wine, ladies?' He seems as if a weight has been lifted now we've established they're leaving soon.

He draws a bottle from the box with a flick of the wrist, and holds it up to Alice as if asking for her approval. He's in wine professional mode, now: the place where he's the expert and where everything fits in neat boxes that he understands. No surprises, no uncomfortable conversations, everything in his control. This is the Ted that I know and love.

She bites her bottom lip and gives an enthusiastic nod.

He holds out his hand for the bottle opener and she starts as if she hadn't realised she was holding it. She places it in his hand and from where I'm standing, I can't tell if she purposefully brushes his fingers with hers.

He grins at her, and suddenly he looks younger. Like he did when we first met.

I watch their wordless interaction with a pang: we were supposed to open the first bottle together, the two of us. I turn away to hide my face and pull an extra wine glass from the cupboard, lining it up on the counter next to the two I found earlier, ready for Ted to pour.

'That looks posh,' Alice says, a question in her voice. She shifts forward on her stool.

Ted nods and pulls the cork from the bottle with a neat *pop*, bringing it to his nose to sniff. 'It was a gift from a client.'

I line up charcuterie: olives, Brie, apples, salami, Cheddar, Stilton, grapes... and a little bowl of macadamia nuts. That will have to do.

She claps a hand to her cheek and leans forward on her stool, a faux-enraptured look on her face. 'I don't even know what you do these days. So strange. Are you a lawyer? Was it a gift from a legal client?' She giggles girlishly and I suppress an eye roll.

I can see what she's doing. I've known women like her, who rely on their looks and their charm to get what they want. And now she's turning those charms on my husband, who can't see how fake it is because he's guileless and kind.

'Sadie, this looks lovely, but could you...' says Ted, eyeing the spread. He points to the Stilton and shakes his head.

Oh, yes. Blue cheese doesn't go well with this wine. He's told me about this before. Something about a compound in the cheese, I think. I should pay more attention. I put the Stilton aside and he smiles at me before pouring a small measure of wine into one glass, takes a sip and rolls it around his mouth, then he swallows and gives a small nod of approval. He fills up the other two glasses and tops up his own, handing one to Alice. 'Not a legal client, no. I never practised law in the end.'

I wait a moment, but Ted doesn't hand me a glass so I reach across him and get my own, throwing him a look as I do. I don't wait to clink glasses, but take a big mouthful, which catches in my throat. I suppress a cough and head to the fridge to see if there's anything else to serve alongside the charcuterie.

'It's a shame you didn't go into law. You were brilliant.' She turns to me. 'He was the best in our class.'

'Oh, yes. He's told me a bit about his time at uni,' I say, showing Alice that Ted hasn't kept secrets from me. *I know everything about him. And you,* I want to say.

But I don't, I realise. Ted told me a few things about their relationship, but he's never gone into detail or told me why it ended. When we first met and briefly discussed exes, he shut it down and said he wanted to focus on our future, not his past. At the time, I thought that was charming. That it showed his focus on the present and how interested he was in me. Now, I'm frustrated that I've been put on the back foot, that I know so little. I have no ammunition or armour against her and their history together. So instead, I decide to change tack and attempt a different approach.

'So you also studied law at Aberdeen, Alice?' I ask nonchalantly, as if I didn't know Alice existed until today.

She pulls her jumper over her head, revealing a strip of bare skin around her midriff. Probably on purpose. 'Sorry, it's lovely and warm in here, isn't it?' She lays the jumper on the kitchen island and smiles at Ted before she looks back at me. 'Ted and I were in the same year. He was a much, much better student than I was.'

He takes a sip of wine and shakes his head half-heartedly, his cheeks flushing with pleasure at the compliment. He glances at me, a kind expression on his face as he tries to draw me back in. 'Sadie was at Aberdeen, too. But a year or two above us.'

Alice raises her eyebrows and looks back to Ted, ignoring his attempt to include me. 'So what do you do that gets you this amazing wine? I really thought you'd become a lawyer, Teddy.'

Teddy. I barely manage to suppress my grimace at the nickname. I find a bread knife and slice a sourdough tiger loaf, lining up the pieces on the wooden board.

He swallows. 'I'm a wine buyer for a big supermarket. I work with winemakers to decide what goes on the shelves. And Sadie's a therapist,' he adds, trying again to bring me into the conversation.

I take another slug of wine. It's really good, even at this slightly colder temperature from its trip in the car. It coats my mouth in tannins and gives off a beautiful dark cherry flavour. 'Lovely wine,' I say. 'I get vanilla on the aftertaste.'

Ted shrugs. 'It needs airing.' He's staring into his glass, which is already empty. Alice's arrival must have shocked him even more than it seemed. Noticing, Alice lifts her glass and drains it, pushing the glass towards Ted with a wink. 'Gotta keep up,' she says, flashing me a snide look that makes me wonder if that's a challenge.

I suppress a shake of my head, eager to hear Ted advise her to slow down, to savour the flavours. But instead he tops up their glasses with a sweep of the wrist, ignoring mine because it's still full.

I pick up the lunch platter and carry it through to the living room. Ted and Alice follow, their cheeks flushed from the warmth and the wine.

The girls pounce on the bread and cheese, Natasha too. Alice nibbles on a couple of slices but mainly sinks the wine and tries to draw Ted into as many reminiscences as she can: their 'hilarious' wild camping trips in the hills, freshers' week drinking games, and the 'brilliant' selfies they used as their Myspace profile pictures back in the day.

Ted and Alice drain the first bottle of wine before I've even finished my first glass, their eyes glassy and their cheeks even more flushed as their laughter gets louder. I sink further and further into myself, refusing to – and unable to – compete for his attention. I think back to the choice I made earlier today: deciding to trust and believe him without question over the claim of a stranger. Would he choose me like that? If you'd asked me a few hours ago, I would have been certain the answer would be yes. Now... I'm not so sure.

The sun has begun to sink towards the horizon as we finish lunch, with only some olive pits and several crusts remaining. My stomach churns and gnaws at the couple of slices of bread I was able to choke down, an underlying anxiety thrumming in my chest like a just-plucked guitar string.

Ted sighs and sits back on the sofa, putting his feet up on the edge of the coffee table. 'That was just what I needed.

Thank you, Sadie,' he says, looking at me for the first time in what feels like hours.

'Yes, thank you,' joins in Alice, and she drains yet another glass of wine. 'I love all the flavours in this wine.'

'Black cherry on the nose and a vanilla aftertaste,' says Ted, as if I didn't say that earlier.

I suppress a sigh as Alice nods indulgently. 'And thank you both so much for making Natasha and me welcome. I know you have so much to do for tomorrow and it's just so nice that you've let us muscle in on your day.'

Ted mumbles a platitude in response. I ignore her and look out through the darkening windows, willing Matt to arrive like a miracle to remove the intruders so I can breathe again.

'Hey,' says Alice, reaching out to touch Ted's shoulder. He flinches slightly, but still turns to her with an engaged smile on his face, eager to relive more of his twenties. 'Do you remember...'

Next to each other on the sofa, Tamara and Charley begin to bicker. They've been sat still long enough.

I stand up, unwilling to hear more of Alice's tipsy chatter. I clap my hands. 'Come on, girls. Let's go upstairs. Maybe Natasha might like to play some board games? I spotted a cupboard full of them: Twister, Buckaroo, Pictionary. All the good ones.' I grab Charley's hand and hold out my other one to Tamara.

The girls scramble to their feet and Natasha flashes me a grateful smile as she stands. I lead the three girls from the room, wondering again what this looks like to her: watching her mother throw herself at someone else's husband. It can't be comfortable to see. Unless she's used to it? Perhaps Alice does this all the time. I toy with the idea as we head to the stairs: a mother dragging her daughter around the country, showing up on the doorsteps of old flames, claiming to be invited. With a knife in her pocket. What is her goal? Does she want money?

Or something even more sinister? Would Natasha even understand what her mother was up to, if that was the case?

For a second I get a flash of an image: my girls lying in their twin beds on crisp once-white sheets, their bloodied throats slashed by Alice's knife. *No.* I shake my head, pushing the thought from my mind. Those kinds of things don't happen in real life.

'How old are you, Natasha?' I ask as we climb the tartan-carpeted stairs to the first floor. A mounted deer head watches from the wall, its shiny eyes following me.

'Fourteen,' she mumbles, and I almost trip on a step.

I gaze at her, my eyes scanning her face. She's got a light dusting of freckles on her nose and her teeth look too large for her features, like a much younger child. I would have put her at twelve, or even eleven.

She grins at me and rolls her eyes. 'I know, I know. I look a lot younger. Everyone's always telling me that. But I'll catch up eventually.'

I give a reassuring smile, help them select a few games and lead them to Tamara and Charley's room, which is quaint and just as Scottish as the rest of the grand house. The windows are framed by heavy velvet curtains, pelmet and tiebacks. The twin beds are clad in red and cream tartan blankets – very festive – with starched white sheets and pillows. It's a faded grandeur, exactly how I imagine the bedrooms might look in Edinburgh's Balmoral Hotel.

To my relief, there are no dead stag heads on the walls in here: just Victorian-looking watercolours of moorland and mountains.

I get the girls settled and head downstairs as quickly as I can. Something tells me not to leave Alice unattended with my husband for more than a few minutes. I heave a sigh of relief as I remember that soon Ted's brother will arrive, ready to take our unwanted guests anywhere else.

On the stairs, my phone chirps for the first time since we arrived: I must have found a small pocket of phone signal on the first floor. I remember I meant to text Matt earlier asking him to bring a can of fuel, but I've had no phone signal ever since. I pause, pulling my mobile from my pocket and clicking through to the new text message. It's from Matt:

Hey S, sorry for late notice. Motorway totally blocked: lorry blown over in the storm. Tailbacks for miles. I've turned around – won't make it for Xmas. Drink my share of the wine and make sure Ted has a wee dram in my honour. Tell Mum & Dad I'll see them in a couple of weeks xx

I hover on the stairs, frozen to the spot as I stare at the phone and try to process what this means. I'm disappointed: Ted's brother is a bundle of fun, and the girls love him. I was relying on him to bring the entertainment: party games and general merriment follow Matt wherever he goes.

While still in the tiny pocket of phone signal on the stairs, I fire off a text to Mum asking her to set off from Crieff as early as she can tomorrow to beat the worst of the weather. Ted's parents are hosting their annual Christmas Eve whist game today so they can't come early, but their journey tomorrow is only twenty minutes or so. As long as they can get past the little bridge over the river, they'll be fine both ways.

But mostly I'm despairing. No one else is due to arrive today: Ted's brother was our only hope to get Alice and Natasha away. With our empty fuel tank and Matt's cancellation, there's no way to get rid of them today. And tomorrow is Christmas Day. An image of Natasha's toothy grin flashes across my mind. Do I have it in my heart to throw a child out on Christmas morning? Do they have anywhere to go?

But unless there's a miracle, Alice and Natasha are here until tomorrow. How do I get through the rest of the day? For a moment I contemplate grabbing a bottle of Baileys from the kitchen and getting into bed with a novel, feigning a headache and just excusing myself until tomorrow morning. But I can't do that to my kids. And I don't want to miss out on their excitement, no matter what it costs me in the meantime.

Thoroughly defeated, I descend the rest of the stairs and cross the hallway into the living room, my phone still in my hand.

'Matt just text—' The words die in my throat and my phone slips from my fingers and lands on the ground with a clatter.

Ted and Alice are standing by the fireplace, her arms wrapped around his shoulders and her lips on his. She's kissing my husband.

5

At the sound of my phone dropping to the ground, Ted and Alice start and leap away from each other, shock on their faces.

'Sadie,' whispers Ted, exposing teeth slightly stained by the red wine he's drunk. His eyes are filled with emotion, a hand reaching towards me.

Alice stays where she is, patting her hair back into place. Her cheeks are flushed, but I don't know whether that's from the wine, the heat from the fire, or much-deserved embarrassment. Again, there's that look of purpose and triumph, quickly hidden as she turns her face away.

For a moment, it's as if I'm watching us from a distance, like we're characters on a TV show. The Christmas album is over and there's no sound except logs popping in the fire and the wind beating against the windowpanes.

The setting is beautiful: the fire crackling in the grate, the overstuffed sofa and armchairs, the tartan cushions, the stormy hills just visible through the windows... and the adulterous couple jumping apart.

And I'm the scorned wife, the one who gets to storm out, to shout and to pummel her husband's broad chest with her fists

while he protests, 'It's not what it looks like, I promise.' And I'm
sure Ted does stammer something like that, but my mind is too
far away to parse it.

It strikes me that this is the moment before reality hits me,
the only time when I can look at this at a remove and see it all
impartially. This is the one moment of calm that I'll get before
the hurt comes crashing into me like an axe to my chest, sucking
the air from my lungs.

I had prepared for disruption after their arrival and some
uncomfortable confusion for Ted, but not this. Never this. My
husband kissed another woman.

I turn away and leave the room, closing the door softly behind
me and striding to the kitchen. I sit on a stool and place my
palms flat on the marble worksurface, feeling its smooth coldness against my skin. It's quiet in here except for the rush of
blood through my veins and the roar of the wind outside. I take
a breath. And another.

I believed him when he told me the invitation didn't come
from him. I believed him when he told me they hadn't spoken
since before Ted and I got together. But to go from almost
strangers earlier today to kissing this afternoon, surely there has
to have been something else at play?

Maybe they've been in touch. Maybe they even met. I
wouldn't know; Ted and I don't snoop in each other's phones or
emails – we trust each other and give each other space, like a
healthy couple. Ted will use my phone to add things to the
Tesco order or whatever. And I know his passwords, his access
codes... but I don't use them. They're for emergencies. But now
I wonder, should I have been more paranoid? Paid more attention? Was he hiding something after all?

And if so, did he ever love me? Was I just a placeholder
until he could find her again and rekindle the love they once

had? No one forgets their first love, and some people do hold onto it like a talisman. She broke his heart, after all – I may not know much about how they broke up, but I do know that.

There's a reason why Friends Reunited ended so many marriages when it first became popular: old sweethearts getting back in touch, realising their current marriages didn't live up to the long-lost young love they once had. Is that how Ted feels about Alice?

Maybe she's his 'one who got away'. A few months after our first date, he confided that I was the first person he'd dated in three years. A nasty break-up, he told me.

He didn't tell me much else – I didn't ask – until we moved in together and I started noticing that he sometimes cried in his sleep. Full body-wracking sobs, and tears running down his cheeks into his ears. If I woke him, the crying would continue. He couldn't leave the dream behind. He told me it was something about his last relationship, but assured me he was over her, that I had nothing to worry about. He assured me I was so special that he gave up his 'no relationships' rule for me. *I'm not crying for her*, he'd say. *Promise you won't hurt me.*

Now, I remember a piece of advice that my grandma used to give: when people show their true colours, believe them. And perhaps what Ted's nightmares were trying to tell me back then was that he wasn't ready for a relationship. Or worse, that he wasn't yet over Alice.

But I wouldn't listen. I wanted him in my life and I couldn't listen. I thought we could make it work, but now I wonder if I made a mistake. My breath shudders from my lungs as I struggle to hold in a sob.

I've never been good at paying attention to my gut. A lonely childhood meant I pounced on love as soon as I found it and was terrified to let go. Perhaps I just refused to see the truth until now. It wouldn't be the first time I've been in denial about something this important, and it certainly won't be the last.

My mind flinches away from what I've seen, what Ted has done. It's all too painful to think about. I've spent my life shoving things down into a little box, and I can do it this time, too. *We have to get through Christmas for our family*, I remind myself.

The wind rattles the extractor fan, and I hear the rustle of the trees surrounding the back of the lodge, just on the other side of the kitchen wall. Suddenly, I feel deeply alone. There are five other people in this house, yet no one for me to talk to.

I can't leave: our car wouldn't get as far as the main road with the tiny speck of fuel we have left in the tank. And we've all been drinking. My phone's still on the living room floor where I dropped it in shock, I realise. And if I did get hold of someone, how would I begin to explain this mess? But even if I had my phone, there's no signal out here. I can't call my mum or text a friend unless I hover on the stairs. Not that I have that many friends, these days: I've been so absorbed with family life and my job that most of them have faded away in the past few years.

My fingers shake as I stare at my pale hands splayed in front of me. The skin looks dry and crinkled, punished by weeks of winter cold. The diamond on my engagement ring glints in the kitchen spotlights, and light catches the little pale feather inclusion deep inside the stone that's been there since it formed – like a diamond's birthmark. It's a flaw that I've always loved because it represents the reality of marriage: even though everything looks perfect from the outside there's always an imperfection or two below the surface. And it turns out I was more right than I wanted to be.

I just want someone to talk to. Anyone. Mum will be here tomorrow, refreshed and happy after a pamper night at Crieff Hydro, my early Christmas present to help her through a tough time of year. At the thought of Mum, my vision blurs as tears fill my eyes. We're not that close, but I'm so glad she'll be here tomorrow. A bit of outside perspective on what has rapidly become the most disastrous family holiday we've ever had. And possibly the last one we'll ever have, too.

Is my marriage over? Do I have a choice? And how would I feel if that is the case?

'Sadie.'

I straighten up at the tentative sound of Ted's voice, my whole body tense.

Tears threaten to spill over and I scrape at my eyes with the heel of my hand. I can't let him see that. I can't show him how hurt I am. The pain is finally here, I can't put it off any longer, and it's searing like a brand to the chest.

I harden my face, pulling my lips tight and my eyebrows low. And I turn to face him.

He looks anguished, his skin grey and cheeks sallow. He looks like *he's* the one who's just lost everything.

'God, Sadie. That was—' He stops, shakes his head. 'I don't know what happened. Alice and I were just chatting... talking about the weather warning, of all things. And then out of nowhere she just...' He takes a huge breath, burying his face in his hands. His shoulders shake; is he crying? I've rarely seen him cry. Not since the girls were born. When he looks up, his face is mottled and his eyes are bloodshot.

I can't look into his eyes right now. I need to hear his words, undistracted by his handsome face. I look down at his hands, taking in the broad strength of his balled fists in his lap. His wedding ring, too, glints in the light. We picked titanium for its durability, knowing it would last for ever without damage or corrosion. *Like our love*, we'd hoped. Once upon a time.

'She just launched herself at me, and I didn't have time to push her away.' His voice is gravelly with stress. 'I would have... I was going to. But then you walked in. What you saw wasn't a kiss, Sadie. It wasn't anything from my side. Please don't make this more than it needs to be.'

I don't move. I shift my gaze and stare at a spot in the corner of the kitchen, where an olive pit lurks next to the skirting board. I must have missed the bin when I was clearing up.

He takes my hand in his, but I can't. I pull it away, curl my fingers in my lap. I need to be contained, alone. If I let him hold my hand, I'll crack and believe him and I don't want to yet. I need a moment to contemplate what the world looks like if I don't believe him. If my husband of ten years was just unfaithful to me with his ex-girlfriend.

'She broke your heart, Ted. She broke your heart and stomped on it and left you a broken person. I had to put you back together when we started dating even though it had been years since she left.' I cross to the kitchen island and pick up a lone glass of wine, abandoned on the counter. 'We had a great marriage and it took a long time to get there, no thanks to her.'

He looks at me, his eyes sad again. 'We *have* a great marriage, Sadie.'

I shake my head, my gut churning. But I sit down on a stool, leaving a gap between us. 'You're not nineteen any more,' I blurt out, a part of me aware that this is a rare moment between us where I can speak my mind without repercussion. After what I just saw, he *owes* me. He has no right to get angry at my words. I can say what I like, for once. And I want to hurt him a little, give him a hint of the sting of rejection that I just felt. 'You're married, no matter what's been going on between us lately. You have kids. A wife. There are consequences to your actions and people get hurt when you don't consider them.'

His face clouds, his eyelids lowering in that expression I know so well. I've pushed a button and he's angry. It's always been tricky, trying to talk to Ted about something he's done wrong. It's worse if he *knows* he's in the wrong: he gets defensive and frustrated – much quicker than if it's a miscommunication or the accusation is unfounded. Shining a spotlight on a misdemeanour makes him angry. Often at this point, I've lost him and there'll be no productive direction in which the conversation can go. He withdraws and gives me the silent treatment, sometimes for days. Until suddenly he snaps out of it as if nothing happened, or finds a way to turn it around and place the blame at my feet.

But I was correct: he knows he has no right to turn it on me today. I watch as he straightens his shoulders and his expression softens. 'It was so sudden, so out of nowhere. We were talking about the *weather*, Sadie.' He leans forward and touches my cheek with his fingertips, gently drawing my head around so I have to look at him. A tear gathers in the corner of his eye. Another tear threatens to spill over. 'Please believe me. I don't know what she's doing, why she's here. But I do believe that she's trying to turn my life upside down.' He pauses for a moment, thinking. His eyes stare into the distance before he realises something and focuses back on me. 'I think she heard you coming down the stairs. I think she wanted you to see that. She timed it so you'd see it before I had the chance to move away.'

My mind flashes back to the look of triumph on Alice's face after she sprang away from Ted when I walked into the room. The way she straightened her T-shirt and glanced down at herself, like an actor on the stage checking they were under the correct spotlight. And again, I think about my earlier choice to believe Ted over this stranger. It felt like the right choice then. *What has changed now?*

There's been more wine and some one-sided flirting from Alice... and that kiss. But he hasn't been flirting back, no matter how hard she tried. And yes, he's drunk a little too much wine. But wouldn't I, if faced with my ex and her child plunged into the centre of my family's holiday?

'I'll tell her to back off,' he says, as if sensing I'm weakening. 'Nothing like this can happen again while she's here.'

'Agreed,' I say.

He slumps in relief, his head resting on my shoulder. I can smell his shampoo: woodsy and fresh.

'And as soon as anyone arrives here with a car, Alice and Natasha are gone. It doesn't matter where they go, but they need to be gone.'

My lip trembles as I remember the text I received just before I saw Alice kissing Ted. 'And Matt's not coming,' I say, my voice shaking with despair. I'd pinned my hopes on Ted's brother getting Alice and Natasha away, no matter how late he arrived.

Ted's eyes widen and he raises his eyebrows in surprise. 'He flaked?'

I shake my head. 'The weather's too bad. The roads are awful. He can't get through.'

'Come here,' he says, pulling me into his arms.

I let him, but I don't wrap my arms around him in return. I'm not there yet. Yes, perhaps this wasn't his fault and he didn't invite it. But why would she think her affections were wanted? People don't kiss people out of nowhere. Even if he's not fifty per cent responsible for that kiss, there *is* a percentage of encouragement which came from him, even if it's just one per cent. That's one too many.

'We'd better go see what the kids are up to. Check they've not destroyed the place,' he says, with a glance to the ceiling.

'Wait,' I say, putting a hand on his knee. 'There's something else.' I draw in a breath and take a moment to think about what we have now. Our life. Our marriage. Our children. Happy, healthy, whole despite everything. I need to take this moment because who knows what exists on the other side. But for now, our family is intact, and our lives are known. I might be about to open a huge fissure: before and after. And I want to stay in the 'before' for a moment or two longer.

He pauses on his way off the stool, one foot on the floor.

I hesitate, gathering myself. I don't know how to broach this but I know I have to. It might even be the reason why Alice is here. I take a big breath and let the words out in a rush. 'I asked Natasha how old she is.'

He turns his head back towards me, a mildly interested look on his face. 'Oh yeah? She's what, like, twelve?'

I shake my head even though he's looking at the ceiling, unaware of what's about to hit. My body fizzes with dread at what I'm about to suggest. The shock and pain of the last half hour pales in significance with the life-changing news we could face soon. For all of us; our whole family. Not just Ted.

'Ted, she's fourteen.' I pause for a moment, letting that sink in.

He straightens up like he's been electrocuted. 'What the...' His eyes flick back and forth as his brain does calculations. His arms are covered in goosebumps. His face is white. 'No. It's not possible. Alice mentioned a dad in the picture. It can't—'

He cuts himself off and rubs his face with both hands. His breath catches in his throat.

'Ted, this is big, if it's true,' I start, my voice trembling.

I watch him closely to see his reaction. Fourteen years ago, Ted and Alice had just broken up. He seems genuinely shocked, and I wonder if Alice kept this a secret from him. Or did he know there was a baby somewhere but chose not to share that with me, and just opted out of the child's life? 'And if she is... it changes our family for ever. The girls need to know each other. It's important.'

He groans into his hands.

Someone clears their throat. 'Sorry, I—'

I turn. Alice. Standing in the doorway, a half-smile on her

face. She has the grace to look sheepish, but it's all an act. I don't
know how long she's been standing there or how much she's
heard. My stomach churns.

'Sorry to interrupt. I was just coming to get a glass of water
and I couldn't help overhearing.' She reaches up and ruffles her
hair again, leaving it sticking up like she's just woken. 'I know
this is weird for all of us—'

'The glasses are over there,' I say, pointing to the cupboard.
I'm not interested in her attempts at charm. It might work on
Ted and other men, but it won't work on me. This fake friendli-
ness and damsel in distress act is unimaginative. I have met
women like her before: women who stand with their backs to
you in circles of friends, trying to freeze you out. Women who
say, 'I don't have many female friends,' in a faux-baffled tone
when it's their own actions which have alienated anyone who
tried to get close. Since she arrived, to her I've been an obstacle
to get around in her pursuit of... what, I'm not sure. Ted, I fear.

Ted looks up from his hunched position, slowly moving his
hands away from his face. 'What was that, Alice? What were
you going to say?' His voice croaks and he looks away from her
again, like he's flinching from what she's about to tell us.

She flashes me a pointed look and then turns back to Ted.
'That it's true.'

'What's true?' Ted says, his voice just a whisper. He doesn't
move, just keeps staring at his feet like a prisoner awaiting a
firing squad. Needing her to say it.

The kitchen clock ticks away the seconds as we wait for the
truth. I brace myself as if I'm about to get hit by a truck. If he
really didn't know, then I've had longer than Ted to prepare for
this, but still I don't think I'd ever be ready.

She crosses to the sink and fills a glass of water, taking a sip
before she speaks again. Her voice is the opposite of Ted's, clear
and crisp. 'It's true. What you were talking about.'

I bite the inside of my cheek so hard I taste blood.

She looks down at the ground and then raises her gaze to Ted. She runs the tip of her tongue across her lip and takes a breath. 'Natasha is your daughter.'

6

Ted stares at Alice, his face ashen. On the edge of the table, I see his fingers twitching, one after another, his lips moving slightly. He's counting. He's doing the same calculations as I am, I know it.

If Natasha's fourteen, that means she was born less than a year after Ted and Alice broke up. It's possible that Alice met someone else and got pregnant soon after they broke up. But it's unlikely.

And then a truly horrifying thought hits me. Did Ted know, back then? Has he known all this time? Can I get over that and move forward, knowing he kept this from me? And our daughters have a half-sister; that's the thing I really couldn't forgive: that keeping his secret was more important to him than letting them get to know their own sister. Family is so important, and I couldn't stand it if he'd kept her from them. They deserved to know.

Ted shakes his head and mutters to himself.

We have to face this. For Tamara and Charley: their family. They're already missing a grandfather on my side, and I'm an only child so they have no aunts, uncles or cousins from my side. And Matt doesn't have kids yet, so no cousins from him either. They can't lose more connections. It feels urgent and important to ensure they miss nothing else in life, that they get to know their sister and they can have as much time with her as possible, starting now. No matter anything else I'm feeling right now – my anger, my resentment and jealousy and hurt – the important thing is our children.

I turn to look at Alice, still hovering by the door. Then I look at Ted, his head still hanging low as he stares at his knees, frozen in place.

'Did you know?' I ask him.

Ted doesn't answer. A stone settles in my stomach.

I close my eyes. I'd been hoping that there's something else, some miraculous other explanation that allows our family to remain an isolated unit, protected from the rest of the world just as we've always been. That Alice never told him. That Natasha was someone else's. Not more lies and secrets. Not for the entire duration of our relationship.

'You'd better tell me what's going on, please,' I say to them both, leaning back and folding my arms. 'No more lies.'

'This isn't Ted's fault.' She turns to me and tries to meet my gaze but I can't let her. 'It was just me, alone. I decided to do this on my own, without Ted.'

I look back at my hands. I think back to the baby days: the sleepless nights, the 3 a.m. feeds, the endless treadmill of feed, change, sleep, repeat. Even with two of us to share the load, there were days when I imagined just walking out of the door and never coming back. The days when we'd get all dressed up to leave, keys in hand, and there'd be a nappy blowout and baby and I would both need a new outfit. The days when Tamara wouldn't nap for hours on end, no matter how much rocking and shushing and patting I did. Teething, tantrums, accidents, coughs and colds, spills... there were so many things I couldn't have coped with by myself. So many days I had to hand over to

Ted because I felt like I'd lose my mind if I didn't have a break. Alice must have so much strength, to choose to bring up a daughter alone when she was barely out of her teens herself.

She climbs on a stool across from Ted and me, like a job candidate facing her interviewers. 'We were so young, neither of us ready to be parents. I thought at least one of us could keep some freedom.'

A flash of realisation crosses Ted's face. 'We were meant to be going travelling. We were going to go Interrailing, work on cruise ships, drive across America...'

She nods, sadly. 'It all seemed so romantic.'

'We wanted to do everything. You did, too. You wanted all that.' He glances up, a flash of pain crossing his face as his eyes meet Alice's. Then he turns to me. 'We were about to buy our first ticket when Alice said she didn't want to go any more. She said we should stay at home, rent a flat, get a job. I couldn't work it out. I was angry. We had all these plans and...' He runs a hand through his hair, ruffling it up, and then he reaches for my hand.

I squeeze his hand and let go. I need to be separate from him while I process all this.

He shakes his head with a rueful smile. 'So I left, went travelling without her. I thought she'd panic as soon as I left and realise staying was a bad idea. But she didn't. She never got in touch. So I travelled alone, and when I got back I couldn't find her.' He looks at Alice for the first time. 'You disappeared.'

She looks up at Ted, studying him as he stares into his lap, his hands balled into fists on his thighs.

I watch as waves of emotion cross Alice's face. 'And now you know for sure. That's why all my plans had to change. Why I couldn't travel. You have another daughter, Ted.'

He shakes his head. 'You should have told me, Alice.'

A flash of anger crosses her face. 'I tried. I wanted to. But you were unsurprisingly difficult to get hold of while you Interrailed around Europe with no phone, having the time of your life. I called your parents' house a couple of times, but I always lost my nerve and hung up. By then, I was deep in the newborn days, and although I could have done with the help, it was hard to admit I needed it.'

Ted straightens up and looks at Alice for the first time. He gives a quick nod, as if accepting his role in everything. 'Does Natasha know?'

Alice shakes her head and closes her eyes against another wave of emotion. Her throat bobs as she swallows. 'Until this week, she believed that Robin was her biological father. She now knows that's not the case, but not much more.'

I sit forward, my elbow on the worktop. I feel a prickle in my scalp, knowing that this might give the answers we've been looking for about what Alice wants from us. 'What happened this week? Why did you come here?'

She huddles into herself, wrapping her arms around her ribs. Her eyes fill with tears as she looks up at me. 'What you saw in there, Sadie' – she points back towards the living room – 'it's not me. I'm not that person. And I'm so sorry. To both of you. I've been going through some awful things lately and I've brought all this baggage with me. Seeing a friendly face and feeling safe, and then the wine... suddenly I just made a stupid error. It was all me and it won't happen again.'

'What happened this week?' I ask again, refusing to let her confuse things and avoid a question, even though her words have soothed something, deep inside. I was right to believe Ted. She's backed him up. It was all her, that kiss. And now I need to know the truth about the other bombshell. I need to know everything. I've had enough of evasion and tricks.

'And as to why we're here, Natasha and I have recently left her dad. It wasn't safe to be there any more. The timing's terrible – at Christmas and everything – but it's better to be away from him than...' She lets her words trail away and I see her hands are shaking as she tucks a strand of hair behind her ear. Her eyes flick to me.

Despite her apparent candour, there's still something sneaky about her, like everything she does and says is calculated to get what she wants. I don't trust her at all. And what *does* she want? I stay silent for a moment, watching her. In therapy, leaving a moment of silence can let a client reach a conclusion on their own, leading them to the realisation they need. Or, in this case, giving them the shovel to continue digging their own grave.

And soon enough, Alice begins again. 'So when I got Ted's invitation, it was like a lifeline. I'm sorry that we've caused so much confusion by being here; if I'd known it would have been so awkward, I would never have come. But honestly, we had nowhere to go when we left Glasgow. The homeless hostels wouldn't take us, as Natasha is under eighteen. She'd have been sent off to a foster family or something. At Christmas. And there are complications with finding housing in this part of Scotland. It's so remote.' She gestures out of the window with frustration. 'And then I remembered Ted's invite and we managed to get the last bus out of Fort William before they stopped for Christmas Eve. We walked the rest of the way. This was the only safe place I could think of.' She glances around the kitchen like it's a palace. 'It's like it was meant to be.'

Is she telling the truth? I don't know. But there's something about her hunched form on that stool, looking so tiny and lost as she hugs herself. I know that look, the look of someone running away. I've seen it before. And I believe her, I realise. I want to, and I need to. She's running from something terrifying, and as inconvenient as it is to have her here, at least she's safe. And so is Ted's daughter.

Ted stands up and fills three glasses with water from the tap as the kitchen door swings open and Natasha slides into the room, followed by Tamara and Charley. Charley's hair is everywhere, and all the girls have flushed cheeks and grins on their faces.

'We've been playing hide and seek,' says Tamara, sidling up next to me and grasping hold of my hand with her warm little fist. I lean over and rest my cheek on the top of her head.

Across from me, I watch as Natasha stands next to Alice. I look between her and Alice. Natasha's wavy hair falls in tangles around her face, and when she's not hunched over and frozen, she's remarkably pretty. Like Alice, she has brown eyes. But that's where the similarity ends. She's got a round face where Alice's is small and heart-shaped, and Natasha's cheeks are pleasantly pink when she's not pale and huddled against the storm. *Does she look like Ted?*

I glance at him and see that he's doing the same thing, his eyes raking Natasha's face, searching for his own likeness. He snaps out of it and places glasses of water in front of me and Alice, just as the doorbell breaks the quiet.

I'm shocked – who could possibly be here? But it's nothing compared to Natasha's reaction.

Natasha looks up at Alice with wide eyes, grabbing a fistful of Alice's T-shirt in her hands. 'Mum. What if it's him?'

Alice jerks, her elbow knocking the water glass in front of her. She jumps off the stool and backs away towards the kitchen door, the one which opens out into the courtyard.

Sensing their fear, Tamara and Charley huddle into me, one on each side. I look down at my two children, my stomach twisting.

'Who is it, Mummy? Who are they scared of?'

7

My hand wrapped around the knife in my pocket, I stride through the hall of the house towards the entrance, Ted's reassuring presence right behind me. A blast of rain hits me and the door is almost thrown against the wall by the wind as I open it. Behind me the curtain ripples and puffs into the house.

'Sadie, love!' shouts a voice and Ted's dad looms out of the grey day, a large box full of beer bottles hefted in both his solid arms. 'Let me in, it's blowing a hoolie out here.'

I step aside and release the knife, shaking off the dread and fear like a heavy coat. It's contagious and cloying, that fear that immediately filled the house as soon as the doorbell rang. And the weather doesn't help. The wind outside roars like a wild animal. I hold the door with both hands to prevent it from banging against the wall.

Neil strides into the house and Patricia – Ted's mum – follows him in, carrying a supermarket bag for life rammed with presents in one hand, and holding her green Barbour coat around her small frame with the other. I slam the door and lock it, grateful to shut out the storm.

'Sadie. Ted. You're both looking well,' Patricia says with a smile. She sets down the bag of presents on top of the beer box, hugs Ted, then kisses me on both cheeks before pulling me into a hug, too. I squeeze her back, grateful that they're here even though we weren't expecting them until tomorrow. I need familiar faces and people on my team in this confusing whirl-wind of secrets and lies.

'I know we're early,' she says as Neil slides her coat from her shoulders. She flashes him a smile, and my heart thrums with appreciation for their loving relationship and the model they set for their sons. I'm lucky to have them as in-laws. 'But our whist players cried off because of the weather and we got a dog sitter until tomorrow. Thought we'd pop over for the night, as Matty texted that he had to stay in Manchester so we knew there's a spare room.'

Ted flicks me a wry smile, pats his dad on the back and grabs the box of beer, slipping away into the kitchen.

'We couldn't wait to see the wee bairns' faces with all the presents we've brought,' she says. She pats her hair, straight-ening the salt-and-pepper bob with both hands. 'They'll be so excited,' she whispers to me, as if sharing a secret.

I smile back, even though the idea of more plastic, noisy toys crammed into our already over-stuffed house fills me with a niggle of anxiety. Ted's mum recently relinquished a lifetime of catalogue shopping and stepped into the digital world, launching herself into online shopping with enthusiasm.

The last few birthdays and Christmases have been filled with oddities from dodgy websites hosted in distant countries: socks without built-in heels, so your feet feel horribly constrained at the ankle; pungent body lotion that smells nothing like the label's claims; nasal pore strips for Ted (that one gave us a laugh); and endless gadgets claiming to make your life easier but which do anything but, and then stop working after a few uses anyway. The gift-giving comes from a good place, but I secretly hope she can channel this newfound fascination for internet shopping in a new direction soon.

Neil hangs Patricia's coat on the rack, followed by his own wax jacket and tweed cap. He's still wearing the gamekeeper's unofficial uniform, even though he's retired. I feel a flush of affection for the pair of them: they've been welcoming and friendly since the first day we met, and although we're not a family that has spirited debates or deep heart-to-hearts, they're the easy, loving family I'd wanted my whole life. They're good, kind people who love their son – and me, too, I believe. And they adore their grandchildren.

Neil removes his hiking boots to reveal mustard socks pulled up over the ankles of his corduroy trousers. 'Aye, haven't seen a storm like this in a fair few years,' he says, glancing around the hall, his eyes trailing across the mounted deer antlers and tartan stair carpet. 'This place is nice.'

Next to him, Patricia nods. 'Och, it's lovely. I've often wondered what it's like inside here as we drive past.' She glances around, running a hand over the flock pattern on the wall. 'What lovely wallpaper too. Looks brand new, but very classic.'

Neil gives me a nod. 'Oh aye, you did well, choosing this place for Christmas. And enough room for everyone, too.'

I beam at them in gratitude for bringing such positivity. They seem to be in good spirits. It must be nice to break tradition and get a year off from hosting Christmas at their house. 'Yes, although it's a shame Matt couldn't make it, isn't it?'

I gather some of their bags in my arms and lead them away from the coat rack and into the hallway, where Patricia stops walking with a gasp, her whole body rigid.

'Pat?' I place a hand on her shoulder and glance up. 'Oh. Alice.'

Alice is hovering outside the kitchen, her arms wrapped around herself and a frightened expression on her face. But when she sees Ted's parents, she steps forward, a huge smile on her face.

Patricia opens and closes her mouth like she's looking at a ghost.

'Patricia, Neil. This is—'

But I don't need to say any more. Patricia opens her arms and Alice rushes forward, almost lifting Patricia off her feet with the force of her hug.

Then it's Neil's turn, and his big face flushes red as Alice wraps her arms around his solid middle and stands on tiptoes to kiss his ruddy cheek. 'Good to see you, lass. You look well.'

I stand alone, arms full of bags, watching. I've been with Ted for over a decade and I've never had a welcome quite like this. It feels like Alice is their daughter-in-law and I am the unexpected stranger, not the other way around. I want to drop the bags at their feet and walk away, but I don't.

'Wee Al!' Patricia's smile is so wide that her eyes are watering. 'What a surprise. Haven't seen you in far too long.'

'Definitely,' says Alice, stepping back from Neil and putting her hands on her hips. 'Where did Ted go? He was here a second ago.' She looks around the entrance hall with wide eyes, as if lost without him.

'I'm here.' Ted emerges from the kitchen, wiping his hands on a tea towel.

Neil and Patricia corner Alice, asking her questions about her life, her family, everything and anything.

Ted and I stand watching the interaction until Ted turns to me and gently pulls me away from the group. He takes the bags from my arms and sets them down on the ground.

'Thank you,' he mutters in my ear, his breath tickling my skin. He wraps an arm around my shoulders and pulls me closer. He smells of washing powder and wood smoke, a heady combination which makes me want to curl up and fall asleep alongside him immediately, closing the door against this strange day.

This time, I don't pull away. So much has happened, so much confusion and horribleness, that I am grateful for the feeling of his touch on my skin, his nearness to me. He's helping me feel like I belong here, that I'm not the outsider, Alice is. 'Thank you for what?' I ask.

'For coping with all this. I know it's a lot. I can't imagine what it must have been like, my ex-girlfriend showing up like that. If it was one of your ex-boyfriends, I don't know how I would have coped. You've been a trouper.'

I turn to him and look into his blue eyes. One of my favourite things about him has always been his eyes; they sparkle with a fierce energy even when he's tired or sad. 'It's a lot for you to cope with, too.'

'And I didn't deal with it very well. The surprise, I mean. I'm not good with surprises. I shut down, panic. You know.' He lifts one shoulder in a shrug. 'I'm processing it all, slowly. You know me.'

And I do, so I smirk along with him. Ted feels things very deeply, but it takes him a long time to process and react to things. Bad news seems to glance off him at first impact, but it's just sinking in, often for days or weeks. Then when the information finally hits, his emotions are just as deep as anyone's. Combined with his avoidance of confrontation in any form, this makes most tricky interactions a lot more difficult. And time-consuming. There are no fast resolutions in our household, that's for sure. But I've got used to this, over the years, and learned to give him the space he needs, understanding he'll come back when he's ready. And recently, more than ever, it's been important for me to cling to that.

'Let's talk about everything when we can,' I mumble.

He nods, looking up at Neil and Patricia chattering away with Alice. His voice is a low rumble in his chest and I lean closer to hear him. His breath tickles my cheek and I shiver. 'One thing we really need to consider is this Robin guy. Alice and Natasha seemed genuinely terrified when the doorbell rang. He must be a real piece of work.' Ted squares his shoulders as he speaks, as if preparing to confront Alice's ex himself.

I feel the weight of Alice's knife in my pocket, and now I think I understand. It's not a weapon she brought to hurt anyone. It must be protection.

Alice glances up at Ted, as if she can hear what he's saying. But then, in a flash, she's absorbed back into jokes with Ted's parents about old camping trips, bothies and deer herds.

'It's definitely a sensitive subject,' I mutter, going back to Alice and Robin as the other conversation lulls.

Ted pulls a hip flask from his pocket, offering it to me with a shaking hand. I shrug and unscrew the metal cap with unsteady fingers, too. I take a swig, and the warm sweetness slides down my throat.

'Mmmm. Sloe gin. I didn't know you had any?' I ask, handing the flask back to Ted. It's not easy to come by in the city, and I haven't tasted it for years. But the taste always flashes me back to years ago, when Ted and I would go for long walks in the hills and he'd hand me stealthy swigs of sloe gin he'd purloined from his dad's annual hedgerow forage.

Now, he flashes me a smile, sharing the memory. It's a welcome moment of closeness after such upheaval. I belong here. Relief loosens the tightness in my chest. This is my family, my husband, my memories. I open my mouth to bring it up, but Alice is too quick.

'Oh my God, is that your dad's sloe gin? I knew I recognised it. God, no one makes it like Neil. I'm having major flashbacks to our misspent youth.' She nudges Ted and winks at Neil.

Neil's eyes twinkle at the compliment.

I close my eyes to hide my irritation. When I open them, I feel a renewed urgency. We're all hovering in the hallway, socked feet chilled on the slate tiles. Now would be the right time to usher everyone into the living room, encourage them to sit down, offer drinks. But there's something about that which would cement Alice's presence here and I just can't bear to do it, especially not after Neil and Patricia's warm welcome. 'Alice, I just wanted to ask about your plans. You know, we've got more family arriving tomorrow and the house will be full.'

Pat smiles broadly as if she's just heard the best news ever. 'Are you staying for Christmas?' she asks.

'We were actually going to ask you about that,' I say, not looking at Alice. *Screw it*, I think. This is my Christmas, too. 'Alice and her daughter need a lift to the nearest hotel—'

'—on us, of course,' Ted adds to Alice with a small smile.

'—and we're low on petrol. We were going to ask Matt but now that he's cancelled... They've got to get going before the storm gets worse.' I let my words hang in the air as Neil and Patricia exchange a glance.

Finally, Patricia waves a hand, dismissing me like a fly. 'Oh, it's just a bit of wind. Nothing's spoiling. Let's talk about all that later.' She links her arm with Alice's and leads her towards the sitting room, still talking to me over her shoulder. 'We need to have a good catch-up first. I want to hear all your stories,' she says to Alice.

I don't follow. I stand in the hallway listening as Tamara and Charley greet their grandma with excited chatter and introduce Natasha.

I bend slowly and gather a couple of bags of groceries, which thump against my leg as I follow Ted towards the kitchen.

Ted's dad hangs back, throwing me a knowing glance before he picks up the bag of presents. 'She's a good lassie, but I'm sure she's nothing on you, Sadie.'

I watch as he joins the others in the living room, but the momentary warm glow at Neil's words fades quickly. It's the first time anyone's acknowledged that this might be a competition, that Alice is a threat to my marriage and life as I know it.

How scared should I be?

8

In the kitchen, I find Ted already wearing a white chef's apron, peeling Brussels sprouts for tomorrow. He turns as I enter the kitchen and flashes me a smile. 'I worked out how to use the oven.'

I can't help but smile back, despite everything. 'Thank goodness. I was anticipating a raw turkey tomorrow.' I walk over to him and he slips his arms around me.

'It's nice that your mum and dad are here,' I mumble into his chest, and he lets go of me, turning to the sink to wash his hands. I look around at the various cabinets, opening a couple of doors. 'I thought I'd get everyone a sherry.' I try to keep the reluctance and dread from my voice. Bringing everyone drinks feels like an invitation for Alice to stay.

He dries his hands with a tea towel and dumps it on the worktop. 'Great idea.'

I give him a pointed look and pick up the towel, hanging it on the little hook next to the Aga. 'Did you mean it about the hotel? We'll pay for it?'

'You heard what Alice said about hostels and foster care stuff. They're not in a good place. But they can't stay here. This is our Christmas. We needed this break. The last couple of months are just a little speed bump, and I'm not going to jeopardise what we have in order for my parents to revisit some nostalgic memories. I don't know what's going on with that invitation or where it came from, but we can fix this.'

I flinch at the mention of what we've been through, the first time we've had a chance to even touch upon it since we arrived here. A speed bump. I want us to talk about it, that was my plan when we rented this place: the first night after the kids were in bed, curled up together in front of the open fire, the Christmas lights twinkling... we'd talk it all through and come out the other side stronger and closer.

To hear him say 'we can fix this' fills me with relief. We can help them and get rid of them at the same time. They'll be in our lives for ever, but we'll get space to enjoy our Christmas, even with Neil and Patricia's early arrival. It's ideal. I try to look sympathetic and reluctant, like this is a decision I don't want to have to make. 'Thank you. Can you go and talk to your parents? Get things moving? I get the feeling that they—'

'Did Mum and Dad meet Natasha?' he interrupts, a concerned look on his face.

'Yes, they're all in the living...' My voice fades away with the realisation of what this means. Patricia and Neil have just met their granddaughter.

Ted pulls the apron over his head, crumpling it into a ball and stuffing it onto the worktop. He bustles from the room, leaving the kitchen door swinging on its hinges. Before the living room door swings shut, I hear him greeting his parents with a faux-jovial, 'Who wants a sherry?'

I close my eyes for a moment, gather myself and then find the sherry and some glasses, including one for Alice. One for the road.

As I'm stacking everything onto a tray, the kitchen door nudges open and Patricia pokes her head inside. 'Helllooooo?'

she hoots, like she's stepping into my territory. 'Just came to see if you needed a hand. Ted mentioned you're getting some drinks.' She glances around the kitchen, taking in the large island, the high ceilings, the dining table and the large sash window. 'Ooh, isn't it lovely? It'll be a pleasure to cook in here.' She runs her hand over the smooth marble worktop, her engagement ring winking in the spotlights. Her knuckles bulge and the skin on the back of her hands is thin enough that I can see the veins snaking under her skin. But her face looks younger than her hands: years of facials, wide-brimmed hats and expensive skin cream have done her favours.

I make a mental note to book myself in for a facial in the new year. It's not lost on me that Alice and I are almost the same age but she looks at least five years younger. But thinking this way isn't helpful or kind to myself. I am who I am, and that person prioritises fun and living life over aesthetics. And I've always been proud of that. I can't doubt myself now. I shake off the creeping insecurity and pick up the tray, the small glasses clinking together. 'You could grab the sherry bottle if that's OK.'

She gives me a nod and picks it up, admiring the blue glass. 'It's not Christmas without Harvey's Bristol Cream, right, Sadie?'

I smile, even though I don't particularly like sherry; it's Ted's parents' tradition, not mine. But traditions are important, so I drink one with them every year and they have no idea that I think it tastes like lighter fuel.

I turn to the door with the tray of glasses in my arms, but before we head into the living room, she stops me with a hand on my forearm. 'Bit strange for you, is it? Having Alice here.' There's a twinkle of amusement in her eye. If we didn't get on so well, I'd worry she was enjoying this. But perhaps this can be interpreted another way: she's so certain that my relationship with Ted is solid that she doesn't have to worry about what Alice's presence might do.

Can I feel the same way? I think back to witnessing Ted and Alice's kiss, and my acceptance of Ted's explanation that he hadn't had time to pull away. And Alice's excuse that she'd made a mistake. Twenty-four hours ago I would have brushed off any concern about our relationship; strained though it was, Ted and I were going to be OK eventually. But now... I don't know which way is up any more.

The glasses clink again, and I pause, resting the tray on the table by the door. I'm grateful that someone has acknowledged how weird this is for me. 'Strange is a word for it, yes. I keep thinking they'll leave, you know, go to their own family for Christmas Day.'

'Must be strange for Ted, too. You know, he broke up with her once and now she's come back years later like nothing's happened, with a daughter in tow.' She fiddles with the cork in the top of the bottle, loosening it in its socket. She glances up at me, assessing my reaction. Then her expression changes to a sympathetic one. 'Alice's family are long gone from these parts, love. I didn't know her parents. She used to stay with her grandma, but Hilda died a few years ago. As far as I know, she's not got anyone here any more. Except for Ted.'

My stomach burns with acid, and I feel it creep up into my throat. I'm so glad we've offered to pay for their hotel. They've got nowhere to go when they leave here. They have no one... except my husband.

In the living room, Neil is sitting on the big sofa, deep in conversation with Alice. On his other side, Tamara is snuggled into her grandpa's jumper and Charley sits next to her. Their eyes are trained on the TV which is playing *The Snowman* at low volume.

'Ah, Pat. And Sadie. Sherry. Lovely,' Neil booms, as I lay the tray on the coffee table and Patricia begins to pour. Neil's cheeks are flushed red with the heat of the fire. He stands up and moves away from the TV, closer to the coffee table and the sherry.

I hand out the glasses and Ted makes eye contact as I pass him his glass. He looks uncomfortable.

I hand Alice her glass. 'One last drink before you and Natasha head off,' I say, pointedly. They've had their catch-up with Ted's parents, and now it's time for them to go. 'Perhaps, Neil, could you take them...?'

Alice's smile doesn't reach her eyes.

'Are you sure, lovey?' asks Patricia, settling into the armchair. She looks tiny, nestled into its wing back. She's already wearing her fluffy slippers, I notice with an inner smile. Patricia doesn't leave her house without her slippers. 'Perhaps they should stay. The weather's getting worse by the minute.'

I raise my eyebrows. *Just a bit of wind*, she'd said earlier.

I grit my teeth and prepare my argument. The cupboards are crammed full of goodies for days of festivities, the fridge bursting with turkey, vegetables, stuffing for Christmas dinner and then pastry for the inevitable leftovers pie. There's a huge sack of presents ready to be stuffed into stockings while the girls sleep upstairs, desperate to wake up and see if Father Christmas has been. Everything is planned. Everything is perfect. It's so different to the Christmases I had, growing up. So carefully and purposefully different. They can't stay. They just can't.

'Natasha, come and join us,' Patricia calls, gesturing at the space on the seat next to her. 'I want to hear all about you. Who you are, what you like to do? Do you watch videos on the YouTube? Or is it that clock thing now? Tick-tock?' she says, emphasising the second word and sounding frankly like an alien trying to assimilate into the human race. 'I've had a little look myself...'

Neil chuckles and sinks his sherry as Patricia tries to engage

Natasha about the internet. 'Aye, it's nice to see our bonus grandchild again, right enough,' he says.

What? The room goes totally still and silent except for the TV playing to its rapt audience of two in the corner. My head snaps up to look at Neil, who's leaning back in his armchair, a huge grin on his flushed face.

Ted looks up too, his knuckles white around his tiny sherry glass. We stare at each other, eyes wide. Ted swallows and blinks slowly, turning to face his dad.

The grin slides from Neil's face as he realises what he's admitted.

'You've met Natasha?' Ted asks in a quiet voice, too low for the girls to hear. 'You both knew I had a child, when I didn't?'

9

I stand up quickly and gesture for the other adults to follow me out of the room. We can't risk the children hearing: that isn't the way that Natasha should find out who her father is, nor the way Tamara and Charley should learn they have a sister.

In the kitchen, Neil and Patricia perch on stools at the central island, Alice across from them.

I hover by the door, an outsider observing the family rift and ready to gather any of the girls and usher them away if they try to interrupt what is clearly going to be an important conversation.

Ted leans against the rail of the Aga, his arms folded and a dark look on his face. He's glaring at his parents, so it surprises me when he rounds on Alice. 'You contacted my parents?' he hisses at her.

Alice flinches at his tone, a shudder wracking her body. I wonder if it's real, or an act. She must have come here knowing that this might happen, that Ted would find out about Natasha. She couldn't have expected this to stay a secret. In fact, I think she seized the chance to tell him as soon as she could.

Patricia frowns at Ted. 'Watch your temper, Ted,' she says in a tone so sharp that I wonder – not for the first time in our marriage – whether her maternal style might be the reason Ted is so conflict-averse. She's always been sweet to me and a lovely grandmother, but Ted has told stories of her strict, distant and sometimes cold mothering that I have often struggled to reconcile with the Patricia I know. But then, people do say that becoming grandparents can change a person. Maybe the arrival of Tamara and Charley softened Patricia.

I wonder again why Alice really responded to Ted's invitation. If I were her, I would have left it unread, blocked the sender and never looked back. Anyone would have. So why is she here? Is it money she wants? Because we can pay backdated child support if that's it. But deep down I know it won't be as simple as that. If there's a child in the world who belongs to Ted, he'll want to make sure she has what she needs, look after her just like he looks after our girls. This isn't as simple as meeting the long-lost daughter and then saying goodbye. I know that. I've known that all along.

Suddenly, things come into utterly clear focus. No, I think I know exactly what Alice wants, and I think it's been plain since the moment she turned up on the doorstep and pushed me out of the way to get to Ted. That was no accident, and nor was the attempted kiss. She wants my husband. She wants to take my place. The hair on my arms stands on end as I watch her from across the room, gazing at Ted with her eyes wide with unconcealed adoration.

Oblivious, Ted turns to his parents. 'How long have you known?'

Neil crosses to the fridge and pulls out two bottles of beer, offering one to Ted.

Ted just glowers at him until Neil shrugs and takes both for himself, pausing at the drawer to pop the tops.

Patricia leans forward, her elbows on the marble worktop, her fingers laced together, ruby-red nails glinting in the spotlights. 'OK, so, we bumped into Alice in Fort William a couple of months ago. She was up here looking for somewhere to live, I think?'

Alice nods in confirmation. 'Robin was making it difficult for me to leave. I kept trying, but there'd always be something that stopped me or sent me back.'

I nod in recognition. I know the statistic: people in abusive relationships often try to leave up to seven times before they're successful. The story certainly makes sense.

'So I was trying to be careful this time. I had to be, especially if I wanted to take Natasha with me. He was prepared to fight for her, and unlike me, he has a lot of money and connections to do so.' She brushes a hand against her cheek. In the harsh kitchen light, she looks tired, her skin grey. Despite everything, I feel a wave of sympathy for what she's been through. 'I'd heard that councils are more likely to offer housing to people if they're originally from that area, so we came up on the train from Glasgow for the day while Robin was away with work. I thought maybe if the council workers saw Natasha, and saw my face, they'd understand a child was involved in a difficult situation. But like I said, it's hard to find housing up here when it's so rural. They didn't have anything. So we were grabbing something to eat before our train back, and—'

'Saw your face?' I ask, not understanding what she means.

Patricia jumps in. 'And we saw them on the street. We were coming out of WHSmith, weren't we, Neil? Alice had a horrible black eye, and Natasha... well—'

Neil swallows a mouthful of beer and takes over from his wife. 'We knew straight away that she was ours. Just look at her, she's the spit of Ted at that age. All big teeth and gangly legs, right enough.' He chuckles and sips his beer.

Alice leans forward and smiles at Ted's parents. 'It was so

lucky, bumping into you that day. It was a little piece of humanity in a dark time. You helped us so, so much. I don't think I'd be here today if it wasn't for you both.'

'So, what? You all went for tea and cake?' Sarcasm drips from Ted's words. 'Played happy families? Laughed about the secrets you were all keeping from stupid old Ted?'

The room falls silent. Neil puts down his beer bottle with a clunk.

'They came back to our place, yes,' says Patricia, her voice steely as she looks at Ted.

And suddenly, I get a flash of memory.

In my mind, I go back to the early days of our relationship when everything was new, meeting Ted's family for the first time and being astounded at the warmth there. His brother Matt still lived at home back then, and visiting Ted's old childhood home was like being plunged into a warm pool: Patricia was always baking, Neil was always nearby to offer a useful piece of advice, and Matt would bound into a room ready to cause chaos and run out again like a playful puppy. It was so overwhelming; different to the quiet sadness in which I grew up, just me and Mum.

But now that memory is shaded in a new, darker filter, knowing that Alice basked in that warmth before I ever stepped inside, and she was equally welcome just a couple of months ago. I don't matter. If I leave my marriage, someone else could walk right in and take my place. Patricia and Neil would be kind because they always are. And that someone could be Alice. That's what she wants. What she's been working towards for a long time, it seems.

Patricia's still explaining as I tune back in. 'We wanted to get to know them, make sure they'd be OK. What would you have us do, walk straight on past and pretend we didn't recognise her? When she's injured? You'd want us to ignore *your* daughter, *our* grandchild?'

Ted stays silent, watching his mother.

Patricia straightens up, sitting tall on the stool. 'We had no say in what happened between you and Alice all those years ago. We didn't even know it was happening. They were abandoned once, when you left. I'll be damned if we'd perpetuate your actions and make this mess even worse. And if that's what you want then you're not the man I thought you were.'

Neil straightens out his waistcoat, smoothing it over his belly. 'You should have faced up to this at the time, Ted. Been a man. Not done a runner.'

I want to step forward and defend Ted, to tell them that he didn't know about Natasha until today. That he would have told me, sought out a relationship with his daughter. That he'd never leave a child behind without a dad. But something stops me. I feel like such an outsider here. This is about Ted's relationship with his parents, with Alice, and with his daughter. I'm not part of this. And it stings.

Ted's shoulders slump and his arms hang by his sides as he looks between his parents. 'I can't talk about this right now,' he says, finally, shoving his hands into his pockets. 'And I understand you wanting to help Alice, to get to know Natasha. But where was your thought for me? Didn't you think I might want to know that I had a child?' He strides to the door. 'Especially now,' he says, with a glance at me before leaving.

We all sit in silence for a moment, the Aga ticking as it warms the room.

'What did he mean, "especially now"?' Patricia asks me.

I shake my head. I can't even begin to explain, especially not in front of Alice. I won't give her any more information to use to try to break up my marriage.

Alice slides down from her stool, pointing at the door, still swinging on its hinges behind Ted, his footsteps receding as he strides away. 'I'll just—'

'No.' I cross the kitchen before she can get there and interfere more in my marriage. 'I'll go. You help yourselves to some food. And get some for the girls, too. It's getting late.'

I find Ted in our bedroom, lying on our tartan-clad bed and staring at the ceiling. I perch on the edge of the mattress. Ted shifts with my weight but doesn't move, his gaze fixed on a point above his head.

'Talk to me, Ted,' I say, resting a hand on his chest. I can feel his heart beating hard and fast against the palm of my hand.

'Come here,' he says, and I lie down next to him, my head on his chest. Finally, he closes his eyes and starts to speak. 'When Tamara and Charley were born, I looked at their little faces and I loved them so fiercely. I would have loved Alice's baby too, just as much. I probably wasn't ready, but I would have got there if I'd had more of a chance.' He covers his face with his hands and lets out a groan. 'And then earlier this year when you—'

My stomach lurches and I lean away from him, shaking my head. 'Ted, don't.'

This, again. I can't go into it all now, what happened to us a couple of months ago. The whole reason we're here in Red Hart Lodge. I booked this getaway as a desperate attempt to pull our marriage back together: the chilled first night, just the four of us until Matty showed up. Then a lovely family Christmas with the grandparents, and then a couple more close family nights before heading back down the road to Edinburgh, restored.

But then Alice arrived.

I clench my teeth and glare up at the dappled glass panes looking out at the fading light outside, the trees whipping and swirling against the indigo sky.

Ted turns to face me and places a hand on my cheek. 'I

could have been a dad to Natasha, and I wasn't. I didn't get that chance.'

I look at his handsome face and gaze into his glistening eyes. I'm bristling with anger at Alice and his parents, but I understand my husband so much more now.

Alice has taken so much from him. And I know now what she wants next.

10

I wake up early on Christmas morning, startled awake by the wind shaking the house and unable to get back to sleep. It's a mixture of excitement and anxiety: I want to create the perfect day for Charley and Tamara, and to do so I have to get going. I lie awake for a moment in the tartan-clad bedroom, my eyes adjusting to the darkness. Outside the window, through a gap in the curtains, the sky is still lush indigo as the sun doesn't show any sign of rising yet.

The rest of Christmas Eve passed in a blur of tiptoeing around the emotional landmines. Eventually, I managed to persuade Ted to come back downstairs to continue the pretence of a happy family celebration, for the children if nothing else. At some point, it became an unspoken agreement that Alice and Natasha would stay the night, and even though I wanted to push against it once again, with everything that had happened that day I was just too exhausted to have that fight again. We watched films in the light of the fire, the adults occasionally breaking the tense silence to talk about logistics: who needed more wine, where everyone would sleep, and what time to be up in the morning. Ted alternated between staring blankly into space and glaring at his parents, and instead of contributing he drank glass after glass of red wine, at one point accidentally breaking his wine glass because he held it so tightly.

I imagined everyone sat in their own bubble of thoughts: Ted steaming with anger at his parents for keeping Natasha from him; Ted's parents delighted at officially adding a third grandchild to their brood; Alice pleased to be warm and safe, scheming on how to further charm Ted away from his wife; and me processing both the addition of a half-sister for our girls and what this means for my marriage, even if Ted manages to withstand Alice's charms. It was a lot. It was exhausting.

So long as I can keep my marriage, there's also part of me that revels in this new complexity, as I remember my own childhood Christmases. How quiet they were, how lonely. How sad I felt, if I saw through someone else's open curtains into their warm, festive living room, as I compared it to my own echoing existence alone with Mum. Because yes, this year is painful and difficult, but that's what families are: they're messy, they're loud, they hurt. But in the end, you're all there for each other when you come out of the other side. You have to be: you're family. And I've never had that before. I just hope we'll make it through this year intact.

Next to me in the bed, Ted snores softly in that way he does when he's been drinking the night before. He's curled up on his side with the covers pulled up to his shoulders. He stayed up late with Alice, reminiscing and drinking yet another bottle of that Malbec. I hope he's not too hung-over to enjoy the day.

I'm glad of my clear head this morning. I went to bed after we hung up the stockings and laid out the presents under the tree, my plans for a cosy couple's night destroyed by Ted's parents' early arrival and Alice watching me with sneaky eyes.

Ted slunk into bed at around midnight, his breath sour with

wine, pulled me close to him under the covers and whispered, 'I love you, Sadie,' before he turned over, accidentally whacked me in the cheekbone with his elbow and began to snore.

I believe he loves me, I think as I rub my sore cheekbone. *I have to.*

Do I love him? Yes, but I can't look too hard at that question right now.

As the sky lightens towards the horizon, I swing my legs over the side of the bed and pull a dressing gown around myself against the early morning chill. I tiptoe from the room, hearing the metallic clicks of the radiators as heat begins to circulate through the house. I offer up a silent thanks that we have central heating; that our sole source of warmth isn't the Aga in the kitchen, like Ted tells me of his childhood home not far from here.

The kitchen is already warm, and while the kettle boils, I bend to stare at the Aga for a few minutes, trying to understand how it operates. I'm so pleased that Ted worked it out yesterday: I hadn't anticipated cooking a Christmas dinner in an incomprehensible oven. I can't even Google it: I still haven't signed into the Wi-Fi and there's no phone signal except on the stairs. Thank goodness Ted's sharing the load, that he doesn't take after his dad and many other men of that generation who believed that anything home-related was 'women's work'.

My cheekbone is still tender from where Ted accidentally knocked me with his elbow as he turned over in bed last night. We've always joked that he's 'all arms and legs' when he drinks: tripping, knocking things over, spilling. Last night was no exception. He'll be so apologetic when I remind him what happened. I poke at my face, feeling the tender bruise with my fingertips. I can see a red and purple mark reflected back to me in the silver shining surface of the hob lid. It'll fade, and I have make-up to cover it if I need to.

When my coffee is ready, I pick up my mug and head to the living room. It's in darkness, the curtains still closed, and it smells of coal ash from the fire, which glows faintly behind the guard. Tamara and Charley's stockings hang on either side of the mantelpiece, bulging with little gifts. Balanced precariously on top of the mantel is one of Ted's hiking socks, also bulging with a few presents repurposed from the girls, but not nearly as festive. Natasha's feeble Christmas stocking.

I place my coffee on the table next to the empty bottle and two glasses left over from Ted and Alice's late-night chat, and then tug open the heavy curtains to let some light in. The curtain rings scrape loudly on the rail.

Without warning, a dark shape leaps up from the sofa, lunging at me with a shriek like an owl on the hunt.

I stifle a scream, and back away towards the windows. My shoulders press against the damp glass, and I raise my hands to my face to protect myself from my attacker, cowering with my eyes closed.

But the screech dies as quickly as it began, and the room descends into silence once more.

Carefully, I open my eyes and remove my hands.

'Natasha.' My voice is breathy with residual fear.

The girl sits on the sofa, wrapped in a blanket, hunched over, eyes huge in her childlike face. She's shivering, I see now, and I don't know if that's with fear or the early morning chill. I must have startled her when I opened the curtains.

'Sorry if I scared you,' she says, a sad smile on her face as she settles back into the cushions. She looks relaxed for the first time since they arrived, and I wonder if that's the brief absence of Alice from her side, or whether it's the feeling of acceptance that comes from knowing she's got Christmas presents on the mantel, just like the other kids. 'What happened to your face?' she asks, her eyebrows drawn together in concern.

I raise my fingertips to the bruise once more, and realise

what this must look like to Natasha. My body shudders with guilt. 'Oh, no, Natasha. It's nothing. Just a silly accident.' She has witnessed violence at such a young age, of course her first thought when seeing an injury is fear and abuse. I gather my dressing gown around me and slump into the armchair by the fire, my heart still pounding from the fright she gave me, and now embarrassment too. 'Did you not sleep upstairs with Alice? That bed was big enough, wasn't it?' We gave them a lovely bedroom with a king-sized bed and a view out to the hills. The one that Ted's brother Matt would have claimed if he'd managed to get here yesterday.

I lean forward and pick up my coffee, bringing the cup to my lips and blowing on the surface.

'She talks in her sleep.'

I frown, remembering Ted's night-time sobs when we first met. I shake the thoughts away. Coincidence, nothing else. 'Merry Christmas.' I nod towards the fireplace. 'Santa has been,' I say with an ironic smile and a knowing look.

She meets my eye and gives me a mischievous grin, then gives a cursory glance to the Christmas tree, where gifts are piled high in their matching wrapping paper. 'Sure has,' she says, and then her eyes alight on Ted's hiking sock and a look of relief and pleasure crosses her face. 'Merry Christmas to you, too. And thank you' – she gestures around the room – 'for everything. I know it wasn't Santa.'

I kneel at the fire and rustle it with the poker, trying to reignite the flames and bring some heat into the room. 'Go and get some more rest, if you can,' I say, nodding upstairs.

'I think I will.' She pulls the blanket tighter around her shoulders, stands and walks to the window, gazing out across the bleak landscape as the sun begins to creep over the horizon, tinting the sky pink. I watch as she gathers herself and takes a deep breath. Bracing for something. Then she crosses to the door. Her hand on the handle, she turns to look at me where I'm still kneeling by the fire. With a very adult sigh, she adds: 'And I'm sorry. About everything.'

I freeze, almost dropping a log on my toes on its way to the fireplace. *What is she sorry for?* That she and Alice came here to interrupt our celebration? Or something worse, some sick scheme still to come?

11

Alone for the first time since we left home, I decide not to dwell on Natasha's words. I don't have the headspace. She's just a teenager, and I remember those days: everything is so embarrassing that you want to apologise for your own existence, and especially that of your parents. I file it away to examine later, and then I shrug it off, determined not to squander this moment of solitude.

On the sideboard I find that laminated piece of paper containing instructions for the rental: use the fireguard, basement door sticks when it's raining, Wi-Fi password... yes. As I'm inputting the characters into my phone, I hear the distant shrill of the doorbell.

Frowning, I pull my dressing gown tighter around myself and head into the hallway, the tiles cold under my bare feet. I tug the curtain and wrench open the front door, almost blowing off my feet in the process.

On the doorstep is my mum, one hand braced against the doorframe to hold her up against the gale. Her hair whips around her head.

'Hello, you,' she says, warmth in every word.

I pull her inside and into my arms, closing the door behind her.

'Merry Christmas, Mum,' I mumble into her hair, which smells of Pantene shampoo and conditioner, the same she's used since I was a child.

She's a little slice of home in this terrible, unfamiliar world that seems to have emerged in the last twenty-four hours, and finally someone is here who will be a hundred per cent on my side.

She pulls away, a delighted smile on her face as she drops bags of wrapped presents at our feet. 'It's nice to see you, my girl,' she says, not wishing me a Merry Christmas back. She never does. She hates Christmas. But she loves me, and that's why she's here. 'I thought I'd get here early,' she says. 'That storm's going to hit properly this morning. Although it seems like it's already here; I could feel the wind trying to tug my car off the road.'

I pull the curtain closed against the wind and help her off with her coat before leading her into the kitchen and switching on the kettle for a second round of coffee. I need to tell her everything, and for that we need coffee.

'Are you OK?' she asks, a frown crossing her brow. 'You look pale. Has something happened?'

You look pale is what Mum says when she can tell something's wrong. There's no getting away from it; once she's asked that she's like a dog with a bone. Avoiding the question is not an option and I have no wish to today.

Coffee made, I grab a bag of potatoes and start to chop them. I take a breath and start from the beginning, when Alice and Natasha turned up on the doorstep yesterday morning. As I talk, I hack the potatoes into pieces so small that I have to downgrade my plans from roast potatoes to mashed.

Mum joins me at the counter and picks up a peeler, drawing it along the length of a carrot. She listens quietly, peeling so many carrots that we'll have leftovers for days. When I'm done talking, she lays down the peeler and reaches out for my knife to cut the carrots. She lays a hand on my arm. 'What a mess. You poor love.'

I swallow a sob. I rub my nose with the back of my hand. 'What gets me the most is that she doesn't have to do anything. And she just sits there, so smug, not leaving. She's in, she just has to wait it out. She has so much control, and I have none.'

Mum doesn't look up, her gaze trained on the carrot and the knife as she slices. Her hands are so familiar, plumper and younger-looking than Patricia's and yet older versions of my own. She has worn no rings since the day she removed her wedding ring, so many years ago now. 'And where does Ted come in all this? He can't want them here?'

'Mostly he seems angry with Alice. But he also wants to get to know Natasha, which I can understand. I said the same thing. We'll have to get a paternity test, of course. We can't trust Alice's word.' I grab the knife from Mum and start slicing carrots into long skinny batons, channelling my frustration into the blade.

She opens the fridge, looking for something else to prep. 'But you trust him? You two are doing OK?' she asks, flicking me a glance, her eyes dropping to the bruise on my cheek.

I nod half-heartedly. She knows we've been struggling a bit lately, but not all the details. I couldn't bring myself to tell her. I still can't.

I clench my jaw and turn back to the carrots, which are nearly all chopped. Some latent rage does wonders for Christmas dinner progress, apparently.

'Any time you need to talk,' she says in a low voice. 'I need you to know I'm here.'

I flinch with guilt. Mum's been trying to coax things out of me for a while now, and I know she'd love to help. I can tell her this, but the last few months are all too much, too raw. And

Alice's arrival has just made it all bigger and scarier. 'I know. And thank you.'

The kettle starts to bubble again, and Mum picks it up and pours the steaming water into the cafetière, making enough coffee for all the adults as the kitchen clock chimes 8 a.m. 'Well, I'll tell you one thing, my love. I can spot a liar and a cheater from a mile away. I lived with one for long enough. This holiday might not be exactly what we planned, but I'm right here with you.'

She gives my hand a reassuring squeeze. 'If Ted or his ex-girlfriend have anything to hide, we'll rat it out and find out the truth. I'll keep an eye on her. We're all stuck here anyway; nothing better to do except watch and wait.'

12

The rest of the morning passes in a blur of excitement and chaos. Tamara and Charley launch themselves downstairs not long after Mum's arrival, shouting, 'Santa's been! He's been! It's Christmas!' Their excitement reaches new heights when they see their other grandma has arrived, too.

Alice joins soon after, her hair ruffled with sleep and her features softer and even more alluring, despite the hangover she must feel. She's wearing one of Ted's T-shirts and a pair of shorts, I notice with a grimace. Natasha slinks into the living room just behind her, and again I study her face, looking for signs of Ted. But there's nothing I recognise.

Ted's quiet, and doesn't make eye contact with either Natasha or Alice. He looks green, like he's trying not to vomit. I wonder if that's a hangover or a reaction to everything that happened yesterday.

And finally, Ted's parents join us, Patricia looking immaculate and dressed in her Sunday best, her bob perfectly smoothed and pearl earrings glowing in her earlobes. Neil looks just like he's about to go out hiking with his dogs: his bulk is a wall of corduroy and tweed.

Mum's quiet and thoughtful this morning, as she always is at Christmas. As I was, too, until I had children of my own. For many years, Christmas was a reminder of what my dad took from us. The year Dad's many flings and affairs evolved into one single relationship with a woman from work, and his so-called 'late nights at the office' became a note left on the sideboard with his wedding ring on top.

The year I turned twelve, when spoiling his only daughter became annual birthday cards through the post – not in person – because he had other children to think about, now. The year Mum stopped baking gingerbread men and singing along to the carol concert on the radio. The year I ate toast at lunchtime and cereal for dinner. No turkey, no roast potatoes, no mince pies. And every year after that, the same desolate loneliness. Mum didn't want to celebrate. She didn't want to remember.

So as soon as Ted and I had children, Christmas became incredibly important to me: a chance to undo the damage of my childhood and re-establish lost traditions. I never want Tamara and Charley to look through tenement windows at other families and wish themselves inside. I want to make the holiday magical for my kids. Even this year, with all its strangeness.

So today, in an effort to get the train back on the tracks, I prepare our traditional breakfast: pancakes for the kids and smoked salmon on crumpets for the adults, with Buck's Fizz. As usual, Charley and Tamara eat about half a pancake before they're jumping up and down with excitement, begging to open presents. We give up on the dining table and carry our plates through to the living room so we can nibble our breakfasts while we distribute and unwrap. The adults don't mention anything that went on yesterday: an unspoken agreement that this morning is about the children, the magic of their Christmas morning.

The girls tear into their stockings and with each small gift, they look up and thank me and Ted, which fills my heart to bursting. Ted smiles and watches, but I can tell he's miles away, tortured with uncertainty and worry. He taps his foot, his fingers white where they grip the arms of the chair.

Over in the corner of the sofa, huddled under a blanket, Natasha unwraps the repurposed gifts I transferred from Tamara and Charley's stockings late last night. My cheeks burn as she unfolds the fluorescent plastic of a My Little Pony figure, but she strokes the technicolour mane and mouths, 'Thank you', before digging her hand back into the sock to discover what other gifts await. They're small, childish things but she admires each present with a smile and a glance of gratitude.

I find myself wondering again if she understands why they're here. If Alice has clued her in on their goal. How she feels about it.

Next to her, Alice leans against her shoulder, legs tucked up underneath her while she sips her drink. Her hair is dishevelled like she just woke up, and she keeps a half-smile on her face as she watches the festivities. I didn't wrap anything for her. There wasn't time, and I hadn't brought anything appropriate – unless she would have been grateful for an egg full of alien slime. Alice chose this, but Natasha didn't.

While the kids open their presents, I top up the adults' coffee cups and ponder my next step. I know that it's important that Ted gets to know his daughter, but that's not something that can be achieved in one day. He's met her, that's the first step achieved. Now they can leave and we'll resume in the new year.

'I saw your new car as I drove in this morning, Neil. Very swish,' Mum says to Ted's dad as we watch the gift carnage.

Neil flushes with pride. 'It's a new electric Merc. Top of the range. Better than a Tesla. Practically drives itself.'

'Good idea to park on the other side of the river. That bridge...' She shakes her head. 'I got across first thing, but if I'd arrived any later I think my car would have been pulled downstream.'

My heart sinks. After Neil and Patricia refused to give Alice and Natasha a lift yesterday, I'd switched my hopes to Mum. But it sounds like there's no way she's going anywhere. She's always been a nervous driver, and wind and potential flooding will just make that worse.

With raised eyebrows, Neil sets down his empty coffee cup. 'How high is the water, Julie?'

'The river's almost reached the bridge's keystone,' Mum says.

'Aye, it looked a bit dodgy when we got here. It'll get worse, right enough,' says Neil, with foreboding in his voice.

I cross to the window and gaze out at the landscape, which seems even more windswept than before, the shrubs like hunched figures huddling against the wind. The hills in the distance are almost invisible, hidden behind a wall of rain sweeping across the horizon on its way towards us. Closer, the river is swollen, the muddy water rushing fast and high, almost bursting its banks. And sure enough, the water has almost reached the keystone at the centre of the bridge.

Neil's new car sits shiny on the far bank, tucked into the side of the lane and out of the way. It was clever of him to leave it there, so they can get away later today, back home to their dogs who'll need letting out and feeding. Maybe there's still hope that he'll give Alice a lift.

I turn back to the room, steeling myself for the same fight again. 'Alice, you and Natasha really ought to get going before the bridge is totally out of commission. Where do you need to get to?' I hope that Neil will offer to drive them somewhere if they need it, taking the opportunity to show off his new retirement-present-to-himself car. Heck, maybe I could borrow Mum's car and take them. Anything. 'That offer of a hotel is still there,' I add, hearing the tone of desperation in my voice.

But Mum's shaking her head, biting her lip. 'I really don't think anyone should be going anywhere. Not in this weather.' Her eyes widen in a silent apology. She knows how much I want them to leave. She'd take them if she could.

Neil clears his throat. 'I have to agree, Julie.' He raises his sleeve and flashes his Apple watch. 'I've just got a notification: they've upgraded the weather warning to red. Everyone needs to stay put where they are.'

I close my eyes and stifle a silent scream. Another day, all cooped up together, unable to let down my guard. My muscles ache with the tension of watching Alice at every turn, tracking where both she and Ted are in the house. Wondering if she'll try to kiss him again, and if he wants that after all. Maybe he'd kiss her back, now he's had time to think about it. Time to prepare. Now he knows they share a child together. Surely that changes things?

I wanted Alice and Natasha gone. I needed to relax. To enjoy my Christmas.

But I have to keep going regardless, for Tamara and Charley. They need the Christmases I never got.

'What will you and Patricia do about getting home?' I ask Neil, who's clicking away on his watch.

He looks up and shrugs. 'It might calm down in a few hours. I've got the winter tyres and we're not too far along the road.'

I clench my fists in my lap and dare to hope. It's still an option for them to take Alice and Natasha with them, surely? I look down at my ridiculous Christmas jumper: a red-and-white Fair Isle pattern with snowflakes from shoulder to shoulder. I'd bought Ted a matching one, but he hasn't put his on today and I haven't the heart to ask him when he's in such a bad mood.

The stockings demolished, I turn to the tree and hand out presents one by one, watching the piles of goodies building next to my two daughters. I wrapped these gifts, I know what they are, so it's easy to pick out a chocolate selection box and quickly pull off the 'Charley' label so that Natasha can open it. Her cheeks flush with delight and I slip the 'Tamara' selection box out of sight as soon as I can so there are no arguments.

Sure enough, Patricia has bought everyone's presents online. And we all have a good-natured laugh at the burger socks, the luminous bath bombs and the nose hair trimmers. To my surprise, Ted has bought me some lovely diamond earrings, and most of the other adults have given each other alcohol: Highland whisky for Neil, Harvey's Bristol Cream for Patricia, matching seaside botanicals gin for me and Mum, and a Mexican tequila for Ted. We're already slightly tipsy from Buck's Fizz, but we exchange enthusiastic intentions to share and taste each other's gifts as soon as we're done opening presents.

'After all, if you can't be drunk before lunch at Christmas, when can you?' asks Neil with a belly laugh, his face flushed.

I watch Alice from the corner of my eye throughout the gift-giving, keeping tabs on her. She sits quietly, sipping her drink, and I'm grateful she doesn't try to muscle in on anything. She hasn't received anything – which does give me a slight pang of guilt – but she also brought nothing, too, not even for her daughter.

Finally, Charley and Tamara open their 'big' present: Charley gets a lifelike baby doll which drinks milk and cries, and Tamara gets an iPad. They're both ecstatic, Charley bottle-feeding her doll while it makes scarily realistic suckling sounds, and Tamara immediately climbs onto Ted's lap so he can help her set up the iPad.

Over on the other sofa, Natasha is eating a Dairy Milk from her selection box. She has carefully unwrapped it and broken each square off the bar, lining them up along the arm of the sofa so she can pop one into her mouth at a time. The movement of her jaw tells me she's sucking them, letting them melt on her tongue. She's watching Tamara and Charley, her eyes skittering over their gifts one by one. Poor girl.

I glance at Alice, who seems so relaxed she looks like she could almost doze off, her eyelids heavy as she watches the kids with a half-smile. She doesn't seem to have noticed Natasha. I feel a rush of hatred for her. She came here with no gifts for her daughter. How can she watch this and not feel even a pang of guilt? She doesn't seem to care. She's so selfish that I can't muster one ounce of sympathy for her in this moment, just latent rage. *Who is this woman?* I wonder how late she stayed up with Ted. I wonder what they talked about. I wonder what she's planning next.

Suddenly, Natasha slides from the sofa and sidles over to Charley. 'What did you get?' she asks, pointing at Charley's doll. She side-eyes Tamara, still sitting on Ted's knee with the new iPad.

With a small smile, Charley holds her doll out to Natasha, who takes it and cradles it like a real baby, cooing. Despite her mother, Natasha seems to be a genuinely kind person, I think as I watch her.

'What's its name?' she asks Charley, an indulgent smile on her face.

A grin breaks over Charley's face as she thinks of a name.

'Can I help with anything today, Sadie?' Alice asks from her perch on the sofa behind me, stretching out her bare legs and rubbing a hand along her shin.

I bristle, tensing against the sing-song sound of her voice. 'Everything's under control, thanks. Mum and I got started on the prep this morning.' I want to tell her to go and get clothes on, to pack her bag and leave.

Charley reaches out and carefully removes her doll from Natasha's hands, hugging it to her small chest possessively.

Ted stands up, shifting Tamara onto his vacated chair. She

barely looks up from her iPad, which Ted had already loaded with age-appropriate games before we wrapped it.

'And Sadie and I can deal with the rest.' He leaves the room, our parents watching him go. The atmosphere lightens as soon as he disappears, and I see Neil and Patricia exchange a look. They're used to him, used to his moods. They know that this is just something we have to wait out, because confronting him or trying to fix it won't help while he's like this. Once he's decided he's angry or upset, that's how he feels until he's processed it all. No exceptions. No shortcuts.

To an extent I'm used to him, and I know how to deal with his shutdowns to protect my own mental health: pretend it's not happening. So today I'm in full denial mode: this Stepford wife is having The Best Christmas and hasn't noticed that her husband has barely said a word. Food arrives on time, drinks never run empty, the table is laid with crackers by each place setting, the tree glistens, the fire crackles in the grate and the music tinkles away in the background. Luckily, everyone else seems on board with the denial, which means the kids can enjoy their Christmas no matter what. That's the most important part.

I gather the discarded wrapping paper and crumple it into a heap next to the fireplace, and follow Ted from the room, leaving Alice curled up on the sofa looking put out. I flash her a little grin of triumph as I leave the room: Ted and I are presenting a united front, no matter what the reality. *Sadie and I can deal with the rest.*

So Ted and I prepare Christmas dinner together and it's nice to be alone with him in companionable silence. We open a bottle of wine and sip it while we cook together, Christmas tunes on the radio. I flit between rooms, topping up sherry glasses and trying to keep the festive mood going. Ted isn't pleasant to spend time with, but I'm grateful that Alice is giving us space and isn't fawning all over him. Perhaps their late-night drinking session got it out of her system.

I try to talk to him, to bring up how he could get things back on track with his parents, but he just shakes his head. 'Not now. Please.'

I don't push it. I know better.

When we sit down at the dinner table, the adults are all rosy-cheeked from the various drinks I've been providing steadily since we finished breakfast. Happily tipsy, I'd say, congratulating myself on a hosting job well done. While cooking, I decided to embrace the festive spirit and drank nearly an entire bottle of Malbec to myself. Now, everything's pleasantly blurry around the edges and I'm happy to sit back, eat, and observe as everyone else takes part in the social part of the meal.

Tamara and Charley pop crackers with everyone possible until each guest wears a colourful party hat. I watch as everyone helps themselves to food, particularly observing Patricia with amusement as she spoons a tiny portion of stuffing onto her plate, which is dotted with tiny amounts of everything, none of them touching each other.

As we enjoy the food, Neil clears his throat. His wine glass is empty again, and I reach forward to top up his Malbec. We've done some damage to that box of wine bottles over the past day and a half.

'Such an excellent spread, thank you, Sadie,' he says. His waistcoat buttons strain against his stomach.

I smile and wipe the side of the bottle with a napkin where a droplet of wine trickles down the neck, staining the label purple. 'Ted did most of it,' I say, leaning towards Ted so my shoulder brushes his. 'We'd have been lost without him knowing how to cook on the Aga.'

Neil ignores that and shoves a forkful of stuffing in his mouth.

'That's nice, isn't it?' Mum says, trying to offset some of the tension, which has come rushing back now that we're all facing each other around a table, the conversation slowed by the food.

'That Sadie and Ted share the domestic duties like that. It's not every man who'll help his wife with Christmas dinner. And there's nothing that says it's all the women's responsibility, is there, Ted?'

I flash her a grateful smile.

Neil lets out a cruel laugh. 'Yes, it's good that he's stepping up now. Better late than never.'

Everyone freezes, listening. Mum's hand, holding her wine glass, hangs suspended halfway to her mouth, her lips half-open ready to drink. Slowly, she lowers the glass.

Patricia puts a warning hand on Neil's arm, but the damage is done. Although we had the confrontation last night in the kitchen, it feels different and more serious now, with my mum there as an additional witness and the children seated at the far end of the table. We'd had an unspoken agreement to push this to the side for today, and Neil just undid everything.

I grit my teeth and close my eyes in disappointment. I brace for impact, and the tipsiness I felt at the start of dinner disappears as if I've drunk nothing all day. All the effort I went through to keep everything together today, to paper over the cracks, and with one throwaway line from my father-in-law, all my efforts are undone. I pick up my wine glass and take a gulp.

Next to me, I can feel Ted seething with rage. 'That's enough,' he hisses. 'Whatever you've got to say, just say it. Clearly you have an issue with something I've done, and I'm damned if I'm going to put up with these pathetic little comments about my need to "step up" and "be a man".'

I chew and swallow a mouthful of sprout and glance down to the end of the table at Tamara, Charley and Natasha. They're not listening, absorbed in the little trinkets that came in their crackers, thank goodness.

'All right. Fine. I'll say it.' Neil drains his wine glass again and wipes his mouth on a napkin. 'You knew Alice was pregnant. And you got on that plane anyway. You walked out on your responsibilities. This is your second chance, son. And I just hope you're a better man now than you were then.'

Ted puts down his knife and fork with a clatter. 'Better than a man who walks out and leaves a baby behind, is that what you mean? Is that what you're saying?'

'Neil,' I say, clearing my throat. 'Ted didn't know about...' I lower my voice. 'About the baby.'

'I'm sorry, Sadie,' Patricia joins in, leaning towards Neil in a show of solidarity. Her party hat slips slightly over her eye and she reaches up to pat it back into place.

I freeze, bracing myself for whatever she's going to say next. *Why would she bring me into this?*

'I don't know what Ted's told you but that's just not true. He knew. And he left. He's our son, and we had to support him and love him, but it doesn't mean we agreed with his actions. So when we bumped into Alice and Natasha, we thought... now's our chance to make amends.'

My dinner turns to stone in my stomach. I think back to yesterday's conversation about this, and when I asked Ted if he'd known, I realise now that he didn't answer. 'I don't understand. Alice said—'

'Alice told us all about it a couple of months ago.' Patricia reaches out and pats Alice's hand. 'Ted knew about the baby. But he left to go on the trip anyway.'

Alice looks up from her plate, her eyes glittering with triumph. This is the drama she wanted to cause, I realise. She came here for destruction; probably a seed planted months ago when she met Ted's parents again. Destruction of a family. My family. That's what she wants. So she can swoop in and pick up the pieces. I marvel at her skill: she just had to show up and line a few things up and everyone else has done the damage for her.

There's a kernel of dread deep in my stomach because the way Ted's reacting implies that even though Alice has been planning this, Ted gave her the ammunition all those years ago.

'Enough.' Ted stands up and throws his napkin onto the table. 'I don't have to listen to this. Mum and Dad, this is absolutely none of your business.' He pushes his chair back and opens the dining-room door. I think he's about to step through it, but then he turns back to the room, his hands balled into fists and his voice scarily quiet and calm. 'This is a discussion for Alice and me. And Sadie,' he adds, as an afterthought. 'Perhaps you felt like you were doing good when you invited Alice into your home and gave her some money. I know it was important to you to get to know Natasha. But you were meddling and interfering in something you know nothing about. And now you've come here to... what? To scold me for my behaviour fifteen years ago without even asking me my perspective? Screw that.'

He holds the door open wider and waves an arm through it, into the hallway. 'I'd like it if you both could leave, please. You need to get home to your dogs before the weather gets worse, anyway, and God knows I need some space from you both right now.'

Ted's parents mumble their protests but stand up from the table.

'What about the red warning?' Mum asks quietly. 'Surely you should stay—'

Neil waves a hand. 'I can't explain a red warning to a pack of spaniels, Julie. They need their dinner. Besides, it's only a quick drive. That's why I parked the car on the other side of the bridge.' I'm impressed at his ability to pretend that leaving is his decision.

Patricia lays her napkin neatly by her plate. This kind of confrontation is unheard of in their family, and it seems like they're both shocked into submission.

'Thank you for a lovely Christmas,' Patricia says to me in a tense voice, with just a quick glance at Ted. 'We'll see you soon.'

At the other end of the table, Tamara and Charley realise

their grandparents are leaving and start to whine. They rush to Patricia and Neil, clinging to them like baby koalas. Natasha is quiet, staring at her plate. I wonder how much she heard, how much she understood. I feel a surge of protective guilt in my chest. That poor girl.

They scoop up the girls and kiss their cheeks, and Natasha even allows them to give her a brief, stiff hug.

In all the bustle and awkwardness, I can't find a way to ask if Neil and Patricia could consider taking Alice and Natasha with them. There's so much going on, so much drama and chaos, that there's no space for that suggestion. And if I even managed to bring it up, I'd just get accused of insensitivity to the situation. How could I cast Alice and Natasha out into the storm when I've just learned the truth about their abandonment by my own husband? I can hear the shrill disgust in Patricia's words without even broaching it.

I watch aghast as Ted sees them out, the wind blowing through the house as he opens the door to the storm. Even from the dining room, I can hear the ferocity of the wind and a rumble of thunder in the distance. The air calms as soon as the storm is locked out once again, and the heavy curtain is pulled across to keep out the draughts.

I stand and look out of the window. The rain is thick, like a grey curtain blocking out the light. The driveway is pitted with puddles, which roil under giant raindrops. I watch Neil gently guiding Patricia, their hooded and hunched forms buckled against the wind. In the distance, the river is even higher than before, and the bridge is almost submerged by the water. They'll be able to cross it on foot, but after that, everyone here will be stuck, at least until tomorrow.

As if on cue, the lights flicker and we're plunged into darkness.

And a blood-curdling scream breaks the silence.

13

Ted rushes back into the room, silhouetted in the doorway. It's not dark outside yet, but the storm has plunged everything into a dusky half-light. 'What's going on? Is everyone OK?'

Suddenly, Tamara rushes into my arms, sobbing and whimpering. 'My iPad is gone.'

I stroke her hair and reassure her that no one would have stolen her iPad, and hand her off to Ted as soon as he steps towards us, his arms open for her. She's always been a Daddy's girl, getting her comfort from him more than me. I feel a rush of gratitude that he'll always protect his children. No matter what happens with our marriage, he's still their dad. He'll be there for them. History will not repeat itself.

'Everyone stay here,' I mutter, turning on my phone torch and inching my way back to the kitchen. The milky beam from my phone lights my way through the dark hallway where the door rattles against its hinges.

I need to get the truth out of Ted at some point, but it's been fourteen years since this happened. More time won't make any difference, even if I feel like it's urgent to understand why he would abandon his baby. *Put it in a box, Sadie. Seal the lid. Bring it out later.*

In the kitchen, the Aga's still running, and I whisper a quiet 'thank you' to the universe that this lodge has its own independent gas supply so we can stay warm no matter how long the power is out. It would be so miserable here with only the fire for warmth, although I suppose that's how people used to live up here in the Highlands, and not that long ago either. My grandma was born in a two-room stone croft with a heather-thatched roof up near Gairloch. She talked about it a lot, especially as she got older and her recent memories began to fail. She told stories of fish-oil lamps, the stinky peat fire, and bedsheets made of old cotton sacks. I shudder to think about it.

With fondness I think about our little insulated mid-terraced house back in Edinburgh, with its wall-to-wall carpets, combi boiler and a radiator in every room. Sure, it's poky and cluttered, but it's warm and there's a shop on the corner if we run out of milk. For the first time since we arrived, I understand why Ted dislikes returning to this area, with its remote stark beauty and bone-chilling cold. There's something dangerous about this place, especially cut off by a storm like this.

I open the cupboard under the sink and find a torch and some candles, lining them up on the worktop.

The door swings open and Mum shuffles in, carrying a tray of empty wine glasses. 'Well that was eventful,' she says, a ghost of a smile playing on her lips. For her, like me, the drama of a large family is new and holds a certain charm, especially for Mum being so removed from it all. For me it's a little more raw, but I see what she's feeling and I understand it. *At least we're not alone*, she's thinking. *Not any more.* 'What do you think of it all?' she asks, her voice full of concern.

I pause. 'I've no idea. I'm going to talk to Ted, in private, when it's all calmed down. But what I do know is that I don't trust Alice.'

Mum nods, unloading the glasses by the sink and replacing them on the tray with a couple of candlesticks and the box of matches. 'Can we be sure Natasha is even Ted's child? Alice might have lied.'

I freeze, contemplating the idea once again as the jigsaw pieces fall into new positions in my mind. My daughters wouldn't have their bonus sibling. But our connection to Alice would be severed and we'd never have to see her again. It was beginning to feel like we'd be stuck with her for ever.

I shake my head and let out an almost hysterical giggle. 'I can't even process that possibility right now. Thanks for that.' My laughter is an inappropriate reaction but I've reached the end of my ability to think about any of this, to understand Alice and what she wants. So I do the only thing I can do, the only right thing: focus on the children. I slip a torch into my pocket, grab the tray and lift it into my arms, nodding at the door. 'Let's go find this iPad before Tamara freaks out even more.'

We search the whole house, the adults armed with torches and the children following behind. I try to make it fun, especially with the power cut: a treasure hunt in the dark. We open the drawers in the leather-topped desk, rifling through old account books and letter sets. We try the locked door to the attic and peek under all the beds, the torch beam landing on only dust. But after a breathless and giggly rush around the house, there's still no tablet.

Back in the living room, Tamara's lip is quivering and her eyes shine in the reflected lights of the candles we've placed around the room.

I put a hand on her skinny shoulder and squeeze. 'We'll find it, Tam. As soon as the lights come on, I bet it'll turn up.'

I look up at Ted and raise my eyebrows. Through the whole making-a-game-of-it search there's been the unsaid thing hanging in the air: who took it? And why? And I can think of two possible culprits without much effort. What kind of person steals a child's Christmas present? Someone desperate, the angel on my shoulder would say. Someone heartless, cruel and self-serving, my other side screeches, as I look up at Alice where she's curled up into the corner of the sofa, a replenished champagne flute in her hand.

Ted won't meet my eyes. I know what he would say. *We can't accuse them. Someone must have moved it by accident.* I try to catch his eye again but he resolutely won't look my way. I lean forward and pick up an armful of wrapping paper, wadding it up and throwing it onto the fire. 'Talk to Alice about the iPad, please,' I hiss over my shoulder to Ted, my voice hidden by the crackling of the flames as they catch on the paper. If I have to search their bags before they leave, I will.

Tamara reaches a hand up to her cheek and subtly wipes away a tear. She sniffs and then gives me a watery smile. I feel a pang of guilt and I close my eyes to silently hope we find her present, and soon. It should be in the house somewhere. Even if it's been moved.

I stand up and clap my hands with feigned glee. 'I know. Let's play a game. Tamara, you can pick.'

She stands up straighter, excited by the responsibility. She crosses to the sideboard and opens a drawer, pulling out a pad of Post-its and a pen. 'I want to play the name game!' She runs over and hands the paper and pen to me.

'Perfect.'

Tamara distributes Post-it notes to everyone and they pass the pen around, taking it in turns to scrawl a name on the paper and stick it to the forehead of the person to their right. The room is eerily silent as everyone thinks of a name, and I can hear the rattle of the windows in their frames, buffeted by the wind. The candles shiver in the draughts that sneak their way under the door and around the windows.

In the moment of quiet while we get set up, I allow my thoughts to stray to what was revealed over dinner: Ted left

Alice behind, knowing she was pregnant. I fall into a daze, considering what this means about my husband.

Did he know? Is it possible that my husband knowingly abandoned his pregnant girlfriend? And if that's the case, who am I married to? I wonder if he's the same person now; if he'd leave me if I became somehow inconvenient to his plans. My mind skips ahead decades in my marriage, to old age, illness and death. Or sooner, an accident that renders me in need of care. Is he the type of man to leave, 'in sickness and in health' be damned?

I've spent this whole holiday intentionally trusting Ted, giving him the benefit of the doubt and relying on over a decade of marriage to keep me bolstered through this storm. But at some point, there has to be a limit. I can't be taken for a fool. Is this the limit? Where *is* my limit?

Ted tries to catch my eye, but I can't look at him. I can't think about what I just learned, what it means about my husband. I cross to the window and look out, trying to spot if Patricia and Neil reached their car unscathed, but surely they're long gone and the daylight has faded rapidly. It's almost pitch-black outside now. I think I can see the faint red glow of their tail lights in the distance but it's too stormy to tell if it's my eyes playing tricks.

I pull the curtains closed and turn back to the room, taking in the names with a smile: Alice is Thomas the Tank Engine, Mum is Barbie, Ted is Hannah Montana, Natasha is Wednesday Addams, and Charley is Ariel from *The Little Mermaid*. Ted pulls Tamara towards him, wrapping a protective arm around her shoulders. She sinks into him, visibly comforted even though we have no answers for her.

Natasha sticks a Post-it to Tamara's head: Kim Kardashian. I splutter and then quickly swallow my amusement. 'Natasha, I don't think she...' I pause, taking in Natasha's face. She's half-smiling, and I don't have the heart to make her change it to something easier for an eight-year-old. I sit down on the sofa, and Charley rushes over and slaps a Post-it on my head. I take a breath. 'You know what? It's OK. Good choices, everyone.'

We go around the circle asking questions and answering with 'yes' or 'no', until we get to Charley.

'Your turn, love.'

'I'm thinking,' she states, authoritatively, hands on her hips. 'Quiet, please, everyone. I need my space.' She stamps her foot on the rug.

Everyone obeys, sitting quietly and glancing at each other's Post-its, sharing smiles. Ted and I glance at each other, amused by her seriousness and – as always – connecting about the joy of our kids over everything else.

Charley takes a breath, ready to ask her question, when there's a loud electronic noise, like a computerised gong.

'What was that?' Ted asks.

'Sounded like a phone,' says Alice. She shrugs.

'Not a noise my phone has made before.' Ted pulls his phone from his pocket. 'Mine's on silent. No signal anyway. Sadie? Julie?'

Mum shrugs and I check my phone too, but the battery is full and it's flashing 'emergency use only' and on silent.

'My iPad!' shrieks Tamara, leaping to her feet and pulling all the cushions off the armchair.

From her seat on the floor with her back leaning against the sofa, Natasha shifts, wrapping her arms around her legs. Her cheeks are red, I notice. I look at her closer, but she doesn't meet my eyes.

Charley stamps an impatient foot again. 'It's my turn. I want to ask a question.'

I put out a soothing hand and lay it on her shoulder. 'Wait a moment, love. I think we might have just solved the treasure hunt. Everybody, I think Tamara's tablet is in this room!'

Charley and Tamara both jump from their seats, pulling

blankets from the sofa and whipping back the curtains. Natasha doesn't move, and I see Alice looking at her, a question in her eyes.

Suddenly, Alice reaches out and grabs Natasha's arm, pulling her up from her seat on the floor. For the first time, Alice's face doesn't look angelic and beautiful – a harsh grimace curls her lip and blemishes her features.

'It's here, isn't it?' she hisses, and reaches under the sofa where Natasha had been sitting. She slides her hand flat along the carpet until I see her fingers catch on something. When she removes her hand, she holds up the iPad, stripped of its wrappings and its box. 'What were you doing?'

The box is gone, along with all the padding we'd intended to keep to protect the iPad on its journey home. 'Where's the rest?' I ask, but Alice waves me away, tapping on the screen.

I hold out a hand. 'Can I just—'

But Alice moves it out of my reach. I open and close my mouth. I can't even protest, I'm so surprised.

What is she doing? This isn't some childish game, this is theft, and Tamara needs her present back.

Tamara and Charley hear the kerfuffle and rush over, clamouring to get hold of the iPad, too.

'Alice, I really would like to check it over and make sure it's fine. It's Tamara's Christmas pr—'

But Alice ignores me, her eyes trained on the iPad screen. She turns away, flapping a hand at me like I'm an annoying fruit fly. Something is open on the screen – a messaging app, I think.

I lean forward, but she flicks me a look of such intensity that I pause.

She raises her head slowly to look at Natasha, and even in the candlelight I can see the colour drain from her face and her pupils dilate. 'Natasha,' she whispers, shaking her head. 'What have you done?'

The room is heavy with quiet. Tamara and Charley take a

step backwards away from Alice, as if instinctively they can tell something's wrong.

Natasha stands up and moves away, huddling up in the armchair as far away from Alice as she can get without leaving the room. There's an odd look on her face, one of guilt combined with shame. Her cheeks are flushed red.

Alice lowers her arm and stares at Natasha, eyes wide open. She doesn't look angry, I realise. She looks terrified. Her mouth opens and shuts a couple of times, her lips quivering, her breath coming in little gasps.

'You told him where we are. He's coming for us.'

14

The lights sputter and suddenly the room is bathed in a warm light as the power returns. Every light in the room comes to life: the lamps, the sconces and the overhead light are almost blinding. Everyone takes a collective sigh of relief. Mum stands up and switches off the overhead light, which someone must have switched on by accident while we were roaming the house in darkness.

But as if jolted by an electric shock, Alice stands up and rushes towards the door, still holding the iPad.

'Where are you going?' shouts Natasha from her curled-up position in the armchair, her voice quavering with uncertainty. Her cheeks are still flushed red from embarrassment.

Ted and I glance at each other, baffled. What could Alice have possibly seen on the iPad to make her react like that? *You told him where we are. He's coming for us.*

I shudder at the threat embedded in those words. Who's coming? And is he coming here? What could he want? I think of the darkness outside, the punishing wind, the driving rain, the rising river and the tiny bridge. Surely no one would be coming here in this weather. I just pray we're safe.

'Here.' Alice turns back and presses the iPad into my hands. 'You'll want to reset it or whatever.'

Tamara claps her hands with glee and reaches out for the iPad, but I hold out a hand to stop her. 'Just a minute, please,' I say quietly, not looking away from Alice, as she rushes out of the door.

Natasha follows closely behind, wailing, 'What are you going to do?'

The living room door slams behind them.

Shocked into silence, Mum, Ted, the kids and I sit quietly, listening. The girls have retreated, huddled up next to Ted, watching with wary eyes. Mum flashes me a knowing smile and leans forward to grab a glass of wine from the coffee table. She takes a sip, her eyes twinkling. I know what she's thinking: this is karma. Alice came to inflict chaos but the tables have turned back on her. I just hope she's right.

We can hear Alice and Natasha in the hallway, the rustle of movement as they pace.

Alice's voice filters through the closed door. 'I'm going to grab our stuff. We have to leave.'

I sit up straighter, tilting my head to hear better. My heart beats faster in my chest at the thought of them leaving. But the weather, and the darkness... I can't let myself hope.

'But why?' Natasha replies, her voice a juvenile whine. 'If he's coming, he can be here with us. For Christmas. There's still time. Don't you—'

Alice's voice gets shrill and she almost shrieks her reply. 'If he's on his way, he could be here any minute. I saw the time-stamp on that message. Hours ago. And when he gets here, we will be gone. OK? Gone.'

Natasha's reply is a squeak I can't interpret, but Alice continues shouting loud enough for everyone to hear clearly: 'Do you think when he gets here he's just going to want to sit down and have a happy little drink with everyone and play pass the goddamn parcel? No. He's not coming here to be with you. He's coming here for revenge.'

I swallow the spit pooling in my mouth. *Revenge*. What does that mean? Suddenly there's no glimmer of hope. Now I'm beginning to feel scared.

'What's happening?' Tamara asks, her bottom lip quivering in fear.

Ted pulls her closer and whispers comforting words in her ear before standing up and crossing to the window, staring out into the darkness.

Mum switches on the TV and finds a kids' film, cranking up the volume. She gathers Tamara and Charley on either side, sitting them on the sofa. She kisses their heads and whispers to them, making sure they're focused on her and can't hear the argument in the hallway.

My stomach twists in sympathy for Natasha. What must it be like for your mother to drag you into a stranger's home at Christmas time? To watch other children open their presents while you have none? To watch your mother attempt to seduce a married man? I wonder if Alice has shared with Natasha what she wants and why they're here. What does the girl know?

I glance down at the iPad in my hands and sure enough, timestamped a couple of hours ago – just as everyone rose to move to the dining room for dinner – there's a Facebook message from Natasha to someone named Robin Kaufman:

Dad, sorry about everything. We love you and we want to be with you for Xmas. Come get us: we're at Red Hart Lodge, some creepy old hunting house with stag skeletons over the walls. It's in the Highlands, nr Fort William. Google it and come, OK?

The profile picture shows a smiling man with a shaved

head, with the slightly squashed broken nose of a rugby player or boxer.

I look up and see Ted still staring out of the window, his hands cupped on either side of his face.

'What's it looking like?'

He swallows, his Adam's apple bobbing up then down. 'I can't see the bridge. But they don't have a hope. The trees are swaying like crazy and the electricity lines look lopsided; I think a pole might have gone over somewhere close.' He pulls his phone from his pocket and opens it to the local news. 'This says the A82 is closed both ways because of debris. There's been a landslide a few miles away. They're not getting anywhere.'

I hold out the iPad to Ted with a feeling of relief in my chest. 'Then I guess this guy isn't getting here either.'

He takes a look. 'Unless he got through before they closed the road.'

The door swings open and Alice and Natasha stand in the doorway, backpacks slung over their shoulders, coats zipped up to their necks. Alice's forehead glistens with a light sheen of sweat, like someone with the flu. She looks wired, her pupils huge and her eyes darting around the room.

Natasha stands next to her, her expression alternating between fear and defiance, like she doesn't know whether to be an adult or a teenager.

Alice shifts from foot to foot, swapping her bag to her other shoulder. 'We'll get going. Thanks for everything. Really. You're all lifesavers.' She speaks quickly, her words clipped with panic.

She steps forward to hug Ted, but stops short when he shakes his head.

I can't believe I'm saying this but I have to speak. 'You can't leave, Alice. The roads are closed and the weather is dire.'

She clenches her fists, bringing them to her forehead, and steps back from him as if afraid he's going to restrain her. 'You don't understand, we can't stay here. We can't let him find us.'

Ted steps forward and puts his hands on her shoulders. I see her body sink into itself under the weight of his hands. He looks deep into her eyes. 'I do understand, Al. But if you leave, you'll both die out there. It's a red warning for a reason: it means if you go out there's danger to life.'

'There's a danger to life if we stay here, Ted.' She turns to Natasha, whose backpack has slipped off her shoulder and is dangling from her hand by her side. 'What were you thinking, telling him where we are?' Alice asks.

Natasha shrugs and looks up at the ceiling with a sigh. But it's bravado; I can see the twinkle of unshed tears in her eyes.

Alice steps forward and grabs Natasha's coat in a balled fist. Her face is blotchy, mottled red and white. For the first time since she arrived, Alice doesn't look beautiful. She looks haunted. 'You know what he's capable of. You know what happened with him.'

Natasha drops her backpack to the floor and wrenches her coat off, leaving it still balled in Alice's fist. The girl's face crumples as she folds her arms around her skinny frame. 'He's my *dad*. Or I thought he was, before you told me everything the other day. Of course I wanted him with us for Christmas.' Her voice is high-pitched and a tear rolls down her cheek. 'Just because you don't love him any more doesn't mean I don't. He needs our help, not for us to just abandon him, Mum.'

Alice's mouth turns down at the corners like she's trying not to cry, too. She holds out the coat to Natasha, willing her to put it back on. When Natasha doesn't move she looks at Ted, her eyes pleading. 'I need you to understand. Robin's not a good man. And he could be here any minute. Better that we're not here and you can just say you have no idea who we are. That you've never seen us before. Then you'll be safe. He won't hurt you if he thinks we're not here. And we will be long gone. Safe, from him.' Her breathing is ragged and wild.

Ted pulls her into his arms. Natasha's coat drops to the floor.

I know Ted's using similar tactics to those he uses when he's trying to calm our kids down from a tantrum: hold them tight, pull them close, let them breathe, give them a moment. It stings for a second. But I've never seen an adult this afraid outside of actors in horror films. What I'm seeing in Alice is pure, animal fear. No one could fake this. I might not believe a lot of what she's told us over the past twenty-four hours, but I believe her that this man is dangerous. And I believe that he's on his way here: if she knows him and knows what he's capable of, they are in danger. *We are in danger too.* I let that thought sink in.

I close my eyes in frustration and resignation. If Alice and her daughter had never come here, we wouldn't be in this situation. I wish I could just send them out into the storm and never see them again. But that would be inhuman.

'Look,' I say, clearing my throat.

Alice looks up and steps away from Ted, wiping a hand across her cheek and taking a shaky breath.

'The bridge is washed out. No cars can cross it. It was pretty much blocked when Ted's parents left, so it'll definitely be gone now. He can't get here. We're safe. You're safe.'

She gives a small nod, but crosses to the window as if to verify what I'm saying. She pulls back the curtain and cups her hands to the dark window. Moments later, she steps back and her body language is different: resigned. Like a prisoner walking to the gallows. 'You're right. The weather's too wild. We can't go out there.' She looks at Natasha. 'We have to take our chances staying here.'

Tamara glances up from the TV. 'We know lots of places to hide, don't we, Natasha?'

The adults exchange amused glances, but there's an undercurrent of uncertainty behind the smiles. We're afraid it might come to that.

Alice removes her coat and we all try to settle back into a game, but the mood has been punctured. Natasha won't look at her mum, and Alice takes ragged breaths, her hands clasped to stop their shaking.

Only Tamara still has her Post-it on her forehead, Kim Kardashian's name smudged to nothing. Alice keeps standing up and pacing, crossing to the window and pulling open the curtains to stare out into the darkness.

Ted glances over and gives me a reassuring half-smile. I can't smile back. All my plans for the perfect Christmas are gone. It's over, replaced by danger and fear. There's no coming back from this.

I look around the room, at the dark wood-panelled walls and the leather-bound books on the shelves flanking the fireplace. At the mounted antlers and the watercolour paintings of the same hills that surround the lodge right now, looming over us in the dark. I begin to feel like I've got cabin fever, like the walls are closing in. It's a big house, with lots of rooms, yet we're all crammed into one, with Alice treading the boundaries like a tiger in a cage.

What are we waiting for? Why aren't we doing anything to protect ourselves, if this Robin guy is so dangerous? Sure, it's unlikely that he'll make it here in this weather, but if he does then we're all trapped. There's no way out, no way to go for help. We're stuck. Sitting ducks, just waiting. I can't stand it.

I get to my feet and cross to the dresser on the far side of the room, picking up the handset of the landline phone, a black old Bakelite with a rotary dial and a curly cord, probably from the sixties. With a rush of relief, I hear the dial tone. The lines are still up; the phones still working. Even if we lose power again and the Wi-Fi shuts down, leaving our mobile phones useless, we can still make outgoing calls.

'What are you doing?' Alice turns back from her lookout at the window, her voice sharp.

'The phone lines are working.' I flip through the information sheet Alice looked at yesterday: fireguard, basement door, Wi-Fi password... bingo. There's a section entitled 'Useful Contacts'. I start to dial, pushing the tip of my index finger into one of the holes and twirling it around to the stopper and back, the memory resurfacing quick as a flash. If you'd asked me two days ago how to dial on an old rotary phone, I'd have told you I had no idea. But it turns out it was buried deep in my memories, reignited as soon as my finger found the first number.

Alice crosses the room to stand by my side, looming at my shoulder. 'Who are you calling?'

I dial the final number and it starts to ring. One ring. Two.

She leans against me, trying to see the information sheet over my shoulder to find out what number I dialled. 'Sadie, please.' She's so close I can smell her fear: the tang of sweat mixed with something else, something more animal.

Three rings. Four.

She puts a hand on my shoulder and I flinch away. I don't want her to touch me. 'The local police station. If this guy's on his way here and he's as dangerous as you say, we'll need help. Authorities.'

Five rings.

She rips the phone from my hand and slams the receiver down hard back onto the body of the phone. Behind her panting breaths, I hear the resonating *ding* of the jostled bell inside the old phone. She's panting hard, staring at me with wild eyes. I'm frozen with shock and fear.

'Alice, what—' Ted stands up and steps towards us.

I don't move, my hand still raised to my ear where I held the phone moments before. I wonder which one of us Ted intends to help. Logically, I assume he's approaching to protect me from Alice, from her sudden movements and erratic behaviour. But part of me also wonders whether his loyalties are shifting; whether his instincts are now to protect her from *me*, as she's the one who seems so helpless right now, so afraid. So beautiful and fragile. So unlike me and my self-sufficient solidity. My whole understanding of the world and how things should be has turned on its head.

Alice grabs the whole phone, tucking it under one arm and following the cable to where it's plugged into the wall. She crouches down and pulls it out of its socket, winding the cable around the phone.

Her eyes are wide, her hair sticking up. She looks like a wild creature, cornered and afraid, with a threat of violence if approached. 'No police.'

Ted crosses the room to Alice and gently removes the phone from her hands, placing it back on the dresser.

She shoves her hands in her pockets to quell their shaking. 'No police,' she repeats again, louder.

Ted wraps an arm around her shoulders and leads her to the sofa.

I look away. He's just being himself: a kind man who wants to care for others. But I want him to distrust her as much as I do, to see all the badness I see as she sniffs back fake tears and nestles into his shoulder. Or is he trying to make amends for abandoning her all those years ago? Perhaps what I have misconstrued as attraction and nostalgia from Ted was actually shame and guilt at how he treated her.

I can't stand it. I need to know. Everything. We all deserve to know what we're dealing with. 'What's happened, Alice?' I ask. 'Why can't we call the police?'

15

Satisfied our girls are engrossed in the film, Mum slips away from them and comes to join the adults and Natasha where they're clustered around the other sofa. 'You have to tell us everything, Alice,' she says. 'It's time. There are kids to think about here.' Mum's tone is kind but her eyes steely.

Ted and I exchange a surprised look. All day, Mum has been very quiet about Alice and Natasha's presence here, except for our conversation in the kitchen when she first arrived. But now, she reaches out and places a hand on Alice's knee. I wonder if she's genuinely sympathetic, or if, like me, her kindness is an attempt to tease out information.

For so long I've seen Mum as a fragile, damaged person: the ghost of who she was before Dad left. I've spent years thinking of her solely as the person who was cheated on, lied to, and disrespected, who then instead of blossoming after he left retreated even further into silence, as if she let him continue to damage her even after he'd gone.

I thought she stayed the same after I left home to go to university, like a bug trapped in amber. I resented her for not pulling herself out of it, for letting abandonment overtake her and ruin our lives. But I see now that I've been wrong: Mum has been slowly rebuilding herself in the years since I left home. Yes, she still hates Christmas – that will never change – but she's a determined, strong person now. And she's been watching Alice, just like I have. And biding her time. She's quiet, yes, but not in a shy, weak way. She's quiet because she waits until it's the right time to speak out.

Ted picks up a tumbler of whisky from the table and hands it to Alice, who takes a grateful sip. She places the tumbler back on the coffee table and inhales deeply, her hands shaking slightly less now. I wonder how much of this is real, and how much is an act or exaggeration, for sympathy. She glances at Natasha, who's still curled up in an armchair, her arms wrapped around herself and a defiant expression on her face.

Mum nods her encouragement.

I perch on the edge of the sofa, leaning forward to hear what Alice has to say. I catch myself and shuffle backwards, looking away. I don't want to give her more attention than she's already getting.

She clears her throat. 'We can't call the police because as soon as they realise who I am, they'll arrest me.'

Natasha rolls her eyes. 'Shut up. It's fine – you said he's on his way here. There's nothing to arrest you for if he's—'

'Tash. It's not just that.' She shakes her head. 'They'll arrest me for child abduction.'

'What the...?' Natasha stands up from her chair, her hands in her hair. 'You didn't kidnap me. I came with you—'

Alice shakes her head slowly. 'It doesn't matter, Tash. If he's still—' She stops herself and swallows, then gives a little nod, almost to herself. 'He'll have reported you missing as soon as he realised we'd gone.'

I watch as a mixture of emotions cross Ted's face as he, too, realises what this means. Surely, if Robin could accuse Alice of kidnapping, then Natasha must be his child. This isn't Ted's child? She's Robin's. Alice and Natasha can just walk away from our lives for ever. We have no ties to them, no loyalty. For a moment, he looks relieved, too. His shoulders unfurl as if he's just removed a heavy backpack.

Our family is safe and whole. Complete.

I want to stand up and roar in triumph and relief.

But then his features twist into an expression of grief and loss, and my relief dissipates. *Oh no.*

He *wanted* a child with Alice, I realise. Natasha represented his second chance, to make things right. He'd been waiting all these years and finally had that chance to connect. And now it's gone.

I pull my eyes away from Ted, unable to look at him any more. I don't want to see that grief.

'I don't understand. How would Robin report you for kidnapping? You're her mother. Surely...'

Ted stops talking as Alice shakes her head again, with a glance at Natasha. 'Her biological dad was never on the birth certificate. Robin adopted her when she was tiny. He has full parental rights.'

Ted and I are quiet as we process this. My stomach plummets. No reprieve. I grieve for the hope I'd held moments ago, that I'd been wrong all along and Natasha isn't Ted's. Ted is Natasha's biological father. And he abandoned her. Something I've still not been able to question him about. Our families remain tied together by blood, united with Alice indefinitely.

Mum leans forward, the only adult in the room capable of speaking at this moment. 'So what happened, Alice? Why did you have to run?'

She uncurls her legs from under her and sits forward, clearing her throat. 'Robin has some problems: anger and drinking, mainly. Shaking hands in the morning, a swig of vodka before lunch. And the arguments...' She shudders, her whole body hunched over and tiny like a child.

As if it's too painful to listen, Natasha looks away, shifting her gaze to the TV which has moved on to another Christmas film with a Plasticine reindeer and elves in a cotton wool landscape. Tamara and Charley are rapt; I'm grateful they aren't listening to this.

'I thought I could help. I went to AA meetings and found other family members of alcoholics, but I didn't tell anyone about the violence. I couldn't. It felt like failure: as if letting him do that to me was somehow my fault. Like I could and should stop him, somehow. And Robin had no interest in stopping drinking, this time.'

My mum closes her eyes and raises a hand to her forehead as if wanting to block out what Alice is saying. I feel a pang of sympathy, as I know listening to this must resonate with her, after some of the things that happened with Dad.

'Of course, there was no sign of that at the beginning. We lived in Glasgow, in a little terrace near Kelvingrove Park. Amazing views. Tash could walk to school and I was close to the gallery where I worked. We were happy. It was small at first: throwing something during an argument, breaking a plate. But then it escalated, of course. I still thought I could fix it; I could remember who he was before, you know? I thought if only he would stop drinking, we could get back there, get back on track. But then, a couple of days ago he almost hit Natasha.'

Everyone in the room freezes. Even the TV goes quiet for a moment.

Natasha raises her chin, a defiant look on her face. For a moment, she looks a little older, the tension around her eyes giving her a haunted, adult look.

Alice rubs her forehead with a shaking hand and looks up, her eyes sparkling with unshed tears. She gazes at Ted, a pleading look in her eyes. 'I just couldn't let an abuser hurt anyone else. And that's how we ended up here. I had to get her away.' She glances at me and then away, unable to make eye contact for more than a second.

'I didn't ask you to get me away from anything,' Natasha hisses, pulling her sleeves over her hands and folding her arms around her body. 'We could have stayed, kicked him out instead. Got him the help he needs.' Her words say one thing, but her frightened body language says another.

Alice shrugs. 'I wasn't thinking straight. I just needed to get away, both of us. And then I remembered your invitation...' She nods at Ted, who stares back at her, a pained look on his face.

The film finishes, and the final credits roll with the festive sparkle of sleigh bells. Both girls clap their hands like two old ladies giving a round of applause in a theatre. They're squashed together on the sofa, their legs entwined, their chubby-cheeked faces glowing in the light of the television. They're so perfect, my two girls, and I just want to scoop them up into my arms and run away so fast.

I need to keep them safe. I want to take them away from Natasha, who stole my child's Christmas present. I want to protect them from Alice, who brought a knife into the house and may have led a monster to our doorstep. I can't let them see the badness that can happen in this world. Violence, abuse, threats. All on their way here. It angers me that we're checking out of the window, imagining figures moving among the trees, peering at the horizon to try to detect if someone is on their way here to cause harm.

Mum leans forward and pats Alice on the knee. 'You did the right thing, love. You protected a child, and that's what matters.'

Alice gives Mum a watery smile and glances at the clock on the mantelpiece. 'Thank you all, so much, for taking us in these last couple of days. And I'm sorry it's been such an imposition. But if he's on his way here and we're not leaving, we need to make sure he can't get in.' She stands up and takes a step towards the door. 'I'm going to check all the outside doors are locked. We need to protect ourselves if he gets here.'

The panic and frustration build up in my chest. My children are in this house. My innocent babies, who have never been hurt or genuinely afraid, except for ordinary childhood fears. How dare she bring this here? And not let me call for help?

Ted shifts, ready to follow her and help. I can't stand it. None of this makes sense. What she's saying just doesn't add up. My heart beats wildly in my chest and the words bubble up in my throat. I'm hot and cold and sick all at the same time.

I stand up. 'Wait,' I say sharply. 'I need to understand, Alice. Fair enough you received this invitation and it was good timing for you. I get that you wanted to get away. To protect yourself and Natasha. But... how?' I point at Tamara and Charley where they're curled up together on the sofa, looking over at me with shocked gazes at my sharp tone. 'How could you bring this here and put these children in danger? And you won't let me call the police?'

'I...' Alice's chin quivers as she glances at the girls. Her eyes brim with tears.

Ted shifts again, leaning towards Alice. 'Sadie,' he says, a warning hidden in his voice.

'No.' There's a ringing in my ears that I can't shake. My heart's thundering against my ribs and I can't catch my breath, but I need to ask these questions. I can't stop them bursting from me like water from a fountain. 'No, I'd like to know. It's not your fault that Robin did this to you, or that he's the way he is. I'm sure you did everything you could, God knows it's so hard to get away.'

I glance at Mum. 'But why not involve the authorities? If not now, then why not then? When he hit you? When he almost hit Natasha? If Robin is abusive, why not stay where you are and call the police? You could have got help. Natasha's right:

he should have been the one to leave, not you. But now my children are in danger too.'

Alice is sobbing now, her face in her hands. I watch her as I catch my breath, and I wonder if the crying is real or fake. I'm looking at this as if through two lenses: the one where everything she's saying is true and she's here out of sheer desperation, and the one where she's here to usurp my role and claim my family as her own. I suppress a twinge of guilt and a surge of anger at once.

Ted crosses to her and puts a hand on her back, then when she doesn't respond he pulls her to his chest and wraps an arm around her shoulders. 'Sadie, she's trying to escape an abuser. An abuser who might be on his way here. Have some empathy. This isn't her fault.'

Alice's sobs subside slightly and she glances up at me, her face angled so Ted can't see. I could swear I see her smile behind her fake tears. This is all for show.

My mouth falls open in shock. My husband has aligned with Alice. I'm losing him. She's winning.

'No, Ted. I don't have a law degree but I know that it's not a crime to take your own child. It's not child abduction if you haven't left the country. But Alice *does* have a law degree. And she probably does know that. What Alice is saying here isn't true. And my primary goal is to protect my children, and apparently there is a violent man on his way here and yet we are not *allowed* to call the police?' I cross to the phone and unwrap the cord from around it, ready to plug it back in. 'And frankly, the explanation we have been given is not good enough. If our children are in danger, Ted, I need to protect them and I will call the police.'

Alice steps towards me and Ted's arm drops away from her shoulders. For a split second, I wonder if she's about to attack me, to hit me in front of my husband and children. Would she? Could she? My mind flashes to the knife still in my pocket, the one she brought here. For protection? Or for something else? I still don't know who she is and what she's capable of, but it seems I do know what she wants: she wants my husband.

I move back, but she reaches forward and puts a hand on the phone. 'Please, Sadie. Don't.'

I cling to the phone, my eyes scanning the skirting board looking for the jack to plug it back in. If she grabs it, I can always run up to the little patch of phone signal on the staircase and call with my mobile. Or even Wi-Fi calling, now that we have power again. She has no hope.

She searches my eyes with hers, her hand resting on the phone. I can see a vein twitching at her temple. 'Sadie,' she says, her voice quiet and clear. She takes a big breath, straightening her shoulders and then she stills, like a lion about to pounce on its prey. Then she speaks again, her voice clean and clear like an axe through the air. 'I hurt Robin back. That's why we ran. And that's why we can't call the police.'

The room is silent as everyone processes what Alice just said. She hurt him back. What does that mean? Has he already called the police? They could be on the way here, too. And the knife, maybe that's what she used. Maybe she stabbed him. And it's in my pocket, covered in my fingerprints and probably wiped clean of her own.

I resist the urge to step away from her. I can't let go of the phone.

'I'm sorry...' Her voice cracks and she clears her throat. 'Ted —' Her eyes flick to the gap in the curtain and she draws in a breath. She crosses the room and pulls the curtains apart with both hands.

She lets out a scream that pierces my ears. And another.

The girls cover their ears, jumping off the sofa to huddle against Ted's side.

I rush across to the rain-streaked window. 'What? What is it? It's too dark to see any—' But my words cut off as I see exactly what is causing her to scream: a set of headlights heading straight towards the lodge.

They're moving slowly, almost walking pace, but they're definitely coming closer. We're the only house at the end of this track: they can only be heading here.

Next to me, Alice almost vibrates with fear. She turns to look at me, her eyes brimming with tears. 'We need weapons. Guns. Are there guns in the house?'

I step back, drawing in a breath. I rush to the phone, shoving the jack back into the socket, but no sound comes from the receiver. 'The phone is dead.'

The windows rattle with a sudden gust of wind and we're plunged into darkness again, the only light the glow from the fire's embers. Another power cut.

Ted lights the torch on his phone, setting it upright on the table, the beam shining at the ceiling and bathing us in a milky light. 'Wi-Fi just dropped, and there's still no mobile signal. We can't call for help.'

Silence.

'I'm scared, Mummy.' Tamara and Charley cement themselves to my sides.

The headlights move closer and I swallow hard.

Me too, I want to tell my girls, but guilt and fear choke my words. What have I done?

This is my fault. What terrible thing did I invite here?

16

TWO MONTHS EARLIER

I walk into our bedroom, holding the white stick between two shaking fingers. Ted's sleeping form shifts as I sit on the edge of our bed, next to him.

I can't understand how this happened. We're careful. So careful.

'Sadie,' he mumbles as he wakes and turns onto his back. His left cheek is wrinkled and pink where the pillow marked his face. 'Good morning.' He reaches out and places a hand on my knee. His face clouds as he sees my expression. 'What's up?'

'Ted,' I say, and he pulls himself into a sitting position, a frown of concern across his brow.

His hair is mussed up, his beard thick and dark. 'Tell me,' he says.

But I don't need to say anything, because he spots the white stick in my hand, its two pink lines on the window signalling the existence of the little ball of cells inside me, rapidly growing and multiplying every moment. 'It's positive,' I say, as if he needed me to clarify.

He takes the pregnancy test and squints at it, clearly unable to process this news so soon in his day. 'Could it be a mistake? A false positive?'

I shake my head. 'I took two. I'm three days late, and I'm never late.'

He places the test on the bedside table and wraps his arms around his legs, shaking his head. With a pang, I remember the previous positive tests we took: one for Tamara and one for Charley. Both of them planned and very much wanted. We'd jumped up and down, hugged each other, wiped away tears of joy. Yes, there was trepidation at how much our lives were about to change, but it was eclipsed by excitement.

And now those two little positive tests are eight and six years old, with their own personalities, interests, passions and opinions. They're fantastic and beautiful and amaze me every single day. The joy I felt when we discovered I was pregnant those times has continued through every moment since those two lines appeared.

We didn't just slide those tests onto the bedside table like a piece of rubbish to be thrown into the bin. We held them aloft, took photographs of those two little pink lines so we could keep them for ever, and waited with excitement for the day we felt safe to tell people. To shout it from the rooftops.

Grief bubbles up in my throat. Because I adore Charley and Tamara. And I know that the little bundle of cells burgeoning inside me right now would bring me so much joy and love, no matter who they turn out to be. I would love this child to the end of my days, just as much as I love my two daughters today. There's enough room in my heart, even if our home and our car might need an upgrade. We can afford another child, and our marriage can survive the newborn days just like it did with our first two. And other families have three children and more; many even plan it that way.

But... I just don't feel it. That joy. I glance over at the test on the table. Today I don't feel happiness. I feel dread.

I would look at that child in five years' time and wonder if they knew that they weren't planned or wanted like their sisters. That their sisters had an advantage over them before they'd even existed outside the womb. Would this baby hate me one day? Resent me?

No, I don't feel joy. I feel fear. I feel disappointment: the family I know and love could change now, becoming unrecognisable from what we have today. The plans we've made, the future I imagined, it's different with a new baby at forty, and a huge age gap between a newborn and my two older kids.

And what if that child had additional needs? It's statistically more likely than it was with my first two pregnancies, considering my age. And yes, I could care for a disabled child, and I would love him or her just as much as I love Tamara and Charley. But I don't think I could cope with the guilt that I would feel about what had been taken away from my two daughters: my time, my attention, and my care, all poured into this new child who needs me more than they do.

Doesn't a child deserve joy? And hope, and excitement? Every child does. Could I bring a child into this family, knowing that our reception of their existence differed so greatly from our reaction to their sisters' conception? It's not fair on that unknown baby. And I know that life isn't fair, but we can at least start them out on an equal footing, can't we?

'Sadie?'

I start, Ted's hand on my shoulder ripping me from my catastrophising thoughts. 'Sorry, I was miles away.'

'I was just saying, this is a surprise.' His eyes are wide as he gazes at me, his eyes flicking back and forth between my own.

I puff my cheeks out, forcing a chuckle of mirth. 'That's an understatement.' He pulls me into a hug and I sink into his chest, grateful for the comfort. I feel brittle, like I could shatter into a million pieces.

'There's no right choice.' My words are muffled against his chest. 'Another child was never part of our plan, Ted,' I whisper, my voice choked.

He shifts slightly, moving his body away from mine so he can see my face. His forehead is furrowed with concern. 'True, but life gets in the way of plans. Life's unexpected sometimes, and that's how it goes. This isn't a terrible thing, Sadie. This is a new and different thing, and one we'll take a while to get our heads around.'

I let myself imagine it for a moment: gathering all the baby stuff again; moving Tamara and Charley into a shared room so there's space for the baby; swapping our car for one with space for booster seats and a baby seat; the night feeds, the burping; the school runs with a baby in tow; drop-offs and pickups at three different places when Tamara starts high school, Charley's still at primary and the baby is at nursery; the weaning, the food throwing, the spit-ups, the sickness bugs, the arguments, the nappy changes, the sheer destruction of pregnancy and birth on my body and my mind.

I've done it twice. It was over. I *thought* it was over. I really don't think I can do it again. I don't want another child. I know it. But what kind of selfish monster would I be if I choose not to go ahead with this pregnancy just because it feels inconvenient?

Grief bubbles up in my throat. 'I hate that we have to make this decision.'

'Make what decision?' His neck turns pink and mottled. 'It's happened. It's a shock, but a new baby is a gift. Our life just took a curveball and the next few years will look different to what we expected.' He glances at me, his gaze hard and steady. 'But there's no *decision* to make.'

My body turns cold, my skin prickling as the hairs on my arms stand on end. I'd just assumed that Ted would be on the same page as me about this. After Charley was born, we'd agreed that our family was complete, that we had everything we wanted. We'd given away all the baby stuff as Charley grew out of it, and even toyed with the idea of a vasectomy, until it dropped out of our heads in the chaos of two under two.

My breath catches in my throat, and I can't breathe. Does he really want to keep this baby? Does he really want to go through everything again, right from the start? How could he want that? He's pro-choice; we've always aligned on issues like that. We've been to marches and held friends' hands with no judgement as they made this very decision. But now when it's our choice, when it's our pregnancy, it seems like there's no choice as far as Ted's concerned.

Except there is. It's my body. And if it comes down to it, the choice is mine.

I straighten up and pull away from him. 'Look, we've had a huge shock this morning. Let's take some time and think about everything, really work out what this means for our family and make sure we're on the same page. We don't have to make any decisions today.'

He stands up and opens the bathroom door. I look over at him, at his naked body: the dusting of dark hair on his chest and thighs, the pale skin and toned stomach of a man who rides his bike fifty miles with his friends every Sunday afternoon. The body of a man who has the time and the headspace to *think* about his body and to take care of it as he ages, in a way that would be ripped from me if we go ahead with this pregnancy.

The body that stands in front of me will stay the same, no matter what decision we make. It's me who is in the crosshairs of this decision, so it's me who gets to make it, no matter what he thinks. And yes, I can wait a couple of weeks while we talk about our options. And I'm not going to try and persuade him either way; we must agree on this based on facts and logic. I'm confident that once I've outlined everything that has flashed through my head in the past few minutes, Ted easily will be on the same page as me. I've got time for him to understand.

But then he switches on the bathroom light, and he's illuminated from behind, his body becoming a dark silhouette as he looks back at me. 'There's no decision to make, Sadie,' he says again. 'I don't repeat my mistakes.'

17

But in the days that follow, Ted's mind doesn't change. In fact, he behaves as if we'd never had that conversation in our bedroom about decisions and choices. I could pretend everything is normal, except that he's quiet, and he avoids me. He goes to bed before me and ensures he's fast asleep when I come upstairs, or waits until I'm asleep before he slides between the covers. He spends more time in the gym, stays late at work, takes the girls swimming and to the park under the pretence of giving me a break, when actually it means that we have no opportunity to speak.

And the pregnancy test sits on his bedside table, the pink lines blurring and bleeding together. Every time I see it, the sick feeling rises in the back of my throat, and it's unclear whether it's the rising anxiety of an unresolved issue getting more and more urgent, or the start of the morning sickness that left me pale and weak in the first months of both of my previous pregnancies.

I continue to churn through the possibilities in my mind: keep the baby, accept the new life I've stumbled into, relinquish my ideas of the future and embrace the new world we'd be stepping into... or make the difficult decision and cling onto the familiar, the carefully planned, the wanted *now* that we chose.

No matter how many times I think about it, and how many angles I look at it from, I still come back to the same conclusion. And after a few days of thinking alone and without Ted's moral support, I hit upon a new layer of clarity: a difficult decision can still be the right one.

Then one day, Ted comes home with a plastic bag, which he leaves on our bed. When I look inside, it's a tiny newborn onesie from Marks & Spencer, with little hand coverings to protect the baby's face from scratchy fingernails, and poppers up the front. I shove it back into the bag as if it's burned my skin.

'No,' I say out loud, rolling up the bag and placing it back on the bed next to me. That 'no' refers to so much: Ted's inability to talk about this, his assumption that we'd keep this baby with no further discussion, and now the outfit that he's bought, as if by avoiding any confrontation he will just keep this train on the rails right to its destination. No to all of it.

I stand up, ready to clatter down the stairs and confront him where he's sitting with the girls, one on either side of him, oblivious bodyguards protecting him from me. Enough. It's time to talk.

But as I step towards the bedroom door, it swings open and Charley stands in the doorway, a funny look on her face. I gather her into my arms. 'Is anything wrong?' I ask quietly.

She shakes her head, but her little body shudders as she starts to cry.

I hold her tight and stay silent until she speaks: 'Why is Daddy so mean?'

'What happened, baby?' I say, keeping my tone neutral. Ted and I have always been careful not to undermine each other's parenting in front of the kids, even if we don't agree with each other's approach in the moment. We've agreed it's important to show a united front where we can. But Charley's words in combination with Ted's recent coldness towards me means I pay special attention this time.

'We were trying to play with the dollies but he kept staring into space. He wouldn't even pretend to change my dolly's nappy or sing her a lullaby like normal.' She sniffs and wipes her tear-stained cheek with her sleeve. 'Then I put the doll on his head and he pushed her off and said I should "Get lost". He said if I'm so interested in babies I should come and ask Mummy because she's the one who doesn't want any.' She shakes her head and pulls her eyebrows down in a frown. 'What does that mean? You play with my baby dolls all the time.'

I pull her towards me and bury my nose in her hair so she can't see my face. I'm livid. It's OK that Ted and I have some speed bumps in our relationship, but it's not OK for the children to be affected by it. And it's certainly not OK for him to make snide little remarks to the kids which give them any indication of what's going on between us. They can't know about my pregnancy at this early stage, no matter what we eventually decide. And they certainly never need to understand the decisions behind it or who feels what.

Through gritted teeth, I comfort her and tell her Daddy's just tired, then when she seems happier I try to lead her out of the room, but she points behind me at the bed. 'What's in the bag?'

I manage to deflect her away from the M&S bag with the onesie inside, and pull a fake smile onto my face to invite Charley and Tamara to help me bake some cupcakes, away from Ted.

But even while I help them crack eggs and show them how to sift flour, my mind is elsewhere. Ted's parting shot from the other day keeps echoing around my brain: *I don't repeat my mistakes.* I still don't know what he meant by that, and it's clear that he's not going to tell me right now.

He's distanced himself so much from me in the last few

days that he's almost a stranger. And now he's broken one of the rules we agreed upon right from the beginning of our family: we don't involve the kids in our conflicts.

I still don't think his behaviour relates to us or our relationship. It's so far removed from any way he's behaved before, and doesn't seem to directly relate to our situation. Sure, we're in a difficult position, but it's not relationship-ending in the way he seems to be behaving. So maybe the answer to Ted's total withdrawal lies somewhere in his past, with some other woman; an old lover, maybe.

As I oversee the chaos of the kids spooning batter into the cupcake tin, I'm newly resolute: something's going on with Ted, and this is the final straw for me. *I don't repeat my mistakes.* What did that mean? I need answers. There would be ways through this if Ted would just engage with me. But he won't. And so I decide to break my own rules about snooping. If Ted won't tell me what's going on, I'll find out myself.

That night, after Ted has taken himself off to the gym and I've put the girls to bed, I make a cup of ginger tea to quell my nausea and look up all his ex-girlfriends on social media, starting with his high-school girlfriend, and ending with the one before me.

Does one of these women hold the key to the 'mistake' he was talking about?

I don't find much. They all look like fairly normal people with ordinary lives, and their privacy settings are high so in most cases I can only see their profile pictures and a couple of JustGiving posts they've made public.

Then I find his girlfriend before me: Alice. Her profile is locked down like the others, with only a photograph of her and her daughter in the circular profile picture, and a few scant details in the 'About' section: Alice's name, her hometown and her year of birth.

This is looking like a futile endeavour. I'm about to switch to another social media platform when the cramps start, and when I look down there's bright red blood on the chair beneath me. My breath catches in my throat as I realise what this probably means.

I don't know what I'm feeling. But silent tears pour down my face as I try to wipe away the blood, the physical confirmation that there will be no baby.

The decision has been made for us.

My emotional reaction to the loss of the pregnancy is complex, and I switch between relief, grief and guilt. But any relief I feel is tempered by Ted's distance as he drifts even further away after my miscarriage. Although he doesn't say it, it feels as if he believes it was somehow my will that caused the pregnancy to end. Like I wanted that. As if I did it *to* him.

I feel so alone and mixed up and I know I need to speak to someone about it all. Not just the pregnancy and my reaction, but also the miscarriage and my confused feelings, and mostly, of course, the state of my marriage after everything we've gone through. I run through my friends in my mind, but to my shock there's no one I feel I could talk to. My 'mum friends' are all parents at the girls' school, providing surface-level entertaining chats about celebrities, our children and vague references to our petty annoyances in our marriages. My before-kids friends wouldn't understand the complexity of this, and they're all a little distant now anyway. And my other so-called friends are the wives and girlfriends of Ted's friends; i.e. totally off-limits.

The final nail in the coffin of my desire to talk is that most of my female friends by our age have gone through various traumatic fertility and birth issues: IVF, secondary infertility, abortions, miscarriages, perimenopause, ectopic pregnancies, PCOS... the list goes on. My unplanned pregnancy and subsequent miscarriage after two healthy children seem like small fry compared to some of the things my friends have endured, and it would feel so selfish to go crying to any of them about this, forcing them to push aside their own trauma to focus on mine.

But as a therapist, I know the value of talking things through, of getting all your tangled thoughts out and letting an impartial third party sift through them until they make sense again. So, I do something I haven't done for a long time and I book myself into therapy with Jean, a former colleague who's never been a friend and who has no friends in common with me.

To my surprise, after I blurt out everything that's happened in the last couple of weeks, we end up talking about my dad. I realise I made a rookie mistake: Jean isn't here to decode Ted, she's here to decode me. So, of course, she has no interest in answering my question of 'What's going on with Ted?' Instead, she asks, 'Why does Ted's behaviour upset you so much?'

And that's how we end up talking about Dad: about how Jean believes that inconsistent parenting and unmet needs in childhood can lead to insecure attachment in later life: namely, a fear of rejection. I'm uncomfortable with Ted's silent treatment because I'm afraid of being abandoned, just like my dad abandoned Mum and me.

As Jean leads me along this path, I play along but, in my mind, I regret attending therapy at all. I respect the work of my fellow therapists, but I've never had much time for attachment-based therapy or psychotherapy. It feels too theoretical, especially as it relies heavily on the unconscious mind. I'm all about the conscious mind and the here and now. My issues are firmly rooted in what's happening this week, this month, today. Not how I felt one December afternoon in 1992 before I could even plait my own hair.

At the end of the session, I'm gathering my stuff and regretting an hour wasted, when Jean sits forward in her seat, a curious look on her face. 'I know you didn't get the answers you wanted today, Sadie,' she says, the corner of her mouth twitching as she pauses to think. 'I know you wanted to dive into Ted's motivations in all of this. I hope what we've talked about has been useful nonetheless.'

I nod and heft my handbag onto my shoulder, mumbling some platitudes about all therapy being useful. As my hand is on the doorknob, she says my name, calling me back – that cliché that doctors speak of all the time when at the last moment their patients blurt out the *actual* ailment they've made the appointment for, except this time it's the patient being called back.

I turn towards her, head tilted and a forced smile on my face.

'He mentioned past mistakes in the context of your pregnancy. Have you considered that the child in his ex's profile picture might be Ted's daughter?'

18

I stumble from the therapist's office in a daze, her question bouncing around my mind like the silver ball in a pinball machine. Because, no, I hadn't considered that Alice's daughter might be Ted's, too. It seems incredibly obvious now, but in the confusion of the pregnancy and then the miscarriage, it's like my brain had to protect me, couldn't let me connect those dots.

As soon as I get to my car, I open up Facebook and search for Alice's profile once again. She pops up straight away, my account remembering my previous search on the day my miscarriage began, pushing everything else to the side.

I peer at my phone screen, at the round photograph of Alice and the little girl. The girl looks young, too young to be Ted's daughter. But it could be an old photo, taken years ago and only uploaded recently. She has wavy hair, the same colour as Ted's. And it's hard to tell but perhaps she has his eyes. *It's possible*, I think to myself as I gaze at the screen.

How would I feel, if Ted has a daughter from a previous relationship? And our girls have a half-sister? My thoughts are complex, and triggered by the therapy session I've just had, I think back to my own childhood: my mum broken and devastated after Dad left, while I had no one to play with. I longed for a sibling so much that I would beg my school friends to pretend we were sisters, or I'd talk to my teddies like they were real. When Ted and I married and had children, I vowed to fight to keep us together, to protect my children in any way possible from the loneliness I felt as a child.

It's possible that this girl – if she *is* Ted's – could fulfil two purposes in our lives. First, Tamara and Charley would have an older sister: a playmate, a confidante, an advisor. A bigger family and another guard against loneliness, for life. And second, another child for Ted right now could save my marriage. Clearly, Ted wanted our baby, and now he's grieving its loss. I know he blames me, even though the doctors said it was no one's fault; just one of those things. Perhaps discovering the existence of this girl might fill that void in Ted's world that ripped open in the last few weeks, and build us back up as a united couple in the process, without the need for me to sacrifice everything I love about our life right now.

My phone slides into my lap as I stare out of the windscreen at the cobbled streets of Edinburgh where I've parked, thinking about how I could approach this. I imagine walking into our house this afternoon, showing Ted the profile picture and announcing that he might have a daughter. If he's even home; if he'll let me talk to him. I imagine his questions: why were you searching for Alice? Who else have you looked up? Why now?

I shake my head and mutter to myself. *No, that's not the way.*

I look out of the windscreen, across the road to a grassy park dotted with trees. It's a lovely autumn afternoon with the low sun colouring everything gold. A couple in their early twenties stroll along a path, holding hands and crunching in fallen leaves. The girl is talking animatedly, waving her free hand with enthusiasm as the boy gazes at her, a happy, indulgent smile on his face. I feel a pang of loneliness, of loss. It's been a long time since I've felt adored like that; since it seemed that I could be unashamedly myself in front of my husband, with no repercussions.

I have to walk on eggshells, to plan ahead, to avoid his triggers. I don't get to crunch my feet in fallen leaves with my husband's hand in mine. I can't even remember the last time he reached for my hand, I realise.

I know instinctively that I can't ask Ted about his ex-girlfriend and her daughter. Ted is angry with me, which is why he's so withdrawn. Bringing this up with him isn't the best way.

Or rather, I am not the best messenger for this information. But if the news could come directly from Alice herself or even the daughter, while I'm an innocent bystander – someone also affected by the bombshell – perhaps it could pull Ted and me back together? Frankly, right now, I'm willing to try anything.

And then I think about it from Alice's perspective. I don't know her life, who she is, where she lives, anything. We're strangers to each other, with no mutual friends, no familiarity at all. Coming from me, any invitation to connect would look like a typical online scam from a stranger. She'd delete the message and block me without a second thought. I can't be the one to contact her, to invite her and her daughter into our lives.

But she knows Ted. She loved Ted, once. It won't look like a scam coming from him. It'll look like it is: an invitation to connect, to let our children get to know each other and extend our family. A barrier against loneliness, for life.

I pick up my phone again and switch Facebook accounts, signing into Ted's. His password is saved on my phone from a day long ago when his phone battery died and he needed to check something. He barely uses this account any more, but it's all still there as usual. It's as simple as the click of a button and I'm in, and typing the invitation.

Hi Alice, I type. My family will be staying at Red Hart Lodge over Christmas this year and if you're in the area…

19

NOW

What have I done? I think, as I watch the car advance along the one-track lane towards Red Hart Lodge. *This is my fault.*

If I hadn't sent that stupid Facebook message to Alice, she wouldn't be here right now, jabbering about guns and dangerous men.

'We need weapons. Guns. Are there guns in the house?' Her voice echoes through the room as we all look at each other in shock.

No, if not for me, Ted and I would be wrapped up together with the fire roaring, sipping Baileys and laughing with our girls. Perhaps things between Ted and I would still be tense, but we'd have fixed it all eventually, after a few days of cosy family time. How could I have made such an error of judgement?

I regretted sending 'Ted's' Facebook message as soon as I pressed send. Alice hadn't replied; I'd checked every day. It had been read, but she never sent a response. By that point I'd found Alice's Instagram, too, and could see she had a partner. I assumed the lack of reply meant she had no interest in recon-necting, and had hoped fervently that maybe that meant the girl wasn't Ted's. If I could have taken that message back, I would have.

And even more recently, I should have closed the door on them when they showed up on the doorstep yesterday. But I was so surprised, I didn't act fast enough. And then they were freezing and drenched. Natasha looked so young. I thought I'd got a reprieve and my goals shifted: help them warm up, confirm she's too young to be Ted's child, send them on their way. But they wouldn't leave, and now we're all stuck here with danger on the way.

I open my mouth, about to apologise. To Ted, to Alice. To anyone who'll listen. This entire debacle is my doing, and I will regret it to the end of my days.

But before I can speak, Ted steps forward.

'Alice, no.' He places a hand on her shoulder and leans towards the glass, cupping his other hand around his face. 'No guns. Even if there were any, we're not going to use them. We'll keep him outside and refuse to open the door, but we're not going to escalate anything.'

His voice wavers and I feel a rush of sympathy for him. He's not a fighter. He hates confrontation in any form. He's way out of his comfort zone, but you'd never know it to look at him: he's decisive and commanding, standing tall and giving instructions. Even though inside he must be quaking, just like me.

The damage is done. Confessing will do no good right now. The spell broken and my confession sucked back down, I gather the girls to me and kiss them both on the tops of their heads. 'We'll be OK, girls. It's just a bit dark. We'll find you somewhere safe if we need to. Like hide and seek.'

Mum crosses to the window and peers through the glass for another moment before she pulls the curtains closed. 'Right. The car has stopped at the bridge. I'm guessing the water is too high to get through.'

Alice paces the room, pulling the zip of her hoodie up and

down, up and down. 'So we've got a few minutes for him to cross the bridge on foot. Before he gets here.'

Mum cups both hands around her face, peeking through a gap in the curtains. 'I see him, I think. He's a big guy. He's on foot, but he's moving slowly. He doesn't have a torch, and it looks like the wind is really slowing him down.'

Alice stops pacing and hunches over, her hands in her hair and her eyes flitting wildly around the room in panic.

Ted crosses to her and places a hand on her back. I flinch. I want to stand up and pull him away but I can't move away from my girls.

'It's OK,' he whispers. 'I'll go and check all the doors.'

Alice straightens up, taking a breath. 'I'll come with you. I need to feel like I'm doing something.' She flaps her hands as if trying to shake off water.

Ted's hand is still on Alice's back and I'm hit with another pang of regret. Another thing I hadn't considered before I stupidly pressed send on that message, and one which has been eating at my soul since the moment her 'Hello, stranger' growled at Ted through the open doorway.

I'd been so arrogant, so comfortable in my marriage, even though it was strained. I thought Ted and I were strong, and that he would want to fight for our marriage as much as I did. It hadn't occurred to me for a moment that Alice might come here with an agenda, and that she'd want to lure Ted for herself. And not for a second had I considered that Ted would ally with her, would wrap his arms around her to protect her, to comfort her. Whether she came here with the explicit conscious aim of stealing my husband or whether it occurred to her while she's been here, she might be succeeding and it's killing me. I brought this on myself. I invited her in. I brought this trouble to our door.

I stand up. 'I'll come, too. Mum, could you—'

But the girls grab my hands, pulling me back down. 'No,

Mummy. Don't leave me,' howls Tamara, tears beginning to form. I lean down and gather her into my arms, and Charley begins to whine in sympathy with her older sister.

Ted leaves Alice and kneels in front of me. 'Go with the girls, Sadie. Find them somewhere safe to hide. Stay with them, OK?'

He knows I want to help, to avoid waiting around helplessly. And we need to talk; I need to understand what happened with Alice all those years ago. *Did* he abandon her when she was pregnant? Is he the man I know, or have I been wrong about him all along? But there's no time, with Robin on his way to do God-knows-what. And Ted's right. The girls need me.

'I'll stay with them, too,' Mum says to Ted. She turns to me. 'We'll stick together.' Her eyes are wide in fear, but her jaw is set. 'You'll keep him out, and he'll soon give up, in this weather. Sounds like a pussy, if you ask me. Hitting a little girl. Pffft,' she scoffs, throwing an affectionate glance at Natasha, who's watching everyone with a look of detachment on her face, as if we're all imagining a threat and only she sees clearly that we're all making a fuss of nothing.

Ted kisses each of us on the cheek, including Mum. 'Go. Be safe.'

I nod and help the girls to their feet. They cling to me like little koalas. Charley smells faintly of chocolate.

'Take Tasha with you,' Alice pleads. 'Keep her safe too.'

'No,' Natasha says, her voice steely. 'I'm going to stay with you. I want to see—'

'Natasha, you will go with Sadie.' Alice's voice is so loud that Natasha takes a step back, bewildered. 'No arguing. You will hide somewhere safe and you will only come out when we say you can.' Alice leans down, her face inches from Natasha's. A vein pulses on her forehead. 'This is not a game, do you hear me?'

Natasha hesitates for a moment and then nods, biting her bottom lip. She shifts to stand next to me, and I lead the girls and Mum from the room, leaving Alice and Ted alone together, checking windows and exchanging whispered instructions.

'We know a good place to hide,' whispers Tamara, her little hand cold in mine. On my other side, Charley is uncharacteristically quiet, her thumb in her mouth. Usually, she's the louder of the two, but the darkness and Alice's shouting have penetrated even her six-year-old sense of adventure.

I nod. 'OK, can you take us there?'

Tamara stands tall, proud to be tasked with a job. Behind me, I hear Mum and Natasha's footsteps, their breath quiet as they follow us close behind.

Tamara leads us out of the living room and into the hallway where she pauses, looking around. My stomach sinks. She doesn't have a plan or an idea. She's my imaginative, wonderful bookworm living in a world of secret passageways and bricked-up rooms. Her promise came from imagination and hope, both of which crumble under pressure in even the strongest adult.

'Tamara?' I say, keeping my voice steady and calm. 'Did you—'

I'm interrupted by a loud *boom-boom-boom* which splits the air.

20

I crumple towards the floor, ushering the girls down with me. We huddle together and the girls shriek with terror. I whirl around, covering mouths and shushing until they're quiet. Tears pour down Tamara and Charley's cheeks as they gaze at me with eyes wide, two hands clamped over their mouths to stem their whimpers of fear.

'He's here,' Mum whispers, and Tamara and Charley shriek in terror again, clinging to my sides.

The knocks on the door accelerate into huge body-blows: he's throwing himself against the door, trying to get inside. We all cluster together, our breathing rapid. Mum clutches Natasha's hand.

I pull Tamara and Charley into me, wrapping my arms around them both. 'It's OK,' I mumble, wondering how I can make that statement true. 'We'll find somewhere to go.'

I try to run through what I know about this man. Robin. He was a good man, until he wasn't. He was sober, until he wasn't. He was a good father, until he wasn't. And now he wants his daughter back, and presumably retaliation on Alice for not only taking Natasha but also for injuring him in the process. He's angry. Probably drunk. And he wants revenge.

From the look of his picture and the heavy sound of his hammering on the door, he's also physically very strong.

The banging starts again, and my stomach clenches in fear. I'm shaking now, and I try very hard to regulate my breathing so the girls don't know how afraid I really am. Even Natasha's quiet, her eyes open wide, shining in the darkness.

Alice and Ted rush out of the living room towards the front door, and brace against the wood, flinching each time the door buckles under the pressure.

'What are you doing?' Ted mouths at me, his back pressed against the door.

Next to him, Alice manages to both hold her weight against the door and cower at the same time. She might be afraid, I think to myself, but she still takes a moment to flick an adoring glance across at Ted.

I close my eyes, dredging up my mental map of the house, of everything I've uncovered while we've been here. Which doors lock, which parts are out of the way enough that we might be safe even if this Robin guy gets inside... then I remember the information sheet: Wi-Fi, fireguard, a door that sticks when it's raining...

'There's a basement,' I call to Ted, hopefully not loud enough to be heard from outside. The banging starts again, echoing through the hallway. I think I hear a shout from outside, and my heart leaps into my throat. The wind batters the windows, throwing rain against the glass like gravel.

'Go. I'll come and let you know when it's safe to come out,' Ted says, and turns back to the door, his palms flat against the wood.

I rush across the hallway and wrench open the basement door. A blast of musty, cold air rushes up from below and hits me in the face. The darkness seems to swirl. I can't see anything beyond the foot of the stairs, except a small patch of bare concrete floor soon swallowed into the darkness. There's no light switch.

I usher everyone onto the stairs, pulling the door shut behind us. Immediately, my nose and mouth fill with the odour of mould and dust, and I suppress a cough.

'Mummy, I don't like it,' Charley whines. 'There are monsters down here. I can smell them.'

I let go of Tamara's hand and draw my phone from my pocket, shining the torch on the dusty stone steps that lead down into the darkness.

I swing the torch around, illuminating the bare stone walls at the top of the stairs, but I still see no light switch. 'Come on, let's go down. Someone will fall if we stand here any longer.'

No one moves, so I push ahead and shine the torch behind me so everyone can see their feet on the stone steps as we descend. The steps look ancient, each one with a worn dip where generations of feet have trod.

Down here, the sound of the wind buffeting the building finally fades. All afternoon it's been a constant backing track to our every moment, building anxiety inside me that I didn't know was there until the sound is finally cut off. I breathe in the dusty air as my feet shuffle down the stone steps, and I focus on releasing the tension in my muscles all over my body. We're safe. I'm with the girls. Alice is far away.

I shuffle forward into the gloom, narrating my thoughts to anyone who'll listen: 'We'll find somewhere comfortable down here to wait out the storm.'

'Wait out my dad, you mean,' Natasha mumbles under her breath.

I ignore her and carry on babbling. 'And then in the morning the weather will be fine, the river level will drop and we can drive Alice and Natasha wherever they want to go.' As long as they go far, far from me and my family, I add silently.

At the bottom of the basement steps, I shine the torch around until the beam lands on a white string hanging from the ceiling. 'Finally,' I say, tugging the cord. It clicks, but no light comes on. Of course. The power is out. *Use your brain, Sadie.*

'All right, everyone. Let's find somewhere to sit.' I take a step forward into the main cavern of the basement, but no one follows. I turn back, shining my torch at our feet. 'Wait here, then. I'll do a recce and come back to tell you what I've found.' I flash the torch behind them. 'Sit on the stairs, maybe?'

Charley whimpers as I walk away, taking the light with me. I feel a pang in my chest. I want to stay with them, and I want to comfort my daughters, but I also want to know where we are and what place we're hiding in. Whether it's full of rusty saw blades or if there's a comfy sofa we could relax on while we wait. If I could leave my phone with them and keep them with some light, I would. But I can't leave it.

My torch alights on the whitewashed stone walls. There's an old workbench running along one wall, stacked high with tools and other maintenance items: an old lamp, rusting varnish cans, and big plastic bins full of tools and screws. And on the wall hang old paintbrushes, a sander, a caulking gun. Satisfied that we haven't stumbled into a serial killer's dissection room, I move onwards, shining my light as far into the basement as I can.

The basement is huge; it must be as large as the footprint of the house itself. I can't see how far it stretches, but I keep creeping forward, stepping around old dining chairs and sagging cardboard boxes. There's nothing here, just old storage. I'm just about to give up and head back to the others when my torch alights on a dark hole in the wall. Another room.

I glance over my shoulder, but the darkness is too thick to see back to the stairs. The stone walls soak up all the sound; it's as if I'm alone down here. But I know they'll be able to see me and my light, that my girls and my mum are reassured I'm here, within sight; that's what matters most.

I turn towards the extra room, and my torchlight touches something white and smooth on the floor. Long, like a broom handle. I take another step forward and angle my torch further into the room. A white curve, pointed at one end.

My torchlight illuminates a vision of sheer horror. Bones, piled to the ceiling, bleached white and clean. Hundreds of them. Countless lives, stacked in a heap.

I begin to shake with fear. I've brought my family into a graveyard. *Will we be next?*

21

I shriek, backing away, but my feet catch on something and I fall backwards, onto a hard object. My shoulder sears with pain.

I can't stop; I shuffle backwards, as far away from that room as I can get.

'Sadie? Is everything OK?' Mum's voice is like a balm through fear.

I pause to catch my breath, clutching my injured shoulder with my other hand. After a moment, the throbbing ebbs away and I tentatively move my arm in its socket. 'I think so,' I call back. 'I tripped, that's all. And...' I'm still shaking, even as I realise the bones must be animal ones. *They have to be.*

My shoulder feels bruised, but no permanent damage. I feel around for my phone in the darkness, finally finding it a few feet away covered in dirt. The torch has switched off. The screen feels shattered and rough under my fingers. It's broken. We have no light.

'Mum?'

'Here.'

I carefully make my way back in the direction of her voice, barely lifting my feet so I don't trip again. Finally, I reach the huddled group, standing together at the foot of the stairs in a tiny pocket of warmth. The girls clutch at me until one of them encounters a cobweb and they shriek in half-glee, half-terror.

'What did you find?' Mum asks, trepidation in her voice. She knows I'm not relating the whole story, but there's no way I'm telling the girls that they're sharing a basement with a deer graveyard, bones and antlers stacked to the ceiling.

'Just a load of old tools. Nothing interesting.' I slide my broken phone into my back pocket and lean against the wall, disregarding the dirt and dust now that I've rolled all over the floor.

There's a moment of quiet, and I focus hard, trying to hear what's going on upstairs. But no sound penetrates the stone walls down here. I step around Natasha's hunched form on the steps. 'I'm just going to listen at the door, see if I can hear what's going on up there.'

At the top of the stairs, I press my ear to the door. I hear running footsteps and a shout. My stomach clenches. Something's going terribly wrong.

Whose are the footsteps? Was it Ted or Alice? Or Robin, having finally broken down the door? And if the man got inside, I don't want to draw attention to the basement door, to lead him to my girls. If he finds Alice, will he leave? Is he here for her, or Natasha?

I hear another muffled shout, but I can't quite make out who it is or what they say. Did I hear it, or are my ears playing tricks? Was it a call for help? I don't know. It's so hard in this blanket of darkness, as if having no visual input is messing with my hearing too. The dust tickles my throat and I suppress a cough.

I wait until things fall quiet again, and I call down the stairs, my voice wavering with every beat of my heart. 'Mum,' I whisper. 'I'm going out there. Look after the girls.'

There's a wail of anguish from Tamara. 'Mummy, don't go.'

But I can't stay. If Ted needs help, I need to be there. I know the girls will be OK with Mum. I don't know if Ted will be OK with Alice and this intruder. Because still, even now, I don't know what Alice wants. Perhaps she's here to get Ted back, or maybe this is an elaborate con: she appears at people's houses, pretends she's left her abusive partner, and then he breaks in and they ransack the place together. And I invited that inside. No matter how precarious mine and Ted's relationship, I don't want him hurt or in danger.

I wrap my fingers around the doorknob and push. As the door begins to open, I whisper back over my shoulder: 'Don't come out until I say it's safe. I love you.'

Out in the hallway, all is quiet except for the howl of the wind outside and the creak of the house getting pummelled by the weather. I pause, listening.

The banging on the door has stopped, and Ted and Alice are nowhere to be seen. I shuffle towards the kitchen and I'm about to open the kitchen door when there's the smashing of glass from the living room, and cold air swirls around my feet. I freeze, terrified.

He's got inside.

I think, trying to work out what to do. Where are Ted and Alice?

I need something in my hands, something that looks threatening, that gives the impression I can defend myself even if I don't use it. I swear under my breath. There's no time. I run towards the front door and grab a walking stick out of the ornamental bucket and hold it in one hand like a baseball bat. That'll do.

I push open the living room door and the wind blasts me in the face, nearly pulling the door from my hands. A windowpane is smashed, and glass sparkles all over the floor. But there's no one here. The pane is big enough to reach a hand through, not to climb inside. The room is empty. Did he smash the window and walk away to the next one?

I wrestle the door closed and run to the kitchen, a feeling of dread mixed with relief that the wind isn't roaring as I push inside. The windows are secure and the door is still closed.

'Hello?' I whisper into the darkness.

There's a movement by the Aga. 'Who's there?' a voice whispers back.

Alice. I close my eyes. 'It's Sadie. Where's Ted?'

Her voice is high with fear. 'He went upstairs. Checking the windows and looking for things we can use to protect the house.'

'He left you down here?'

'He knows I can look after myself.'

'What's been happening? I heard shouting.'

There's a heavy clunk as she lays something on the table. I see the glint of a blade. An axe. Alice has got an axe. No wonder Ted thought it would be safe to leave her. No wonder she said she could look after herself, with a sharp weapon in her hand.

I stand on the other side of the table, still clutching the walking stick, which feels ridiculously light and ineffectual in comparison to Alice's weapon. But I still have her knife, I remind myself, feeling the weight of the blade in my pocket.

Her words come fast and breathy, strangled with fear. 'Robin gave up on the front door. We thought he'd come to this door next, but he's disappeared. He might be trying to get into one of the outbuildings, maybe. If he doesn't know the building, it'd be easy to mistake those doors for other entrances.'

'A window has been smashed in the living room. Maybe he's trying to break his way in?'

Her breath shudders.

There's a thud from above our heads. A creak: footsteps on floorboards. We both freeze, listening. Perhaps he got inside. But no more sounds come.

After a moment I hear her rub her face, the scrape of skin against skin. 'He's not giving up, Sadie. He's like a machine, once he has an idea in his head. He'll wait us out until morning if he has to, even in this weather.'

I roll my eyes, knowing she can't see me in the darkness. How dare she warn me like this, when it's her fault he's here? And she wouldn't let me call for help. I grit my teeth and try to affect a concerned tone. 'What does he want?'

She sniffs. 'Natasha, probably. And revenge on me.'

I knew it. I wrap my fingers around the walking stick and feel its smooth surface against my palms. 'Revenge?'

She doesn't reply.

I turn around and look in the direction of the rest of the house. 'I need to go and find Ted.'

'Where are the others? Natasha and the girls,' she asks.

'Down in the basement. They're safe.'

'You left them.'

'I wanted to check on Ted. I thought I heard shouting.'

She leaves a pause, making a point. 'Ted told you not to leave them.'

I feel a burst of frustration. I'm done pretending to be hospitable, and Ted's absence makes it easier. 'I don't need your opinion, Alice. You're the reason this is happening in the first place. All this upheaval and danger, you brought this here. You put my kids in danger, brought all this to our doorstep and then made it our problem. We didn't ask for this.'

She scoffs, her derision palpable even in the darkness. 'You don't know your husband, Sadie. You don't know him at all.'

'Really.' It's not a question. I'm not interested in her opinions on my marriage. 'This is my family's Christmas. And as much as Ted is pleased to see you, you're not part of his life any more. Your relationship is over and has been for years. Ted is married; he has children. We are his family now, not you.'

I want to leave, to go find Ted. But I don't move from my

position standing by the table, the smooth oak surface a barrier between me and her. I wait to hear what she's going to say next.

She takes in a sharp breath as if I've slapped her. But she recovers quickly.

I hear the rustle of her clothes and the creak of the table as she leans over it, her tone hushed and secretive. 'Last night, when we stayed up drinking, he told me he still thinks about the family we could have had. The regret he feels about the way he handled things with me, back then.' Her voice is urgent now, and she speaks quickly. 'I was always his first choice, Sadie. He doesn't want you, he wants me. That's why he invited me here.'

Her words punch me in the gut, but she's shown her hand. She's lying.

I let her keep talking, digging herself into a hole. She doesn't see my incredulous look and doesn't stop to hear my response, preferring to provoke me, to hurt me more.

'He told me he'd looked for me for years, even after he married you. You were his second choice, Sadie. His backup plan. I was the one who got away.'

I swallow the saliva building in my mouth. I want to tell her it's a lie. But my stomach clenches and I suppress the bile rising in my throat. Part of me wonders if what she's saying is true. If he doesn't love me at all, but always loved Alice. I think back to all the wine he's drunk over the past couple of days, drowning his sorrows, making decisions. How far away from me he's felt. How distant he's been, even with our girls. His silences, for weeks now.

And of course, I know he didn't invite Alice here, even though she's claiming he did. But have I just played right into both of their hands?

I know with a sinking feeling that I made a massive mistake in that split second after my therapy appointment. That was the moment that set everything in motion to bring us to this point. No matter how angry I am with Ted or how resentful of Alice I feel, truly at its root this is all my fault. And there's no turning back.

But still, Ted's betrayal stings, if what Alice says is true. I wish he was here, in this kitchen. Not so I could know he was safe, but so I could ask him why he would take me for such a fool.

She shrugs as a cloud shifts and the moonlight illuminates a mock-innocent smile on her face. 'If he wants me, you should step aside. You want him to be happy, don't you, Sadie? Don't get in the way if that's what he wants.'

I clench my fingers around the walking stick again and spit out a mirthless laugh. 'You don't know what Ted wants.'

She laughs too, a hollow laugh matches the howl of the wind. 'And you think you do?'

And now it's my turn to show my cards. I lay my hands out on the table between us, palms flat against the wood. I tick off each point with the tap of a finger. 'You're completely delusional. Ted didn't invite you, Alice. He never wanted you back. He was telling the truth; he had no idea about that Facebook message. I sent it. It was me.'

The kitchen is silent except for the howl of the wind outside, dry leaves hitting the window. 'What? Why?' she says eventually. 'Why would you do that?'

I shrug, a half-smile playing on my lips. I'm enjoying this, I realise. Since Alice arrived it's felt like everything was out of my control, and now I have the upper hand and it feels good. 'I had good intentions,' I say, my tone unconvincing. 'I knew that the only way I'd get you to come would be if I impersonated Ted. But I realise now that inviting you was a mistake. Look at all the baggage you dragged in with you. I've tried my best, but you're bad news, Alice, and we don't need it.'

She opens her mouth, but there's a sound from outside. The crunch of footsteps on gravel. We both freeze, listening.

The door handle rattles. Then it begins to turn.

22

There's a muffled shout of frustration from outside when it's clear that the door is locked. Then there's a *bang-bang-bang* of fists on wood, followed by the same shoulder barge he'd been doing on the front door.

This man is a machine. Why isn't he getting tired? Fear clutches at my heart.

Alice moves quickly, a chair falling backwards onto the tiles with a clatter.

At the sound, the banging stops. 'Open the door,' a man's voice bellows from outside. 'I know you're in there.'

Alice shrieks, muffling the sound with her hands. I can see her shaking, even in the half-light.

My muscles tense and I will myself to move. My mouth fills with saliva and I swallow it down.

'Come on.' I reach out and grab her shoulder, pushing her ahead of me and out of the kitchen, my movements much bolder than I feel. She opens her mouth to protest, but I shove her forward, rough enough that she's surprised and she closes her mouth again. 'Go and hide somewhere. Go in the basement with the others.'

'But—'

'You're here because of me. And it's you he's come for. Go. Find somewhere to hide.' I close my eyes with immediate regret. I don't want to be alone. Even Alice is better than no one. 'Run,' I hiss, fear giving my voice a ragged edge.

More pounding comes from behind us and her face changes again, pure fear crossing her brow. At the sight of her distress, I push down my own terror.

'Give me the axe.' I wrench it from her hands and push her into the hallway. Finally, she runs away into the darkness of the house, her footsteps fading as she moves from the slate tiles onto the stair carpet. She's gone to find Ted, I know it. But it's out of my hands.

I turn back to the kitchen, the axe heavy and cold in my hands.

Suddenly, the body blows start again on the other side of the kitchen door, huge creaking thumps as the monster on the other side throws his entire weight against the door. 'Let me in, for God's sake,' comes a muffled shout from outside.

I freeze at the sound of his voice, that vicious snarl in the dark. The banging on the doors was scary enough, but hearing that angry voice on the other side of the door emphasises that there's a human being out there, trying to get in. Someone who wants to hurt us.

I suppress a shriek and force myself to stand still, to run through my options. I'm strong, I'm resilient. I'm no coward. My life hasn't been easy but I got to where I am today as a whole, complete person and I can face whatever life throws at me. And that includes some drunk abuser who thinks of hitting little girls. And I need to protect my own girls, no matter how terrified I am.

The basement door is feet away, my girls on the other side, safe with Mum. I could go in there, huddle up with them and wait out the storm. Leave Ted and Alice up here to fend for themselves. A two-person front against the intruder. But no matter whether I've lost Ted for ever, I still want him to be safe. And I need to protect my kids.

The world around me tilts as I realise that there's no reason to fight this any more. Robin wants Alice and Natasha, and after what Alice just said, I want them gone. I made a stupid mistake inviting them, but I had no idea what terrors they would bring with them. I hate myself for thinking this, but if it's us or them, I know who I choose.

I feel a burst of anger, which spurs me forwards, towards the door. None of this should be happening. I'm angry with Ted and with Alice, but with myself most of all. If it wasn't for me, Alice and Natasha would be miles away right now, doing who-knows-what with who-knows-who. Getting the help they needed instead of running to us. They'd never know about Red Hart Lodge, and our Christmas plans would be intact. My children and Mum would be safe and warm, not huddled in a dark basement.

I shoulder the axe, blade cool against my cheekbone. I still have a chance.

There's a moment of quiet, as soon as I make this decision. Like I'm in the centre of a tornado. The eye of the storm. All around me is chaos and danger, but for now there's an eerie tranquillity, made more precious by its fragility.

I breathe, filling my lungs with air. In for four, out for four.

If he gets past me, he'll have Alice and Ted to contend with before he gets to the children. A wild, hopeful thought fills my chest: maybe he'll find Alice immediately and take her and go.

Whatever happens next, I can't live in this limbo any longer, with everything out of my control and no idea what will happen next. I need to take charge.

I stride to the door, reach out and turn the old-fashioned key, listening to the mechanical clicks as the lock is released. And I slide the bolt free. The door rattles in its frame, released from the locks. I could run away, to hide in the basement with the others while Robin rampages around the lodge, trying to find Alice. Or I could stay here and fight.

Who am I? What does Sadie choose? I'm a wife in an unhappy marriage, who made a stupid mistake trying to fix things for the children. I'm a person who fights for what she wants. Who protects her family, even if her methods are sometimes misjudged. I don't run away and leave everyone I love alone to pick up the pieces, not like my dad. I don't leave. I stay and fight.

There's a creaking of wood, and my heart leaps into my mouth. The door is opening.

A mud-covered boot steps through the gap.

I'm not ready. This was a stupid thing to do.

But I grab the axe with both hands and raise it, my hands shaking and slipping on the handle.

The door opens further, a silhouetted head and shoulders appearing through the gap. I bring the axe down and it makes contact with a sickening crunch.

'What—' There's a yelp and a shout of pain, and my blood turns cold. *What have I done?*

23

The figure stands in the doorway, his hands raised in surrender like there's a gun pointed at him. He's big, like Mum described.

'Put the axe down before you do something stupid,' says an indignant voice as the figure strides into the kitchen, bringing with him the smell of decaying leaves and rain.

I know that voice. It's not a stranger, not Robin.

It's Ted's dad.

I step back, away from the axe which is still reverberating, its blade embedded in the wood of the door. I missed him, thank God. My hands tingle from the shock of hitting the wood.

'We've only been gone a couple of hours and it's descended into *Lord of the Flies* around here.' His voice is clipped and short.

'Neil? I'm so sorry. We thought...' My hands hang limp by my sides, adrenaline still coursing through my veins. Can I even begin to explain? I lead Ted's dad into the living room and get him settled on the sofa, a blanket around his shoulders. 'I'll explain in a minute. Let's get you warm and dry first.'

I stride over to the basement and open the door.

'Mum?' I call down the steps, and there's a squeal of relief.

Charley and Tamara scramble up the stairs, closely followed by Mum. They all look a little dusty but not worse for wear for their adventure. Charley is grinning, her left cheek smudged with dirt.

'Oh, I'm so glad to see you're OK. What happened?' Mum asks, brushing dust from the back of her trousers.

The girls cuddle into me, burying their faces in my stomach. Ted and Alice appear at the top of the stairs, and Ted rushes down and strokes both of them on their heads. His face is craggy with exhaustion, and grey with worry. His jaw is dotted with salt and pepper stubble, which he rubs with his hand. He looks his age for the first time since we met. 'What's going on? Why are the kids up here?'

I pause, unable to tell them everything all at once. 'There was no intruder,' I settle on. It's true, in a way. I explain about finding Ted's dad on the back doorstep, about nearly decapitating him with the axe. My breath shudders as I contemplate what could have happened if there had been a little more light to see where I was swinging the blade.

'Where's Natasha?' Alice says, scanning each of our faces.

Mum shakes her head in disapproval. 'I told her, stay here where it's safe. But she wasn't having any of it and I couldn't stop her.'

Charley and Tamara step back, and Charley hops on the spot with glee. She's covered in dust, her face smudged and her hair tangled. 'She was so naughty, Mummy. She kept wandering off in the dark even though it wasn't safe. She was looking for something. And then she just didn't come back.'

'She said she wanted to go and find her dad,' adds Tamara, biting her lip. 'That no one needed to hide from him, and that it was stupid.'

I frown, glancing at my Mum. 'So she came up here? How long ago?'

Mum shakes her head. 'It was hard to track time down

there. Maybe ten minutes ago? But she didn't come up here. She was shuffling around down the far end of the basement. I could hear her... until I couldn't.'

'So she could still be down there?' I step towards the door and peer down into the darkness.

Mum shrugs helplessly.

'Oh my God,' Alice says, and pushes past me to get to the basement, her shoulder knocking against mine. I wince but don't respond. She's trying to get a reaction out of me, just like she was when she tried to tell me that Ted had invited her here because he wants her back. I won't give her the satisfaction.

Mum grabs a spare torch and takes Tamara and Charley upstairs through the dark house to wash and change. We leave the basement door open and I put the kettle on the Aga to make some tea.

Once the tea is ready, I carry it on a tray to the living room, to find Ted's dad alone on the sofa, still wrapped in the blanket.

'You doing OK?' I set the tea on the coffee table in front of the sofa and sit across from him.

'Cold and a little bruised, but thankfully not injured.' He pauses and raises an eyebrow at me. 'What was going on there, Sadie? I was shouting and practically hammering the door down trying to get you to open it. The weather out there is the worst I've ever seen. And I've seen some bad storms. Who knows what could have happened.'

I shudder at the thought of *what could have happened* if I had been a little more accurate with the axe. 'Where's Ted gone?'

'Thankfully, Patricia has her audiobook thingy so she just sat in the car, keeping warm. It's got a good battery on it as it's so new. Ted's gone to get her now.'

I nod and lean forward to pour the tea. 'We thought you were an intruder,' I explain, choosing my words carefully. I explain about Alice's ex potentially being on his way here.

Neil frowns, his forehead corrugating. 'Poor wee Al. What's the world coming to, I say. These men with their anger problems, and no one able to trust another soul enough to open the door to them in a storm, right enough.' He shakes his head, and I notice something on the side of his neck, like fingernail scratch marks.

I frown, leaning forward. It's hard to see in the dark. It could be mud or it could be blood. 'What happened to your neck, Neil? Do you need something for that?'

He frowns, raising a hand to it and wincing as he touches it. 'Ah, yes. Must be the adrenaline that I'd forgotten about it, you know. The same thing used to happen on a shoot; I'd get all scratched up by the trees and I wouldn't notice until I got in the shower hours later.' He presses his palm to the wound. 'The wind was so strong that it was whipping branches through the air. One of them got me as I rounded the house. Smashed the window, too. Just a scratch, though.'

'I've got some first aid supplies upstairs. I'll get them as soon as Ted and Patricia come back,' I say.

The door opens and Ted enters, closely followed by his mum, whose salt-and-pepper bob is only slightly out of place.

I hold out a hand. 'Ted, can I use your torch? Natasha—'

'How could you?' Patricia hisses, her voice quivering with anger. She steps around Ted and rushes over to Neil, wrapping an arm around his shoulders. She glares at me, her eyes flicking to Ted and then back to me. 'How could you do that to an elderly man? He's seventy-five years old.'

My mouth falls open and I drop my hand.

She folds her arms across her narrow chest and glances at Neil, who stares down at his knees, shaking his head. 'Look at him, all scratched up and freezing cold,' she says. 'He's not the strong man he once was, you know. And you're barricading him out and making him run around in a storm.'

Neil straightens up and pushes the blanket off his shoulders. 'Pat, I don't want to—'

She cuts him off with a hand on his shoulder. 'No, Neil. They can't treat you this way.' She gets a tissue from her pocket and dabs at the scratch on her husband's neck.

He flinches and bats her away. 'Leave it,' he whispers. 'It's fine.'

Ted slumps into an armchair. 'How could we know you'd turned back? Look, I'm sorry. If we'd known it was Dad we'd have let him in straight away. Mum, you know that. We're all freaked out, here in the dark with the wind howling.' He clears his throat and leans forward. 'There's something you need to know.' And he explains what Alice had confided about Robin, Natasha's message leading him to them, and Alice's pure fear.

Patricia listens with pursed lips, shaking her head occasionally in sympathy. When Ted finishes, she's quiet for a moment and then looks up at him with an accepting smile, but it doesn't reach her eyes. 'Where is Alice now?' she asks, a hopeful look on her face.

I lift one shoulder in a half-shrug, realising that Patricia and Neil have no idea of the contagious terror that swept through everyone when Alice found that message on the iPad and we saw those headlights heading towards the house. They couldn't understand what that was like, seeing the terror in Alice's eyes.

Ted makes to join me on the sofa and I stand before he can pretend to be couiley in front of his parents. 'I'm going to go and find Natasha,' I say. 'And I'll bring the first aid kit and some dry clothes, too.'

Ted nods, but as I approach the door, the room lights up and the TV comes to life with a whirr.

'Perfect timing,' says Patricia, leaning forward to pour herself a tea.

But Ted doesn't hear her, his face white as snow as he gazes at the TV, flashing images reflecting blue in his eyes.

'What—' I start, but the words turn to ash in my mouth as I see what he's looking at on the screen.

The TV has come on to the national news, a ticker-tape red strip running the headlines across the bottom, and a newsreader talking to the camera on one half of the screen. On the other half, a man's face stares out at us, frozen in a passport-style photograph.

It's a familiar face, one that I've seen in the last few hours on a screen not dissimilar to this. Shaved head, rugby player nose. It's Robin.

But instead of 'wanted for domestic violence' or whatever I expect it to say, the headline across the bottom of the screen reads INJURED MAN LEFT FOR DEAD IN GLASGOW FLAT. PARTNER SOUGHT FOR QUES-TIONING.

24

We all freeze in silence, staring at the screen as the newsreader moves onto the next story.

The only person who doesn't seem fazed is Patricia, who is adding milk to her tea and stirring. She picks up her mug and sips her tea, still not looking at the TV. 'We set off home, but honestly, the car was practically being blown off the road, wasn't it, Neil? And we thought, better that we're alive to go back to our dogs when the storm's over than dead in a ditch. And then there was a tree across the road, so we turned back, but by that time the water was up over the bridge. Good old Neil waded across and left me to keep warm, bless him. But I was getting worried when he came back and said no one was answering the doors, poor love. We couldn't work out what was going on.'

Ted and I exchange a look. His eyes are wide, and I can see him processing the same information I am. Slowly, he lifts the remote and mutes the TV.

Neil looks from me to Ted, and back again, before turning his attention back to his wife. 'See what else is on, love. The news on Christmas Day is always a scam. Slimy politicians trying to hide the big stuff.'

Patricia looks from Neil to Ted, confused, as she reaches for the remote.

Ted leads me into the hallway, leaving his dad to explain. It's such a relief to have lights on, to see where I'm walking, to look at my husband's face. The whole house feels warmer, somehow.

The basement door still stands open, the darkness below impenetrable even though the ground floor is now illuminated.

'Natasha? Alice?' I call, and pause to listen. Nothing. 'There's a pull cord light at the bottom of the stairs,' I say to Ted. 'I'll be able to see if I go down and switch it on.' I glance again into the darkness with dread. I don't want to go down there again, but Natasha might need help. Especially now we know the truth about why Alice was running away. Whatever Robin has done, she can't be trusted. Not even with her own daughter.

Ted shakes his head and grabs my arm. 'I'll go. You stay with the girls.'

I pull away, still galvanised by my decision to open the door to Ted's dad. It was the right one, and I don't intend to relinquish control over my life any more. No more sitting back and letting things happen. I want to do this. This is my fault, and I will fix it.

I stride into the kitchen, pull the axe from the door and approach the basement, Ted following close behind, ready to argue.

I turn to him, exasperated. 'We need to find Alice. And the kids are upstairs, alone.' I pause at the top of the basement steps, the axe in both hands. 'You're a big guy. There are a lot of people in this house that need your protection if...' I stop myself before I say any more. Because I have no idea what might happen. I try to communicate the urgency with my eyes: if Alice tried to kill Robin, we need to protect the family from a potential murderer. It's more important that Ted is here, with Tamara and Charley. 'The people we love are in this house. Look after them.'

His shoulders sag and he nods, accepting what I'm saying. Agreeing that Alice is dangerous. Finally. Finally, he sees what I saw from the start.

I close my eyes briefly, knowing that this is the only way. I have to go back down into the basement to look for Natasha and Alice.

There's a shout as Mum shepherds Tamara and Charley down the stairs, the girls changed into clean pyjamas, their hair brushed and their faces washed. 'Thank you,' I say to Mum.

Ted turns to Mum and the girls. 'Go into the living room. There's tea and you can get the fire going again. Grandma and Grandpa are here; they came back.' He forces a jovial tone, and the girls shriek with glee at the thought of more time with their grandparents, before bundling through the door. 'You, too, Julie,' he says to Mum. 'Go take a break. We'll find Alice and Natasha.'

She gives us a grateful look and joins them in the living room. As the door begins to close, I catch a glimpse of the warm, well-lit and comfortable room and I yearn to join them. I don't want to descend into the bowels of the house once more. My stomach roils.

Ted looks at me, his ice-blue eyes holding mine. I wish none of this had happened. I want my husband back, the one I married ten years ago. As if he can read my thoughts, he holds out his arms for me and I step into them. After a moment, I pull back, my eyes prickling with self-pity. I take a shaky breath, shouldering my weapon. 'This wasn't the Christmas I imagined, Ted.'

Despite everything, we both laugh. For a moment, we're *us* again, before everything: sneaking Chinese takeaway into the cinema to watch the newest James Bond film, or hopping across moss-slick stepping stones on one of our first dates. It's such a relief to laugh with him, a release of the tension that's built up over the last thirty-six hours.

But as soon as it began, the laughter stops and the smiles slide from our faces. There's a bad person in this house, and we have to find her. And no one will be safe until we do.

I leave the door open, letting the light from the hallway guide my tentative footsteps as I descend. It's even dustier than earlier; Mum and the girls must have kicked up new plumes of dust with their movements. Coughing, I lift my jumper over my face as I reach the bottom level and peer into the darkness.

I pause for a moment, listening. The silence is heavy. If I had to put money on it, I'd bet there was no one down here. You can sense a person's presence, I've always felt. Even if they're perfectly still and silent, there's an aura about a room that contains another human being. And this basement feels deserted, except for me.

Where are Natasha and Alice?

Still, I make tentative steps forward and tug on the light cord. There's a heavy *click,* but for a moment nothing happens, the darkness remains. Then, slowly, there's a *buzz* and a *hum* and then a strip light flashes on, bathing the room in a pallid, cold wash. It's dim, but for the first time, I can see the shape of everything: the tool bench, the rusting lawnmower, the old sacks of desiccated soil. Lots of gardening equipment.

I circle the room, stepping over the sagging cardboard boxes and peering behind stacked dining chairs.

I pause outside the room that's full of deer antlers, but I can't bring myself to go inside. It's too creepy. There's no way Natasha went in there, surely?

Inside the room, the bones almost glow in the distant light from the main basement. I can see a skull or two, all bleached white like they've been treated with something. What kind of person collects these, and stores them? What are they for? I shudder and back away, swallowing the bile which rises in my throat.

Ready to give up and return to the main house, I pull the cord and the light goes out, but the light from the hallway is off now. The stairs ahead of me plunge into darkness as my eyes struggle to adjust.

I squint and see a shadowy figure at the top of the stairs. Looking down at me through the part-open door.

I can barely see their features, but I'm certain I see the flash of teeth as she grins at me. Alice.

Before I can call out, the door swings closed, slamming into the frame.

I'm trapped in pitch-darkness.

25

'No!' I call. I drop the axe with a clatter and rush up the steps, almost tripping over my feet in the hurry. I throw my weight against the door, hammering my hands on the wood, but it doesn't budge. I peer through the gap in the frame and can see the narrow shaft of a bolt or a lock. She's locked me in.

I'm trapped in here.

A draught rushes through the gap, making an eerie moaning before the cold air hits my cheek. I pull back and bang my hands on the door, bruising them and scraping my knuckles.

'Alice! Don't do this,' I shout. There's no sound from the other side.

I sink to my haunches, my back against the door.

'Ted?' I shout, but no one replies. 'Alice? Let me out.'

I hear a movement on the other side of the door. 'Open the door,' I shout, as loud as I can.

Then I hear a quiet voice from the corridor outside: 'No.'

And then footsteps walk away, gradually fading into silence.

I bang on the door again, trying to attract someone's attention. But no luck. No one can hear me through this thick door and the howl of the wind.

My hands are cold, the skin red and raw from hammering at the bare wood. I pull my phone from my pocket again, jab at the screen and poke at the buttons on the side, but it's totally done. No response.

I shove my phone back in my pocket and pull my jumper sleeves over my hands, suppressing a shiver. I've been so suffused with adrenaline over the past hour or so, protecting the house from what we thought was Robin, that I haven't noticed how cold I am, how hungry. How exhausted. And the ghost of a headache throbs behind my eyes; the inevitable hangover from all the wine I downed at lunch.

I'm shaking all over. I wrap my arms around myself, taking deep breaths to try to calm myself down. Ted knows where I went. He'll come looking for me eventually. Unless Alice finds him first and does something to him, too.

Suddenly, an image fills my head of Ted, lying on the floor in a pool of blood. She's done it once, wouldn't she do it again? Sure, she came here to find Ted, to seduce him and make him her ticket to a new life now that she'd literally destroyed her old one, but if it's not going her way who knows what she'd do to get away? Especially if she finds out that Ted knows what she did to Robin.

She just locked me in the basement. She could be capable of anything. I can't let this happen. My kids are up there, my mum, Ted's parents... and Ted. I can't just sit here, mouldering in the basement, waiting for someone to realise I'm gone.

I descend the stairs, arms outstretched in the pitch dark, adrenaline coursing through my system once more. I reach up and paw blindly at the air until I find the cord and pull it again. The strip light clicks and hums. Then it flashes on, blinding me. I squint until my eyes adjust to the orange strip light, and I scan the stuff down there, looking for something I can use to prise open the door. There's so much old gardening equipment, there must be a crowbar or something heavy enough... I've still got the axe, which I pick up from the floor where I dropped it. I wouldn't hesitate to hack the door to pieces if I need to.

Yet there's no sign of Natasha. Where is she? She was down here, and then she wasn't.

Unless she sneaked past Mum, Charley and Tamara in the basement to climb the stairs and opened the sticky door undetected to escape into the ground floor of the house, she must have found another way out of the basement. And now that I've scoured the perimeter of the room, the only possibility is that either she's hiding in the room with the deer antlers, or the bones are obscuring a way out.

The stored gardening equipment only makes sense if this space was once used by a gardener before they started storing deer carcasses down here. There's no way they'd carry a rusty old lawnmower through the main house and down the stairs. There must be a way out down here, into the garden.

I grit my teeth and approach the yawning doorway, beyond which the bones glow like a light comes from within.

Now I look at them, discarded in the damp and cold under the house, and I feel such grief for these wild creatures that were hunted and their bodies hoarded.

When I step into the room, I see that it isn't stacked wall-to-wall with bones, as it looked from the outside. There's a narrow path along one side, leading into blackness.

I shove my hands into my pockets and hunch my shoulders, gazing into the dark. There's nothing but silence, and the tickle of dust in my nose.

Tentatively, I take my first step into the bone room, the light fading as I move further into the ten-foot-wide space. The walls seem to narrow around me as I walk forward, sliding my feet along the ground to avoid tripping on anything.

There's a sudden movement to my right.

I freeze as a skull slides from the pile and into my path, its antlers snagging on other bones on its way down. It skitters to a stop, followed by an avalanche of other bones – they look like leg bones. Now still, the skull's vacant eyeholes stare blankly up at me from the ground.

I stand for a moment, staring, waiting for my heart rate to slow. Then I step over the fallen bones and further away from the light. I reach out with my left hand, running it against the stone wall to feel my way forward. Did Natasha do this, too? How was she brave enough? I'm a grown adult and I'm terrified.

She must have been desperate, I realise. I know I am. You'd have to be, to come in here in the pitch-black, alone. Now I know who Alice is, what she's been hiding – what they've *both* been hiding – I understand why Natasha would try to get away. Maybe she thought she could run, get free of Alice. I think back to her huddled form when they first arrived yesterday, her hood up to obscure her face. Did she seem afraid? Was she trying to tell me something?

Perhaps she needed help. Her ominous silence, her hunched posture, her isolation... all the hallmarks of a child desperate for help, for an adult to realise what she's going through. And we all missed it.

She was practically kidnapped, and no one knew.

So she had to stumble into this horrifying room, in the pitch-black, in an attempt to save herself.

The room is silent. She's not here, I know it. She's gone. And I need to find her – before Alice does – and help her.

I hope she's safe. I hope she got out and found shelter to hide from the storm. The only way I'll find out is by pushing on and leaving the light behind.

I step forward, one hand on the wall and the other stretched out blindly in front of me, groping at the air.

Then my hand touches something warm and wet.

I shriek and step backwards, my back hitting the stone wall. I flap my hand, my face contorted in disgust and horror. What is that? Blood. It's blood. Natasha is dead, her still-warm blood splattered on the wall and now all over my hands.

I listen, and I think I can hear a faint *hiss* above the silence. I raise my hand to my nose, but it's scentless. It doesn't have the iron tang of blood.

I regulate my breathing, trying to take deep breaths in and out, suppressing the shaking of my whole body and the spasms in my lungs.

I reach out with a shaking hand, returning my fingers to the liquid, which runs over my nails, warming them with its heat. It's water. Just water. There's a leaking pipe above my head, a trickle of water running down the wall. It's not blood.

It's not blood.

I wipe my hand on my jeans and continue, my steps even slower now, my heart beating out of my chest. Then, finally, my hand touches wood. A door.

'Thank God,' I whisper to no one. My voice is whipped away by the silence. My ears ring with it.

I feel around until my fingers encounter a cold metal ring. I twist it, and the telltale *clunk* tells me I've found Natasha's trail. This is a way out.

But what is waiting for me on the other side?

26

As I push the door I see faint light for the first time in what feels like hours. I hear the rush of wind through the trees above me in the night sky, and there behind the door is a stone staircase, leading up towards the sky. I'm free.

I run up the stairs like I'm being chased, desperate to put as much distance between me and the darkness of the basement as possible. As I reach the top, I'm immediately buffeted by the wind, which rips through my jumper as if the fabric isn't there at all. There's an icy sting to it, and it pricks at my cheeks and tears at my hair. The rain is hard, like little marbles hitting my body. It might even be hail, I can't see in this soupy darkness. If there's a moon, it's hidden behind thick cloud.

My feet ache with the cold, the rainwater and mud soaking through my wool socks in moments. The bare trees tower over me, and I can hear branches smashing together above my head. Beyond, the mountains loom, dark and threatening. It's such a dangerous beauty, this harsh landscape.

To my right is the house, and I'm grateful for the golden glow spilling from the windows and lighting my way through the storm. I'm in the walled herb garden at the back of the house, the little raised beds casting shadows across the gravel ahead of me. They once contained fresh herbs; I can see the faded paint on the wood: *mint, rosemary, thyme.* The soil is bare, with dead leaves decaying in the corners. The ghost of the estate's kitchen garden. Beyond that is the wall, and then the river.

I'm alone.

I turn into the wind, towards the house. I need to get back inside, to warn them that Alice's intentions are clear now. That she's willing to stop at nothing to get what she wants. She abandoned her search for her daughter and locked me in a basement.

I peer through the darkness, looking for a silhouette or anything that tells me where Natasha went after she left the basement. And whether Alice was right behind her.

The stones dig into the soles of my feet. Hunched over, I trudge across the gravel drive. I'm out of breath and there's a thin sheen of sweat across my skin, despite the cold.

I glance up, back towards the house, and gasp, the axe slipping from my hands and dropping to the ground. I stare, frozen in place, as a shaft of light slices across the gravel drive ahead of me, two shadows cutting across it. The front door opens, and two people step out. Then the light disappears as the door closes once more.

It's Alice and Natasha, clad in their coats and boots. I'm so confused about timelines and locations, and the wind just won't stop, messing with my thoughts and my ability to reason. They must have got back into the house somehow, if they ever left through the basement to begin with.

But it doesn't matter where they were or where they've been. All I know is that they're getting away. For so long, I've wanted them to leave, but now, we can't let them. We can't let Alice take that child with her. Their figures stop occasionally and glance around, checking they haven't been detected. My stomach churns.

What have they done, while I was trapped in the basement? Did Alice trap me to remove an obstacle? But an obstacle to what? Now we know she's capable of violence, it's not just my marriage that's under threat. It's the safety of my entire family.

My heart is pounding, my breath emerging in steamy puffs that are whipped away within moments. As Alice and Natasha lean into the wind and turn away from the house, I grab the axe from where it fell and pick my way through the kitchen garden in a crouch, ready to drop down behind a planter if they turn my way. But they don't. They seem to know exactly where they're going. They're heading towards the bridge.

I rush to the back door. Where Ted's dad entered. I wrap my fingers around the doorknob and utter a silent prayer that in the rush and confusion no one thought to lock it again.

The doorknob turns, and there's a telltale *click*. With a rush of relief, I push the door open. I'm inside.

I rush into the living room, a sob rising in my chest. They're all there, huddled together on the sofa. Safe.

The girls look up from the TV, their faces transformed into smiles of joy at the sight of me. 'Mummy!' shouts Charley, and both girls jump up and rush towards me.

I crouch to their level, opening my arms to them. It feels like I've been away for weeks. For years. I bury my nose in their hair, inhaling their familiar scent one after the other. They're safe. They're warm. They're dry.

But Natasha isn't. She's out there in the storm. Alice has dragged her out into danger.

'Mummy, you're wet,' Tamara giggles, pushing me away. 'And your hair is messy.'

Ted looks as dishevelled as I do, and exhausted too. His hair sticks up, and I know he's been pulling at it with stress. I stand up and cross to him, and he pulls me into a hug before holding

me away from him, checking me over with his eyes. 'Are you
OK? What happened? You've been gone ages.' He touches my
shoulder. 'Your clothes are wet.'

I straighten up, smoothing my hair down with my hands,
and glance towards all three grandparents. They're looking at
me, their faces marred with a concern they can't voice in front
of the girls. I must look a state, covered in dust and dirt,
drenched by the rain, buffeted by the wind.

Mum stands up and hovers next to me, hopping from foot to
foot. 'What happened to you?' she whispers.

I lower my voice so the girls can't hear, and I tell them about
watching the hooded figures leave through the front door just
moments ago. Patricia looks at me, wide-eyed, but with understanding, and I know that Ted must have brought her up to
speed somehow, without the girls hearing. I tell them through
heaving breaths about Alice at the top of the basement stairs,
closing me in and refusing to open the door.

Neil and Patricia listen from their seats on the sofa, but they
don't stand up to check if I'm OK. I wonder whether they're
still on Alice's side, or if they're now embarrassed that they gave
more credence to a long-gone ex-girlfriend than to the woman
their son has been with for twelve years and the mother of their
grandchildren. I hope they have the grace to feel guilt, but as I
stare at their rigid forms listening to my latest update, I highly
doubt it.

Ted pulls me into another hug. 'That must have been terrifying. Thank God you got out. What is she playing at?'

Mum gathers a blanket in her arms and wraps it around my
shoulders like I'm a child again. I didn't realise I'm still shivering, my teeth chattering so hard I can barely speak. 'You must
be freezing, poor thing. Let me get you a cup of tea.'

'And a wee dram, too. That'll warm you right up,' adds Neil.

I give a grateful nod and cross to the window, my throat
swollen with anxiety.

Through the gap in the curtain, I can only see a few feet over the gravel drive where the light from the house falls. Everything beyond is darkness. I stare for a moment, my eyes drifting out of focus. I'm about to turn away from the window when a cloud suddenly shifts, and the moon becomes visible, bathing the landscape in a milky light.

I can see the river, wider and faster than ever before, the wind buffeting its surface and making it roil like the sea. Beyond, I can see the outline of Neil's car on the other side of the bridge.

The bridge itself is almost obscured by water, almost over the top. I stare at it, trying to see how much higher the water has to rise before the bridge is completely obscured. It's like a moving wall, barricading us in with its force.

Are my eyes playing tricks? I blink, once. Twice. Three times. It's not an illusion.

I cover my mouth with my free hand, silencing my sharp intake of breath.

I gasp. I reach up and pull the curtains open, fully exposing the window. Cold air hits me like a wave, seeping through the broken windowpane, which I see someone has patched up with a flattened wine box and some tape.

'What is it?' Ted's parents bustle over, closely followed by my mum.

What I see at the river makes my blood run cold. *Will they make it out of here alive?*

27

Two huddled figures sway as they trudge towards the river, buffeted by the wind. Their hoods are drawn up around their heads, and their arms folded around their waists. With every step, they look like they could be tugged into the rushing water and swept away into the ether. Gone for ever.

Neil, Patricia and Mum usher me out of the way and crowd at the glass.

'They'll get swept away,' Patricia says, panic in her voice.

Ted rushes to the other window and pulls open those curtains too. He cups his hands around his face, staring into the darkness. We're all silent, trying to work out what they're doing.

I join Ted at his window, scrunching up my eyes to see better.

Mum pulls away from the window. 'What are they doing? They'll kill themselves.'

As Mum says it, Natasha topples sideways as if she's about to fall into the river. We all freeze, holding our breath until she leans back again, righting herself with her hands on the side of the stone bridge. The water is past her knees and rising, obscuring the road surface so that only the bridge's walls are visible above the rushing dark water.

'We need to go and get them,' I say, pulling at Ted's arm. But he doesn't move, still staring out of the window.

'Ted,' I say, my voice getting higher and more urgent. I don't care about Alice – ideally we'd leave her out there – but Natasha is innocent. Natasha doesn't deserve this fate.

Charley and Tamara look up from their TV show, their faces drawn with worry. I force a smile. 'It's OK, girls. Don't worry.' I turn back to Ted, who's pointing now, his fingertip white against the glass.

'What can you see?' I ask in a low voice.

I follow the direction of his finger with my gaze.

'What are they doing?' he asks, and squints, moving his face closer to the glass. 'Are they going to try to walk somewhere?'

'In this weather? Surely not,' whispers Mum, shaking her head in disapproval.

Neil makes a sudden noise, an intake of breath.

Patricia looks up at him, concern on her face. 'You don't think they'd...' She shakes her head. 'They couldn't, surely?'

Neil steps away from the window, his hands rifling through his pockets, his face reddening. 'My keys.' A vein protrudes on his forehead.

Ted tears his gaze from the window. 'They took your car keys?'

Neil nods, circling the sofa and scanning the floor while patting each pocket in turn. 'Or I dropped them somewhere, while I was...' He gestures around, indicating the perimeter of the house. 'You know.'

Ted lets out a groan.

'They're going for the car?' asks Patricia, her voice louder than normal. 'She wouldn't...'

'If they take it, we're screwed. It's our only way out while the river's like this,' Ted mutters, shaking his head in frustration. 'We'll be stuck for days.'

There's a sense of purpose in Patricia's voice as she holds out a hand to Neil, palm up. 'Give me your phone, please.'

With a baffled look on his face, Neil reaches into his pocket and unlocks his phone, handing it to his wife.

She crosses to the sofa and sits down, slides her reading glasses onto her nose and taps at the screen, running through apps until she finds the one that she wants. 'Now, where is it?'

We watch in silence, occasionally glancing at each other in puzzlement.

I wrap the blanket around my shoulders and try desperately to warm up, to think. Finally, my shivering begins to subside. But with it comes fear and concern for Alice and Natasha. As much as I wanted Alice to leave, I didn't want either of them to be out in this weather. Especially not Natasha. Aside from us being stuck here if they take the car, I'm seriously concerned that they'll have an accident if they try to drive through the storm.

Mum turns back to the window. 'They're almost across the bridge. The water's rising quickly; it's almost to their thighs.'

'Be my eyes at the window. I need my glasses to see the phone, but I can't see out the window with them on,' says Patricia, in her new commanding voice. 'Tell me when they get into the car and they've shut the doors.'

'What are you doing, Mum?' Ted asks, drifting between the window and his mum.

Patricia's finger hovers over the screen, like a soldier waiting for the command to detonate a bomb.

'I was waiting in that car for a long time this afternoon, while Neil tried to get your attention in here. I found the car manual in the glove compartment and managed to read the whole thing. And there was this bit—'

'The car's unlocked. They're opening the doors. It looks like they're searching the boot,' says Mum.

I join her at the window and watch as the interior lights of the car glow warm through the storm. They're hunched over the boot, moving things around. 'Probably looking for coats and blankets,' I say, thinking how cold Natasha must be after being out in the storm for so long. I shudder in sympathy. Poor girl.

'They're closing the boot now,' I say, glancing back at Patricia. 'Moving to get inside.'

She nods, her face steely, and I turn back to the window. She gets up and joins us at the window, shoulder to shoulder with Mum and me, so close I can smell her perfume, floral and spiced.

Mum's almost bouncing up and down, a sports commentator documenting a world-record race time. 'They're inside...' She holds up an arm, one finger pointing into the air. And then with a little leap, she drops her arm as if starting a race. 'And the doors are closed.'

Immediately, Patricia presses something on the phone and the screen turns red.

'*Automobile disabled,*' says a mechanical voice from the phone's speaker. '*Door locks activated. Manual override OFF.*'

The interior lights of the car switch on, illuminating Natasha and Alice's figures in the car, their movements frantic as they realise they can't start the car and they can't open the doors from the inside. I watch as Alice clambers over the seats and into the back of the car, trying to open both rear doors. I feel a twinge of sympathy for her before triumph overrides it.

We win.

28

The irony is not lost on me that I've spent the last two days wishing Alice and Natasha would leave, and now I'm celebrating that they *can't*. I sigh and turn away from the window.

Ted and his dad both look at Patricia in admiration.

'There's a setting on your car that immobilises it and locks the doors. It's part of the security system,' she says, pushing her reading glasses back onto the top of her head and handing the phone back to Neil.

'It's a very high-spec car,' adds Neil, as if he invented the whole thing instead of just buying it for himself from his retirement fund. He slides his phone carefully onto the coffee table, afraid to touch the screen and accidentally unlock the car again.

'The feature is supposed to activate if someone's breaking into it, but you can also switch it on manually using the app. I had a lot of time in the car this afternoon, so I distracted myself by reading that manual. I wondered if you could disable it *while* someone's inside. Turns out, you can.' Patricia's cheeks glow red with pride.

Ted gives her another nod of thanks and then strides towards the door. 'I'd better go out there and get them.'

I reach out and put a hand on his arm, feeling the firmness of his tense bicep through his jumper. 'Ted.'

He stops walking and turns to look at me.

'We could just leave them there until we can contact the police?'

Mum mumbles in agreement. 'No need to bring them back inside the house, surely.' She nods towards the girls, who are half-watching another cartoon. Tamara keeps glancing over, nosy about what the adults are doing. 'She's a wanted criminal, Ted.'

Ted hesitates. 'We can't leave them too long. It's freezing out there. It's inhumane. And criminal in itself.'

Mum sits on the sofa next to Tamara and leans towards us. 'Why can't we call the police now? Neil's phone must have a signal if that app worked.'

Patricia hands Neil's phone back to him and he clicks past the lock screen with a shake of his head. 'Still no signal at all, it says. The app must work with some other tech, like AirDrop or Bluetooth or something. Still, I'll give it a go...' He clicks on his keypad and dials 999, holding the phone to his ear.

Moments later, he presses the red button and shakes his head. 'Nothing. Total silence.'

'Can I?' I hold my hand out for the phone and Neil passes it over. Without explaining myself, I leave the room, heading to the pocket of signal I found on the stairs hours ago. But the 'no service' symbol doesn't budge, no matter where I stand. The mast that provided the scrap of connection earlier must have been affected by the storm. I return to the living room and hand the phone back to Neil with a shake of my head.

We all exchange glances, wide-eyed. The fire crackles in the grate and a squeaky cartoon voice chirps out of the TV.

I clear my throat. 'None of us asked for this.'

Ted looks at me, mouth open in disgust.

Frustrated, I pull the blanket tight around my shoulders,

squeezing until I'm almost breathless. 'I'm not saying we should leave them there to get hypothermia, Ted. But we've inadvertently stumbled into this strange situation and we're now keeping two women captive in a locked car. And one of them is probably violent—'

'Shhh,' Mum says, leaning across Tamara to grab the remote and turning up the volume on their cartoon.

She stands up and comes to perch on the arm of my chair, and us adults huddle together to exchange quiet words out of child earshot.

'I'm just saying we don't have to rush this. We've got time to work out what we do next.'

Ted runs his hands through his hair. 'We have to bring them inside. I don't know what we need to discuss.'

I stand up and cross to the landline phone, lifting the receiver to my ear. 'Still dead,' I mutter, and slam it down too hard, jangling the bells inside. 'We just need a way to contact the police.'

'Before they freeze to death,' Ted mumbles. He crosses to the coffee table and tops up a tumbler with whisky, his hands shaking. 'Anyone else?' he asks, scanning the group. Neil nods. Mum and Patricia shake their heads and reach for a mug of tea.

'I'll have one, too, please,' I say, and Ted looks up with surprise. I never drink whisky. I shrug at him and rub my temples, where the hangover headache is still blooming. 'If there's a day for it...'

A joyless smirk crosses his face as he hands out the tumblers.

Neil sips his like an expert. I down mine, and Ted follows before turning back to the window.

The whisky's peaty heat warms me inside faster than the log fire could, and I'm grateful for it. For the first time in hours, my shivering limbs still. Out of the corner of my eye, I see a similar reaction in Ted as his shoulders unfurl slightly.

Tamara glances up, and I see that her eyes are glassy with exhaustion. Next to her, Charley doesn't move, her gaze locked on the TV. 'You two should be getting to bed soon, it's very late,' I say with a forced smile.

'I'll take them up,' Mum says, clapping her hands together.

'Please can we finish this episode?' Tamara asks, big eyes glistening in the Christmas lights.

Charley joins in with the begging, adding, 'Can we watch this much TV every Christmas, Mummy?'

I shrug at Mum and give a vague nod. *What's five more minutes in a day so off the rails already?* We all agree to decide about Natasha and Alice after we take the girls up to bed. The grandparents join Charley and Tamara on the sofa, and, for a few minutes, life returns to almost normal.

I get up and cross to Ted where he's still standing staring out at the car in the darkness. I lean my head against his shoulder and he shifts his weight away from me. But then he wraps his arm around my shoulder and pulls me close. Has he returned to me? Is all the damage over, now that Alice has been unmasked, now that her true colours are visible?

He kisses my forehead and I try not to flinch away. I'm happy for his affection, especially in front of the girls, but maybe the answer to my question lies with me, not Ted: maybe he has returned to me, but can I return to him? If what Alice told me is true, can I forgive that he thought about it? That he wanted her? That for a moment, the memories of his first love were stronger than the reality of his current life? I don't know if I can. I don't know if she was telling the truth. I don't know what to believe.

'Ted,' I mumble, my mouth half-buried in his jumper. 'What does all this mean, for us?'

I glance back over my shoulder and see that the grandpar-

ents are absorbed in the kids' TV show, commenting on its
bright colours and reminiscing about the black-and-white
puppet shows they watched in comparison. No one is listening.

He looks down at me, his blue eyes glistening in the firelight, reflecting its embers. Part of me wants to kiss him, but also
I want to back away and never look at him again. We came here
to fix things, but instead everything has unravelled even further.
What if this isn't fixable any more? I feel a shell hardening
around me as a small part of my brain imagines life without
him. Single parenthood. Child handovers. Lawyers. Alternating
Christmases.

His eyebrows pull together, ploughing deep furrows down
his forehead. Confusion.

'I know that it must have been so confusing to find out
Natasha is yours. Of course you'd have loyalty to Alice, and
you'd want to create some kind of relationship. I can't even
imagine everything that's been going through your head the past
couple of days.'

He closes his eyes and nods once. He opens his mouth but I
keep going. I need to say this.

'But you let them stay and take over our Christmas, when
you know how important Christmas is to me, after everything.' I
take a breath. 'I think on some level you wanted Alice to stay.'

He starts to speak but I hold out a hand.

'You've barely spoken to me for days. Barely looked at me.
Barely touched me. It's like I don't exist when she's around.
And that distance has given me some clarity, if I'm honest.' I
step out of his comforting hold, needing my own space.

He flinches, visibly hurt.

Alice's words ring through my head, burned into my brain
for ever. *He looked for me for years, even after he married you.
You were his second choice, Sadie. His backup plan.*

I don't trust her, and I know she'd say anything to get what
she wants, but there's a ring of truth there. Instinctively, I know

that Ted said some of those things to her last night, over that bottle of wine they shared. I know because I could hear the memory of his voice in hers when she told me. And an echo of my own memories, too: he said things like that to me when we first got together: comparing me to the ones who went before, telling me why I was so much more special than anyone else. More special than Alice.

'I've just been...' His words falter and he stops talking, his expression pained.

'You could have pushed it with your parents, asked them to take Alice and Natasha with them when they left after lunch. Asked to borrow a car, Mum's or your parents. Anything to prioritise our family, our marriage, our Christmas.'

Behind us, there's a bustling as Mum and Patricia usher the girls out of the room, to get them ready for bed. Neil follows them, carrying a refreshed whisky tumbler.

And we're finally alone.

29

'They had nowhere to go. What would you have me do, shove them out into the storm?' A dark look crosses his face as his hurt turns to anger. His voice becomes louder now it's just the two of us in the room. 'Or just lock them in a car for a couple of days, so you can have a nice holiday without interrupting your perfect plans?' His frown is gone, replaced with a sneer.

'That's not fair, Ted.'

'Isn't it? What are you *thinking*, Sadie?'

'She's a criminal, Ted. The police are searching for her right now. She's on the news. What were *you* thinking?'

'We didn't know that when they arrived.'

'We knew *something*, though. I knew there was something off about her, that she wasn't a good person. That she was planning something horrible, and we were going to be the victims of whatever it was. She brought a knife into this house. She tried to kiss you. No one listened, and everyone dismissed me each time I tried to say something. And look.' I open my hands and gesture around the empty room, the detritus of our nightmare Christmas scattered around us. 'I was right. About everything. Our Christmas is ruined.' My voice catches in my throat and I swallow hard. 'Our family has been turned upside down. I nearly attacked your dad with an axe. And it's all because of her. It's what she wanted when she came here. She came here for you, and she's got you, hasn't she?'

He sinks to the sofa, his head in his hands. 'What are you talking about?'

'She told me all about your cosy chats last night, how you told her you missed her, that you still looked for her after you married me. Would you have left me if you'd found her, back then? What if I was pregnant, Ted? Or if our kids had been babies? Would you still have left me?'

He doesn't move from his seat hunched on the sofa.

'Are you planning to leave me now?' I ask, my voice a whisper.

The room fills with silence, the only sound is the wind outside, still buffeting the walls of the house, still rattling the windows in their frames.

Ted looks up, his eyes filled with tears. 'You are the love of my life, Sadie. *You.* Not Alice.' He swipes at his cheek with a balled fist.

'I don't feel loved, Ted.' My chest feels hollow. It's the truth, and one I've been avoiding for a very long time. Long before this. But how far back, I don't know; it's too much to face right now so I tug my thoughts back into the present, back to the original conversation: Alice. 'You looked for her while you were supposed to love me.'

He glowers at me. 'To check she was OK. To find out if I had a child. Because I'm a good man, Sadie. If there was a child in the world who belonged to me, I wanted to make sure they had what they needed. Pay child support. Look after them just like I look after our girls.'

I pause, picking at the skin around my nails, feeling the sting. Part of me wants to know, and part of me wants to run away. But I have to ask. I have to know. 'Did you know Alice was pregnant, Ted? When you left her behind to go on your trip?' I hold my breath and close my eyes.

Ted doesn't respond. He's so silent that eventually I open my eyes again to check he's still there. He sits on the sofa with his head in his hands.

I slump down next to him, but we don't touch. I can't bear to feel the warmth of his body that was once so familiar. 'Ted,' I whisper.

Alice had said Ted knew nothing... hadn't she? But no, I realise now. She'd skirted around those words, choosing instead to say it was her decision to raise the baby alone. But they were words carefully chosen to keep Ted on her good side, until it suited her to let the truth come out and really wreak havoc on my marriage, once she was safely ensconced at Red Hart Lodge with no danger of being turned out into the storm. And her plan worked, because I haven't been able to get this out of my head since it all came out. And she's still here, her claws dug deep into my life.

He sighs, a deep, lung-wracking sigh that rattles in his chest. 'I made a huge mistake, Sadie. I saw the pregnancy test and freaked out. I assumed she'd get an abortion if I left, and I thought that was the best option. A way to solve the problem without looking at it directly. I ran away without ever talking with her about it. But I wondered, yes, and that's why I searched.'

I raise my palms to my face and smooth out my forehead with my fingertips, trying to take in what this means, about Ted and who he is, about our marriage. About me, if I can move on from this. 'Oh, Ted.'

'I'm not proud of it,' he says, his voice hardening as his defences rise. 'I regretted it every day. I looked for her. To make amends.'

I don't reply.

I now have more information than I have since all of our

marital troubles began a couple of months ago. It's clearer, what happened when I got that positive test. Why Ted freaked out when I said I didn't want another baby, not with a six- and an eight-year-old already. Why he refused to speak to me for days after I made the appointment. And why he barely looked me in the eye when I began to cramp and bleed, days before I had to make a final decision.

I didn't have a teammate for one of the most heart-wrenching moments of my life, and it's all because Ted decided to run away from his responsibilities fifteen years ago. At a time when I should have had support from my husband, he was silently reliving something he should have got over decades ago, something he had wanted then more than he'd realised. Instead, Ted pulled further and further away while I lost our baby and tried not to cry in front of our children. He didn't trust me, and I couldn't work out why. Before, I felt abandoned and alone, left confused to deal with the loss of something I didn't even think I wanted. Now, at least, I understand why he couldn't be there for me. He was so haunted by his past, he couldn't manage the present.

'Sadie, please. I grew up. I've worked on myself. I'm still the man you married. The person who left Alice was young and naive. I made a bad choice and learned from it.'

I move my hands and look at him. *Really* look at him. His gaze searches my face, his eyes pleading.

I've barely moved for minutes, and now I sit up, easing the notches in my spine. 'Ted, I'm not sure you've changed as much as you think,' I say in a quiet voice, thinking about the last couple of months and how miserable and alone I've been when I should have had support, someone to lean on. And instead, Ted was nowhere. Actively avoiding me. 'You left Alice when she needed you most. And still now, you avoid your problems, you flinch away from confrontation. You don't face anything important. You wouldn't talk to me for days when I got pregnant. And then when it suits you, you show up and you're upset that the world kept turning while you were gone. It's not OK, Ted. *I'm* not OK.'

'What does this mean, Sadie? What are you saying?'

I shrug, exhausted. I have no idea. All I know is that I need to confront him and face all this if I ever have a chance of fixing our marriage.

He splutters and blusters, shaking his head. 'You're acting like our whole marriage was a sham, like I faked loving you for a decade.'

'It has seemed like that, the last couple of days.' *Longer*, I think, but I can't say it right now. 'Maybe it's just not—'

His whole body shudders, as if he can't hold in his feelings any more. 'I'm not *him*, Sadie.' He flinches as soon as the words leave his mouth, and I know he's shocked himself.

His shoulders deflate and I can tell that he's been holding onto this conviction for a long time, bubbling with resentment at the assumption I'd been comparing them. But only now has he had the guts to say it.

'He wasn't a good man. I won't hurt you like he did. I'm not going to leave you. I'm not your dad.'

And suddenly Ted isn't the only one thrown back into the past.

At Ted's words, grief wracks my body. Not grief for the Sadie of today, but for Sadie of three decades ago who woke up on Christmas morning to find my dad had cleared out his side of the wardrobe and gone to live with a woman from his office he'd got pregnant. He was immediately subsumed into a new family and never looked back, while Mum cried herself to sleep and I scrabbled to find enough coins for the electricity meter. Although Mum gradually became a stronger, wiser person, Christmas was still hard. The damage was done, to both of us.

Since that therapy session a couple of months ago, I've pushed all my feelings about Dad into a little box, along with everything about the pregnancy, the miscarriage, and Ted's subsequent silent treatment.

I don't want to talk about Dad. I spend a lot of effort every day actively trying not to think about him. Ted bringing him up now is a gut punch I'm not prepared for.

'You're not my dad,' I repeat in a whisper, the realisation hitting me like an express train. All the air leaves my lungs in a whoosh and I slump to the sofa, curled up in a ball. I can't catch my breath. How has it taken so long to realise that's what I've been dreading, that Ted could hurt me just as much as Dad had once hurt Mum?

I close my eyes as I realise I don't know whether I believe him when he says he won't hurt me. Especially after what I've seen between him and Alice over the last couple of days. And I wonder if that therapist was right when she told me that my fear of rejection had led me to accept more than I should.

Ted sees me wavering, lost in my thoughts. He gently takes my hand in his. I let him, but I don't intertwine my fingers in his. I glance up at his ice-blue eyes and then look away again with a flinch as soon as my gaze meets his.

'Look at me, Sadie,' he says, but I can't.

I don't move, staring at my hands. My finger is indented where my rings sit. Maybe if I took them off, my finger would eventually return to its old shape. Or maybe it's permanently changed.

'Sadie, please. Tell me you love me.'

I don't know. Am I seeing my father in Ted when he doesn't deserve it? Can we fix this, now we've finally started talking? I know I want to. And doesn't Ted deserve another chance?

30

His fingers envelop mine, his palm warm and firm against my own. 'I choose you, Sadie. You're my world, you and the girls. I screwed up the last couple of days, got lost in reminiscing with Alice and then drowned in fear and guilt when I realised Natasha was mine. But I climbed out of it. I'm back now and I'm still yours. That will never change.'

Ted pours us both another dram of whisky and clinks his glass against mine. 'Cheers,' he whispers, and leans forward to kiss me. It's a slow, tender kiss, the first real kiss we've had since arriving in this house.

Tell me you love me, he'd asked. I break off the kiss and look up at him. I open my mouth and close it again. I do... want to.

Ted feels my hesitation, pulling away from me and standing up, frustration in the set of his shoulders. He walks to the window.

I stare at the golden liquid swirling about in my glass, its peaty scent reaching my nostrils. I lift the glass to my lips and tip it into my mouth, feeling it burn all the way down my gullet.

Looking back, I can't kid myself that it has just been the last couple of months; things between us have been difficult for a while. And if Ted sensed it too... perhaps he panicked. Perhaps, like me with my invitation to Alice, Ted resorted to desperate measures to keep our family together. Desperate measures that leveraged what he knew about my past, my childhood, my father. He knew I wouldn't break up our family. Especially if there was a new baby in the mix. I was committed to not letting history repeat itself for Tamara and Charley, no matter what. And Ted knew that. Is there more to this than I thought?

My face grows hot and itchy all over, and my scalp prickles. What if my pregnancy hadn't been such a surprise for him? He buys our condoms, he stores them in his bedside drawer. I wonder if he sensed my unhappiness and sabotaged one of them, or perhaps just forgot to use one. Felt me pulling away and decided to lay a trap, whether conscious or not. Or at least an incredibly misjudged attempt at keeping us together.

'Ted,' I say quietly without looking up. I want to tear off my skin. It's like I spent the last few weeks at the highest point of a roller coaster, waiting for the carriage to tip over and speed down the steep incline with a whoosh. 'Did you want me to get pregnant? Did you... do something?'

There's a silence.

I look up, and Ted's still standing at the window, staring out into the darkness, his shoulders wide and unmoving.

My stomach clenches.

He turns slowly to look at me.

I expected anger. I expected an argument and defensiveness. But the calm look on his face is even more unnerving, as if he didn't hear me.

He steps forward and I try not to flinch away. 'It looks like the wind is finally dying down. Maybe they'll send someone out to fix the phone mast in the next few hours. We'll be able to call for help.' He turns back to the window.

Speechless, I top up my whisky with shaking hands and sip the new glass. My heart is racing and the drink's initial warming effect has faded; now it just burns my tongue and throat. I can already feel the headache creeping back up my temples, stronger than ever, like always happens with whisky. I lean forward and sit my glass on the table. I feel like I might be sick. Did he even hear me? Maybe I was too quiet. Oh God, the anguish and uncertainty of asking the question out loud, of making that accusation of my own husband. The love of my life. Now it feels like a misfire when a gun is held to your temple.

I'm probably wrong. He wouldn't force a pregnancy on me. And even if he did, he probably thought he was saving our marriage. Doing the right thing for everyone. But still, I need to know. If I am going to give us another chance, I need to know. 'Ted?' I ask, turning to look at him and raising my voice. 'Did you get me pregnant on purpose?'

He's unnaturally still, looking out at the car. He doesn't seem to hear me. He doesn't move, his hand gripping the edge of the window frame, knuckles white.

My stomach fizzes with anxiety. *What's he looking at?*

I stand up and join him at the window, standing far enough away from him that he can't touch me. I think back to his reaction when I got the positive pregnancy test. 'This is a surprise,' he'd said. But was he telling the truth? I was so wrapped up in my own shock that I barely registered his response.

To have asked him and then... nothing. No reaction. I can't bear this suspense. It feels like I've lit a touchpaper and I'm waiting for the explosion. But what will his answer be? And what do I want it to be?

'Sadie, look.' He points out into the darkness, at the barely visible glow of the car's interior lights on the other side of the bridge.

Inside the car, all I can see is a blurry shadow of one person, a silhouette in the rear window. Two hands banging on the glass, over and over. Desperation in their every move.

'Something's wrong,' Ted whispers, not taking his eyes away from the window for a moment.

'They're probably just panicking because they're stuck,' I say, but even as the words leave my mouth I know I don't believe them.

There's blood on the glass, smeared all over. The figure's mouth is open, screaming.

31

'Where's Alice?' he adds, with a shake of his head, his breath fogging the window. 'What's happening?'

I squint, trying to see detail, but the figure is just an outline. 'Is it Natasha?'

He tears his eyes away from the car and glances at me, then he strides away, towards the door. 'We need to go and get them. They need help.'

I follow him in a daze, a fizzing, bubbling feeling of panic still deep in my chest.

In the kitchen, Neil is making cheese on toast while Mum and Patricia potter around, cleaning up and brewing tea. The girls must already be in bed. The smell of melted cheese fills my nostrils and my stomach clenches in hunger mixed with nausea. I wish I could pull out a stool and join everyone, eat cheesy toast washed down with a glass of milk and then climb into bed, feeling satisfied at another Christmas successfully celebrated. I feel another pang of anger at what has been taken from me, not just this year, but every year. What I've been chasing, trying to replace and replicate for my whole life.

'Dad, I need you to unlock the car,' says Ted. And I'm dragged back into the present, into this nightmare. 'It's urgent.'

'Everything OK?' Mum asks, her sleeves rolled up past her elbows as she transfers clean pots from the dishwasher into various cupboards and drawers.

Neil holds out his hands, palms up. 'I told you, they have my keys.'

'Well, clearly the keys aren't working for them,' says Ted, frustrated.

'There's a way, using the app,' Patricia says, holding out a hand for Neil's phone.

'Wait,' Mum says, her voice loud. She turns to the rest of us, her voice more controlled. 'We can't just let them out. We don't know what's going on out there, or what they'll do.'

But even as she speaks, the image of that screaming silhouette, bloodied hands banging against the car window, flashes across the back of my eyelids. Natasha is innocent in this. A victim of domestic violence, kidnapping, and maybe worse. And now she's trapped in that car, begging for help. She might be in danger. No matter my churning doubts about my marriage, I need to push my own stuff to the side. I'm good at that.

Ted sighs. 'What do you suggest, then? Natasha is clearly distressed, and we can't leave her trapped in that car with Alice. There's a lot we don't know. And no matter what Alice has done, we don't have the right to keep her prisoner either.'

I shake my head and lean against the kitchen counter, the marble surface cold against the small of my back. 'What if Ted goes out there and we watch from here, make sure he's safe?' As soon as I suggest it, my whole body relaxes in response to the idea of him being out of the house, even for a short time. *Space to think.* I nod, trying to garner their agreement. 'He can talk to them through the car window, check they're OK. And then if there's some kind of emergency and they need to get out urgently, he can signal to us and we'll unlock the car.'

'What if he needs help?' asks Patricia, her face pale. 'There are two of them and one of him.'

There's silence. But then Natasha's childlike face flashes across the back of my eyelids again. 'I'll go, too.' Dread pools in my stomach as I remember the wind and the cold as I ran from my basement prison. And the thought of being alone out there in the dark with Ted, after what I just asked him. After his reaction. I add a caveat: 'I'll go if he needs help.'

Mum strides across the kitchen and puts a hand on my arm. 'Don't both of you go out there.' She nods upstairs. 'The girls need you. But the storm's still raging and Alice is... you know. We just don't know what might happen.'

'I'll take the axe,' says Ted. 'But enough talking. I need to go, now.'

I swallow, bile rising in my throat. 'I'll put on my shoes and coat. I'll be ready to run out and help if you need me.'

Ted nods to me.

I hope we can somehow keep Alice locked away until help comes. For everyone's safety.

Patricia and I head into the living room with Neil's phone, leaving Neil and Mum in the kitchen. I feel lighter now, as if Ted has taken my pregnancy suspicions with him. It's a momentary relief before I remember Natasha trapped in the car with Alice, the blood on the car window, the man left for dead in his Glasgow flat, and my innocent children sleeping upstairs.

Patricia sits on the sofa, the phone on her lap and her reading glasses back on her nose. Her legs are shaking a little, and I'm not sure if it's the chill in the room, exhaustion from the late hour, or fear at what we might be about to do: her son is knowingly approaching a potentially violent woman, and she might have to unlock the car to let her out. It's a lot for anyone, but especially a woman who's lived her whole life in the rural quiet of the Highlands, keeping house for a family of four.

'Not your usual Christmas break?' I ask as I turn off the lights, plunging the room into a darkness lit only by the glowing coals in the fireplace. That way I can see out of the window much better.

I feel strangely calm, now that we're doing something and Ted is outside. We have the upper hand and a plan; we know more than Alice does, and finally it feels like the light is at the end of the tunnel. Soon we can call the police, get them out of the house and I can start putting my life back together, somehow. It's hard to believe we've been here at Red Hart Lodge less than thirty-six hours.

Patricia lets out a breathy laugh and places her palms on her knees to still her shaking. 'I regret not taking Neil up on his offer of whisky now. Dutch courage and all that.'

I cup my hands around my face and peer through the glass into the storm. The trees still sway in the wind, but the violence of their movement has abated slightly. It's still dangerous out there, but less risk of flying debris.

I squint my eyes and watch as Ted pushes forward, hunched against the wind, his hood over his head. He slows as he approaches the bridge, and I can tell by his stride that he's wading: the river has burst its banks and the water is up to his shins.

He crosses the bridge and I see the flash of the white soles of his shoes: he's on the lane on the other side, the swollen river behind him. He reaches the car where it's parked to the side of the narrow road, tucked into the hedge, and leans down to the passenger window. The car is dark now, the interior lights have gone out. I can't see if he's talking, and I can't see any movement inside the car.

'What's going on?' asks Patricia, holding the phone in both hands. 'Do I need to—'

'Wait,' I whisper, squinting my eyes to see through the darkness as a cloud crosses over the moon.

Ted straightens up and looks towards the house. He turns back to the car and leans his hands on the roof, bending at the waist to see into the vehicle. Then he turns and waves both arms at the house, indicating he needs us to unlock the car.

I wince. I hesitate.

But Ted knows me. He knows I would hesitate. He raises his arms in the air one more time and waves for help. The international distress signal.

I close my eyes. I have to say it. 'Unlock the car.'

There's a movement behind me as Patricia fumbles with the phone, and then I watch as the car's interior lights flash on once more.

The passenger door flies open, pushing Ted backwards. He stumbles but rights himself quickly.

A dark figure bolts from the open door, just as the back door opens too. Both figures run into the darkness, away from the house.

After a moment's hesitation, Ted straightens up and sprints after them.

I stand, open mouthed and staring, my fingers gripping the cold window sill. Every muscle in my body is tensed and on alert. My stomach curdles with fear. All I can see is an illuminated empty car, its doors standing open. No one in sight.

32

The living-room door opens and Neil and Mum walk in, Mum carrying a tray with a steaming teapot and mugs. They stop at the sight of my face.

'What happened?' Mum asks, putting the tray on the coffee table and crossing to stand next to me by the window. 'Is everyone OK? Did something happen?'

I don't answer, turning back to stare out into the darkness with my hands cupped around my face. There's a shuffling sound as Patricia stands up and she and Neil pull back the curtains at the other window.

'I can't see a thing,' says Neil.

He's right: through the gap in the curtain, I can only see a few feet over the gravel drive where the light from the house falls. A cloud has covered the moon once more and everything beyond is darkness. I stare for a moment, my eyes drifting out of focus. I'm about to turn away from the window when the cloud suddenly shifts again, and the moon becomes visible, bathing the landscape in a milky light.

I can see the river, wider and faster than ever before, the wind buffeting its surface and making it roil like the sea.

Beyond, I can see the outline of Neil's car on the other side of the bridge, its interior lights on and its doors standing open, moving slightly in the wind.

'They ran off as soon as Patricia unlocked it. He chased after them.'

The bridge itself is almost obscured by water, almost over the top. I stare at it, trying to see how much higher the water has to rise before the bridge is completely obscured. The river has barricaded us in with its force.

There's a silence and I feel Patricia's eyes on me. I turn.

'Shouldn't you go out there, then? Isn't that what you agreed?'

I close my eyes in dread and pull my coat around myself. She's right.

'It's OK, Pat. I'll go,' Neil blusters, but Patricia puts a hand on his arm.

'You've already been out in this weather for far longer than you should have. She's young and strong.' She looks at me, her expression beseeching. 'He's my son, Sadie. Go and see if he needs help. Please. She hurt someone. She could...'

Her eyes are large and pleading, and I take a moment to imagine how I'd feel if this was Charley or Tamara, if their partner was hesitant to go to their aid. I'd hate them. The person you choose to spend your life with should be there for you, should want to help you. Ted's parents are good people who don't know anything that's been going on between us, or what I've just realised. And I can't begin to explain now. All they would see is their child's wife refusing to run to him when he's in need. And I've always wanted Ted and me to be there for each other. Through thick and thin.

And there's Natasha. I remember her reaching out to cradle Charley's doll in her arms on Christmas morning, her blissful face as she let that chocolate melt on her tongue while watching my girls play with their presents. Her dad in the hospital, her mum dragging her here... I can't leave her lost out in the storm.

Without saying a word, I zip up my coat, head to the front door and pull back the heavy curtain. As my hand closes around the doorknob, I mentally step back and look at this whole situation from afar. The world swirls around me. What am I doing? What waits for me out there in the biting wind? Alice, lurking in the dark, waiting for me to stumble into her path? Alice, who tried to murder her partner and then headed straight here intending to cause chaos. And Ted took the axe. If Alice managed to grab it...

'You don't have to do this, Sadie,' Mum hisses as I pull open the door and the wind hits me in the face. She's been thinking the same thing. She puts out a hand and pushes the door closed again. A dark look crosses her face. 'Better keep the devil at the door than have to turn him out of the house. You remember that one?'

I raise my eyebrows, remembering the moment Alice's foot shot out and blocked me from closing this door against her. The moment everything took a wrong turn. Or do I need to go back further to find that moment? Right back to the day I hit 'send' on that message. 'Is that one of Granny's sayings?'

Mum nods.

'She wasn't wrong.'

'She had a lot of them. Better to be alone than in bad company, that's another,' she says, with a meaningful glance.

I hesitate. I've been trying to get rid of Alice and Natasha since they arrived. And with Ted's absence from the house it feels like a weight has been lifted from my shoulders. What if I just... didn't go outside to find them? What would happen?

Alice and Natasha are probably running along that dirt track, Ted close behind them. There's nowhere for them to go. Eventually they'll get to the main road, but it's almost midnight on Christmas Day; there won't be anyone to pick them up and take them on their way. They'll just be lost out in the darkness and the rain. They'll find shelter eventually; an old croft house or a rickety barn. Ted will give up and turn back, returning to the lodge cold but unhurt. Why should I follow? What will I gain?

A look passes between Mum and me, and her hand drops from the door.

I've decided.

I start to close it, but then I freeze.

I hear the crunch of gravel from outside, and the breathless shouts: 'Help. Julie, Sadie. Please help.'

I pull open the door and the light illuminates the two hooded figures of Alice and Natasha, their arms outstretched towards me. Natasha's hand is covered in blood, a gash across her palm. She must have cut herself somewhere between the basement and the car. That explains the blood smeared on the car window.

For a wild moment I get a flash of an image: closing the door and locking it before they reach me.

But Alice's beseeching call carries towards me over the wind: 'Please help. It's Ted. He slipped and fell in the river. He's gone.'

33

'Ted's gone? What does she mean?' Neil's shout startles me as he strides from the living room and pulls the door open, wrenching it from my hands. He reaches forward and grabs Alice by the arm, pulling her and Natasha into the hallway. He shoves the door closed and finally the roar of the wind is gone. 'What happened, girl?'

I stand, mute and frozen, staring at Alice and Natasha's shivering drenched forms.

Gone. What does that mean? *What did Alice do to him?* My breath catches in my throat. *Slipped and fell into the river.* The freezing, dark water rushing past faster than a racing car. My strong, warm husband.

My eyes burn and I wonder if I'm going to cry at the injustice. The opportunity to understand my husband, to really know him inside out, has been wrenched from me.

Yes, we have problems, but they're fixable. Therapy, communication, confrontation and openness, maybe that's all we need. In my mind, during the last couple of hours I'd been ripping off the bandage so that the wound could get exposure to the air. To heal our marriage and our own battle scars in a healthy way now we'd laid it all out in the open. And now I might never have that chance.

Patricia stumbles from the living room, her arms wrapped around herself and an anguished wail rising from her throat. She looks haggard.

'The river. He...' Alice slumps to the church pew bench, catching her breath. She's glistening, the raindrops on her skin reflecting the light of the hallway. Her hair is matted to her forehead and mascara streaks down her cheeks.

'What happened?' Patricia drops to her knees in front of Alice and grabs at her hands. 'Please, Alice?'

'There's no time, Patricia. The water will be freezing. He's got minutes, at best.' Neil drags his wax jacket from the hook and shoves his arms into the sleeves. 'Take us to the river, Alice.'

I realise I'm still standing by the door, in my coat and boots. And of course Ted's wife would want to go and try to find him. To help. I'm expected to rush out into the storm, shouting his name. To put my own life in danger to save his. And I want to, I realise. I need to find him.

Neil corrals me with his arm, ushering me towards the door. I'm ready.

Alice stands up and turns to Natasha. 'Stay here, Tash. Get warm. Look after Patricia.'

I nod at Mum, too. I need her to stay. There's no point all of us endangering ourselves out in the storm.

Natasha starts to tell Patricia about Ted, her voice wavering with cold and fear: I hear her talk about him tripping over the submerged bridge wall. Did he fall? I wonder. Or did Alice push him? And where's the axe he took with him?

Mum wraps her arms around me one last time and looks me in the eye.

'The first aid kit is in the living room. Please help Natasha with her hand.' And I know, from the steadiness of Mum's gaze, that she's thinking of the girls, too. *Don't leave them. Don't put yourself in danger where you might not come back.* 'I will be careful. I promise.'

I rush to the front door and wrench it open. Alice runs on ahead through the storm and we cross the gravel drive towards the bridge. The gravel turns to standing water, then shallow pools, the moving surface dotted with raindrops until the surface breaks and churns as Alice pushes forward towards the river.

Neil follows close behind me, his breath huffing as he runs in his unlaced hiking boots.

I slow as we reach the water. The river is freezing as it seeps into my boots and soaks my socks. The current threatens to tug my legs out from under me, but I push on, following Alice's figure, barely able to see the stone walls that indicate where the bridge once was.

'Ted!' I call, but my voice is whipped away by the wind. My breath heaves, and I don't know whether it's the exertion or the emotion of the possibility that my husband might have drowned. What if he's in the river, dragged downstream? I swallow the saliva pooling in my mouth. I would be a widow. A lone parent. I never wanted this.

I move onwards, the water dragging at my thighs as I push my legs through the river. I finally reach what's left of the bridge and follow Alice across to the other side, careful not to step close to the parapet and risk being swept away by the current. The bridge's walls are so obscured by water that it's hard to tell where the bridge starts and the river begins.

'Ted?' I shout again. He can't be gone. There's so much left to say.

Next to me, Alice leans forward and points down under the bridge. 'He stumbled here,' she shouts over the wind, her breaths rattling in her throat. 'He went over the wall and got pulled under. And then we lost sight of him.'

I stare into the darkness, hoping my eyes will adjust. But I can't see a thing. My ears are full of noise: the rushing of the water tugging at our legs, the wind, the breath in my lungs. The sounds combine to create an all-encompassing roar that blocks out almost all other sound, like an aural panic attack.

I try to remember what I know about first aid when someone's fallen into freezing water, but all I can think of is something from a kid's film where someone falls through the ice. You're supposed to strip their wet clothes from them and give them dry ones, but Alice, Neil and I have nothing but more wet clothes.

It's hopeless, I think. Ted will be dragged for miles along this swollen river made of thawed snow and ice from the top of the hills. He'll be dead within minutes.

But I can't dwell on that; I can't let myself sink beneath the shock and grief. There's no time. I shake the thought away. Around our legs, the river rushes past and seems to rise higher every moment. Soon the bridge itself will be useless.

I hear Alice try to steady her breath, inhaling longer and exhaling slowly. Is she concerned for Ted? Does she still believe he wants her? That he'll leave me? Or is she worried we'll find him alive after all; terrified he'll tell the truth about how he ended up in the river? That she pushed him. Or stole the axe and hit him with it.

I step away from her, far enough that she can't shove me in, too.

Neil catches up, his breath wheezing in his chest as he approaches us at the bridge wall. 'He fell in?' he pants. 'Here?' He leans over, his hands on his knees. He straightens up and pulls a torch from his pocket and lights it up, the blood-red beam trembling in his hands. It's one of those giant red spotlights, the ones they use for night hunting because the animals can't see the colour. He shines it over the bridge wall and into the river. Ahead of us, the light stains branches and a trunk like blood: a tree has fallen across the river.

'There!' he shouts, pointing with his free hand. I can hear him breathing next to me, laboured breaths like he's still running. He crosses the bridge and wades further along the bank to get a closer look at the fallen tree. His torch light bobs as he strides away, leaving Alice and me in almost-darkness.

I lean forward, peering towards the branches. Can I see a shape? Is it Ted's coat, tangled in the tree? Is it possible he's survived this? My eyes fill with tears of relief, sorrow or something else entirely.

But before I have time to think, a hand shoves hard between my shoulder blades and I pitch forward.

I flail my arms, trying to grip something – anything – to stop my fall. My fingers find fabric and I clutch at it with both hands, gathering the material in my fingers. As I fall, I don't let go, and I feel the tug as another body plunges after me into the icy water.

Alice pushed me in. But I took her with me.

34

I'm going to die. I know it.

As soon as my body hits the icy water, all air is forced from my lungs. I'm breathless in shock as I'm submerged under the dark water, storm debris tugging at my clothes and scratching my skin. I try to swim upwards, but the current tugs at my arms and legs, turning me around and around until I don't know which way is up and which way is down. Everything is darkness and cold.

I finally break the surface and fill my lungs with air, reaching out towards where I think might be the bank. But then there's a hand on my head, on my shoulders, pulling me down, thrusting me back under the water. Panic seeps across my chest as the water soaks through my clothes and weighs me down. I struggle to the surface once more and suck in air.

'You'll die here. And then they're all mine,' a voice hisses in my ear, just audible over the rush of the river.

She's in the water with me. She's still trying to kill me.

I can't believe she did this. I knew Alice was bad, I knew she wanted my life, and I knew she was capable of hurting me just like she hurt others before. But, I think, as my flailing slows in the cold and my lungs burn in their emptiness, I didn't think she was capable of murder.

I thrust and grab as my body is hauled downstream, trying to find something to hold onto: a tree branch or the bank. But all my hands find are twigs and mud, and I'm pummelled against the riverbed over and over. Every time my head breaks the surface, she's there pushing me back under, a cold hand on my skull and a forceful shove. I'm helpless.

This can't be it. I can't leave my daughters. I can't leave them with Ted, without their mother. They're so little; there's still so much I want to experience with them. Charley's first lost tooth, explaining to them about boys, periods, and life. More Christmases and birthdays. Revision, exam results, parties, new friends. Seeing them through the end of school, university, their first jobs, loves, and heartbreaks. Helping them get settled in their first homes, their weddings, and their children. My grand-children.

I'm getting tired, now. All fight is gone. No breath. No warmth.

But I can't leave them. They need me.

Tamara's so responsible, so kind and caring of others. I wanted to help her assert herself and find the fun in life. To learn to lose control sometimes and do the daring thing, the rebellious thing. I wanted her to know she doesn't always have to follow the rules.

And her opposite, my little wild child Charley. Always undone, untied, untethered. So much joy. She needs me to catch her when she falls, to remind her to watch where she's going and look before she jumps.

As my shoulder hits the river bed once again, I manage to get my legs underneath me and I kick out with all the strength left in my body, willing my body to the surface, praying I'm pushing in the right direction: up.

If I die now, I lose the opportunity to give them the happy childhood that I needed but which was denied to me.

If I die now, I don't just leave them to a broken home like I experienced; I might leave them with Alice as their stepmother. There are worse things than separation and divorce, I know now. There are worse things than what I experienced.

My lungs burn and my legs kick out, their movements slowed by the sodden fabric of my jeans. I'm desperate for oxygen, and my hands grasp at my throat, covering my mouth to try to stop myself inhaling the water surrounding me. *Hold on.* I suddenly feel the weight of the water all around me, pushing in on me and crushing me. It's dark and solid, like tar.

I imagine them alongside Ted at my funeral, Alice sitting in the pew behind them, waiting for her turn to step forward and take my place. Their tiny forms dressed in black, holding hands as they gaze at my coffin and say goodbye to their mother. No child should have to experience that.

If I die, Alice gets what she wanted all along. She gets my family.

I can't hold it any more. My lungs are on fire, like I'm being burned from the inside out. Almost on instinct, my mouth opens and I try to breathe. The water floods my mouth and nose, sinking into my lungs and filling them with weight. I feel the sting of the cold against my teeth and the mud-tinged taste on my tongue. I'm getting heavier too, the weight of the water pulling me further and further down and away from safety, from the air.

I'm so disoriented, and the world starts to tilt to the side as dizziness takes over. I thought I was moving upwards, but now I'm sinking again.

But suddenly, it doesn't matter. Nothing matters. I'm calm, like I'm waking from a long, deep sleep. There's nothing else I can do.

I stop fighting. I let the current pull me along, the twigs and branches tearing at my clothes.

I'm alone. No one is going to save me. Not Ted, who floats somewhere else in this river, possibly dead at Alice's hands. Not Alice, who wanted me dead all along.

I open my eyes and where before was the darkness of the water and the night, now I can see swirls of colour dancing in front of my eyes. Hallucinations, I realise. My brain is failing. I am dying.

I send up one last wish for my family. To my daughters, Ted, Mum, Neil and Patricia. All of them. Stay safe, live well.

I loved you so much.

35

A hand clasps my shoulder and my near-death calm dissipates for a moment. Here she is again. Alice, here to deliver the final blow. Will she hold me down, making sure I'm really gone? Or will I feel an axe blade hacking into my skull?

But it's two hands, under my armpits, tugging me up. Pulling me out? Someone is saving me. *Neil?*

My head breaks the surface and the wind hits my face, waking me up. The pain is huge: my lungs still burn, my skin feels raw where the rocks scraped and tore.

I try to breathe, instead vomiting water over and over until it feels like I'm suffocating again. I hack and cough until my lungs are raw, but then finally I can breathe.

My head lolls, my neck not strong enough to hold up the weight of my skull. My back is against something hard. The tree that fell across the river.

The hands are still under my arms, holding part of my body out of the water, my legs still submerged, the current still trying to drag me downstream. I listen for Neil's voice, expecting to hear his heavy breathing. I try to open my eyes to see who has tugged my head and shoulders out of the water.

'Shhh,' a quiet voice says over the rushing of the river. There's a soft hand on my face, holding me steady through my shudders and shivers, every muscle in my body vibrating in the cold. 'Try to stay still.'

I drag air into my sore lungs and freeze at the sound of the voice. It's Alice. Why has she pulled me from the water? Just to prolong the torture?

I try to pull away but she holds me tighter. I turn my head and see her crouched on the tree, her eyes wide in fear.

'Don't speak,' she hisses. 'He'll hear you. He's still in the water.'

36

I freeze at the sound of Alice's words, my breath ragged in my tired lungs. *He's still in the water.*

Who? Did Neil fall into the river too?

But no. The fear on her face says something different. She's terrified of something. Of some*one*. And she's trying to get me away from them, too.

She shifts to gain a better position on the fallen tree and pulls me up and out of the water. The wind hits my chilled body and sodden clothes, and I'm incapacitated with shivering. She pauses and waits for it to pass.

Why is Alice pulling me from the river, when she tried so hard to drown me just moments ago?

Thoughts drift across my exhausted mind and I can't grasp any truth.

Then I'm blinded, blood searing across my retinas. I can't see anything, the dark of the night is replaced with searing red light. Did I die after all? Is this the light everyone says to walk towards? Perhaps I'm still under the water, and this is the next phase of death.

But I raise a shaking hand to cover my eyes and in the

momentary relief I see that it's Neil's powerful red hunting torch, aiming at us from the bridge. He's back standing there, and now he's lighting the way so we can climb along the tree and out to safety.

So if Neil's still on the bridge, who was Alice talking about? *He's still in the water.* I think back to the hands on my body, pushing me under the water over and over.

My blood turns to ice.

When I felt that shove between my shoulder blades, my instinct was immediate: *take her with you.* I'd flailed and grabbed at Alice, pulling her over the bridge wall and into the river with me. But instead she's now up on the fallen tree, her hair damp with rain yet not soaking wet like I am. She's not incapacitated with the cold, because she didn't fall in the river. I didn't pull her in with me. Because Alice didn't push me in. Someone else did. So it was someone else I grabbed as I fell into the freezing water. And he's still down there.

That voice I heard, before I was pushed under once again. It was a harsh whisper and it was almost obscured by the sound of the river rushing past, but now I realise it wasn't Alice. It was Ted. It was my husband.

You'll die here. And then they're all mine. Above me, Alice hooks a leg around a branch on the fallen tree to anchor herself so she can pull me further out. She gives a shout and hauls me up, so that I'm almost sitting on the tree next to her. I'm safe. Saved by the person I thought was my enemy.

I'll see my children again. And it's all thanks to Alice.

But even as Alice's hands tug my shoulders up to safety, from below a clawed hand wraps itself around my ankle and tugs down, trying to pull me back into the freezing cold water. I'm slipping again, my hands scrabbling and sliding on the slick moss-covered tree trunk. I flail, unable to get a grip. My feet hit the water and I kick out, but my muscles are chilled, weak and oxygen-deprived. I can barely move.

His hand tightens, his fingertips digging into my flesh.
Please no, don't let me die here.

It's Ted, his hair plastered to his head and his eyes bloodshot with the cold. His face is red raw and his lips are blue. He looks monstrous as he tugs at my leg, pulling me back into the water.

You'll die here.

I scream. Alice yells in shock and pulls me back, groaning and gasping with the effort. She manages to stop my slide into the water, holding me steady while he yanks at me from below.

'Come on, Sadie,' she screams. 'Fight. Don't let him win. Stay with me.'

Her hands dig into my arms as she pulls me up out of the water once again, trying to get me out of Ted's reach. She's trying to save me.

The world stops. Darkness descends. Sound disappears. All my senses pause as I realise the truth.

Alice is trying to save me from Ted. My husband is trying to drown me, trying to pull me back down into the depths of the dark, freezing water. My own husband. He was the one who pushed me into the water in the first place; his snagged coat on the branches was just a decoy. Bait.

While I've been trying to fix our marriage, he's been trying to kill me.

I'm immobilised with shock. 'Better to be alone than in bad company,' Mum said just before I left the lodge to enter the storm. Her comment was truer than she knew.

My thoughts move at a hundred miles an hour as I struggle to stay above the water, the tree slick beneath me and Ted's fist wrapped around my ankle. Part of me guessed Ted wasn't a good man. Part of me was afraid of him, but I had no idea he was capable of this. I ignored those parts, still trying desperately to fix our marriage. To have the family I wanted. Before, it was all psychological or implied. So clever, so measured: enough to warn me but not enough for me to confront or ask anyone for help. This is a whole new level, brought out of him by my questions and uncertainty.

Perhaps he was waiting for me in the darkness by the bridge, trying to lure me out and planning to push me in all along. Like he's sending me the message, '*If I can't have you, no one can.*' Subconsciously, it's probably why I'd chosen now to ask the questions I hadn't dared to before: witnesses. Moral support. Protection. Much safer than being alone at home with no other adults nearby. Or so I'd thought.

Ted's hand tightens around my ankle and he yanks hard.

There's a shout from the bridge. It's Neil, his voice broken, pleading. 'Save him, please!' The desperate cry of a parent who will do anything for their child.

He has no idea. To him it looks like Ted's begging for our help, trying to pull himself out of the river. Not trying to pull me back in.

The red light shifts as Neil rushes across the bridge and towards the riverbank, trying to get to us.

As the torch's beam moves away, I kick out, once, twice. Ted's grip loosens but he manages to retain his hold.

I can feel Alice's grip on me slipping. Then she turns to me. 'If anything happens, look after Natasha. You're a good person. I've known it all along. That's why I came here.'

I can't believe she's the one trying to save me. Who is this person? I've hated her, I've resented her, I've mistrusted her. But now she's trying to save me from my own husband. I got it all wrong, I realise.

Her words from yesterday echo around my mind, crossing over with Ted's and blurring together into a confusing mess. What did she say? Yes, that's it. *I just couldn't let an abuser hurt anyone else. And that's how we ended up here.* She wasn't just talking about getting away from Robin. Alice came here to save me from Ted.

And, I now realise, I think I invited her here for that reason, too. I needed her help to get away. I just didn't know it.

'Please,' shouts Ted, holding out a hand. His other hand is still wrapped around my ankle, his knuckles white. It's a fitting image that represents the way he's been with me for a long time: one hand reaching out, the other squeezing and threatening. Never causing damage, never leaving marks. Always deniable or explainable. Mind tricks, manipulation, plausible deniability. And then apologies and utter adoration; a suffocating blanket of love until I can't think straight.

Ted's eyes flit between me and Alice. He doesn't know who to beg, I realise. Does he plead forgiveness from his wife who might want to leave him, or his ex who seemed to want him back? He drops his hand, trying to grasp onto the slick surface of the tree trunk, but the wet moss has no grip and he yelps in panic. I can see him fighting against the current tugging him away, into the deep water that flows beneath the tree and away downstream. 'Alice,' he begs. 'Sadie?'

I shift up the tree, trying to get out of his reach.

'Think of the girls,' he says, before his hand slips again and he lunges for a branch, his eyes wide in fear. I can hear his teeth chattering together and his blue lips are an echo of his wine-stained teeth earlier on Christmas Eve.

My own teeth are chattering too, every muscle in my body unwieldy and weak as they shudder in the cold. My jaw is clenched, the muscles tight and unyielding. All my movements are slow, like I'm wading through tar. My eyelids float closed for a moment. I can't move my arms or legs. They're frozen.

Next to me, Alice heaves me up further, right to the top of the tree. Safe from Ted.

'Sadie,' he begs again, holding out a shaking hand. His figure shifts slightly as the current gets stronger, and I can see that he's losing his strength in the cold and the force of the water flowing past.

He's still the father of my children. They love him. Their faces light up when he bursts through the door after work and sweeps them into his arms. Tamara particularly turns to him for comfort when she's upset, burrowing her head into his chest. They need their daddy, both of our daughters. I can't let this happen to them. Maybe I can fight. We can go to couples' counselling, I can learn his triggers and work out how to bypass them. Anything.

I try to move towards him, but Alice places a hand on my shoulder and secures me next to her on the horizontal tree trunk. She shakes her head. 'Don't,' she hisses at me. 'Leave him.'

I don't have the strength to argue. I can't save him myself. I'm too weak.

He realises we're not going to help him, his pupils huge and snake-like as they gaze at us both through the intermittent darkness peppered with flashes of red as Neil runs towards us with the torch. 'I'll kill you both,' he snarls. 'I should have done it a long time ago.'

My breath catches in my throat at the sound of the hatred and evil in his voice: his true personality embodied in the rasp of that threat. No, there's no hope for couples' counselling here. No way to learn to tiptoe around his triggers. This isn't my fault, and nor is it my responsibility to fix, hide or finesse.

Everything he hid of his poisonous character is oozing out right now when he can't get what he wants. I'd seen small signs of it before now, a sharp look that chilled my blood, a rapid movement that implied he'd been tempted to slap or punch. But he'd always managed to hold it in, so I'd brushed away my fears and told myself it was my imagination. But not any more.

And now here it is: Ted's true self staring up at me from the black water. Begging me to save him in one breath and threatening to kill me in the next. The push-pull, love-hate of an abuser. I can finally see it clearly.

'Let him go.' Alice's voice is low as Neil's shouts grow closer, the light bobbing as he runs along the submerged riverbank towards us. 'He's done enough to both of us,' she says, watching and holding me back as Ted's grip loosens on the tree and his head slips under the water.

Ted is dead.

Even through my brain fog and hypothermia, I know that's a fact. I saw his blue lips, his red-raw skin. I don't know how long he'd been in the water, but as soon as the current dragged him under the fallen tree and downstream, I knew he was gone.

My own arms and legs are numb and lifeless with cold. I can barely walk as Alice and Neil help me back to Red Hart Lodge, an arm around each of their shoulders. Neil doesn't say a word, his jaw set in grief. And I know that if Ted was experiencing even a percentage of the cold that I am, there's no way he'd be able to swim or haul himself out of the river. He's dead.

I'm alive.

It's surprisingly easy to feign grief while you're in the grip of hypothermia. As soon as I hear Patricia's wail of devastation, my already stinging eyes fill with tears. Neil and Patricia huddle together in the kitchen, unable to compute the scale of their loss. I feel it with them. I cannot imagine how it feels to lose a child.

No one expects me to speak, as Mum leads me to the fireplace, throws logs onto the flames and strips off my sodden clothes. She wraps my quivering form in towels and blankets, pulls woolly socks onto my feet and then wraps herself around me.

'He's dead,' I try to say, but I'm shivering too much to speak. My jaw is still locked shut, all my muscles vibrating.

'Better to be alone than in bad company,' she mutters again, as she pulls a hat onto my head and gloves onto my clawed hands, her mouth a thin line of worry. She's been saying thinly veiled things like this for a couple of years now, as if she's sensed the low buzz of panic at the edge of my consciousness as Ted and I drifted further apart. Slightly coded comments that could be brushed off or interpreted differently, but leaving space for me to grab onto the offered life raft if I wanted to. I'd always ignored them.

But she knew, before even I did.

I look around the room, lit by soft lamplight and the flames. It's empty except for Mum and me. Neil and Patricia must still be in the kitchen, locked together in mourning. Who's looking after Alice? Where's Natasha?

'Alice,' I mumble, but Mum shushes me.

'Don't try to speak, love. Conserve your energy.'

I shake my head and try again. 'Alice.' This time I'm intelligible, and a dark look crosses Mum's face.

She shrugs.

Alice must be freezing, too: soaked by rain and splashed by the icy river. She saved me. But, of course, Mum has no idea of any of this. I grab her hand with my gloved fingers and look her in the eye, my gaze imploring. 'Please,' I say through my chattering teeth.

Mum nods in understanding and stands, leaving me on the hearthrug before the fire. 'Natasha was getting her some dry clothes. I'll go make sure she's OK. And I'll put the kettle on for hot drinks while I'm there.'

I nod in thanks and stare into the flames as the blood slowly begins to circulate through my extremities once more, bringing with it a horrific prickling deep inside my muscles, and a painful burning on the surface of my skin.

The pain feels welcome, somehow. It's a balance, a debt I have to pay. I'm a widow. Ted is dead. But I don't feel sad. I feel free. So I relish the physical pain, knowing I have been spared the mental pain a wife should feel in this moment.

But then I think of the girls, and my eyes fill with genuine tears. Tamara and Charley lost their daddy today – although they don't know it yet – and I know that pain. I would have done anything to avoid it for my own children. Indeed, the reason I denied Ted's true nature for so long – and stayed long after any other abuse victim would or should stay – was for them. To avoid this loss. And now it's happened anyway.

I told myself throughout our time at Red Hart Lodge – and throughout our marriage – that Ted was just being Ted: looking after people, making sure they're OK, following up on his responsibilities, loving intensely and being true to himself. I willed myself not to take his actions personally: convincing myself that his fierce avoidance of confrontation and conflict weren't a decision or a choice, they were just part of him. I know *him*, I'd tell myself. He's not Dad. Have faith in him.

I did love him, once. I loved when he wrapped me in his arms and his chest was warm against my cheek, his shirt tickling my nose. Curling up beside him in bed in the morning, our bodies still warm with sleep as I breathed him in. He smelled like home, back then. He *was* home. I adored seeing him hold our babies for the first time, watching the wonder in his eyes as he drank them in.

I even once loved comforting him when he was angry: holding him and feeling the tension in his body, all his muscles taut and quivering like a horse at the end of a race, until I heard his breath regulate and some tension release. I thought I was special, somehow, because I could talk him down from that high place. But as our marriage progressed, I stopped being able to calm him and started being the cause of his frustrations. And soon the highs became less frequent and the lows became lower.

There was a quiet part of me, deep down, which wondered if the kind, beautiful soul I saw could be a cunning mask, covering the face of a monster just like my dad. That the goodness I was seeing was a carefully constructed shell designed to distract, deflect and manipulate. I'd get a brief flash of suspicion: maybe I had been tricking myself all along, seeing what I wanted to see. But then I'd shake it away. Denial. Avoidance.

It took me a long time to realise what had happened and where things had gone wrong. Too long. And now we're here.

The door creaks open and Alice sidles inside, a half-smile on her face and a steaming mug of tea in each hand. Like me, she's bundled up in layers including a hat and gloves.

For a moment, I get a flash of the old resentment and distrust her presence elicited inside me over the past couple of days. *She's dangerous*, my slow, hypothermic brain sirens. My mind flashes to the knife, still zipped into the pocket of my discarded jumper, sodden and in a heap next to me where Mum stripped it from my shuddering, frozen body. I hear the memory of the basement door's slam as she locked me down there. Or did she? I saw a silhouette, but it could have been anyone. I heard a voice, but it could have been the wind. And the basement door sticks when it's raining.

And then, like a sped-up film reel, everything in my brain realigns and I remember her pulling me from the water, dragging me away from Ted's grasping hands. *She's not who you thought she was. Everything is different now.*

I sigh in relief that she's OK. She seems to be recovering quicker than I am – I'm still stiff and numb. But then she wasn't submerged under the water, I think. It's hard to remember what happened, everything was so dark and disorienting.

'How are you doing?' she asks as she holds out the tea to me.

I take it in both of my gloved hands, watching the surface of the liquid carefully to make sure I don't spill with my shivering. She joins me in front of the fire, her back against the seat of the armchair.

'Warming up slowly,' I manage to hiss through still-clenched teeth. 'You?'

She raises the mug to her lips and blows on the hot liquid. 'Getting there. I put two sugars in our teas. We'll need it.'

We sit in silence for a minute, the only sound is the popping and crackling of the logs on the fire. There's so much we need to say, but we don't need to rush it. I've spent the last two days trying to push and pull: to prise information out of Alice, to get her out of the house, to push her towards Ted and then to pull her away again when I realised what a mistake this all was. So it's nice, this companionable quiet.

Eventually, I lean down and reach into my pocket, my fingers closing around the ridged handle of the knife. It feels strange to hand a weapon to Alice, even now. Just a few hours ago I would have baulked at the idea of returning this to her. But now I know it's the right thing to do.

I hold it out to Alice and she takes it with a grateful smile, wrapping her long fingers around the handle. Her fingernails are still tinged blue with cold. 'Thank you. Natasha will be grateful. It's her dad's – well, Robin's. A fishing knife. It's important to her. Or it was, once. I'll let her decide whether that's still the case.'

Poor Natasha. Both father figures in her life turned out to be monstrous. I resolve to be there for her, to continue to give her lifelong family connections with Tamara and Charley; and me, if she wants that. One thing at a time, though. She needs to learn the truth about Ted, first. Both her paternity, and his true nature, if Alice decides to share that. But those are discussions for another time.

Alice slides the knife into her own pocket and stares into

the flames of the fireplace before talking again. 'Neil managed to get through to the police and the ambulance,' she says after a moment. 'The mobile mast must be back up and running.'

I nod and place my tea on the hearth, raising my knees to my chest and wrapping my arms around myself.

'Neil and Patricia have gone back out. They're trying to find him.'

'He'll be miles downstream by now.'

'And there's no way he survived more than a few minutes in that temperature,' she says.

'What happened out there?' My memories are blurred and chaotic, a rush of panic and shouts, fear and near-death.

She shakes her head, incredulous. 'I didn't think he'd ever do something like...' She swallows, as if unable to voice the truth we both know now about the person Ted is. *Was*. 'When Natasha and I rushed back here for help, I did think he'd fallen into the river. There was a shout and a splash. The wind was deafening, and it was so dark out there. I knew we'd need help if he'd fallen in. And fast. I didn't push him into the river. Not that time.'

Not that time. I frown, staring at her tiny frame. I question again what she's capable of. How hard she'd fight to save herself, if she had to.

'But now I wonder if he'd planned it. You know, faked falling in to lure you out there on purpose.' She wraps her arms around herself to suppress a shudder. 'On the bridge I saw him run at us and then he pushed you over the wall. It was instinct, and I just...' She mimes a shove and I suck in air through my teeth.

My mouth drops open as I remember grabbing behind me, thinking I was pulling Alice into the river with me as I plummeted. But I was wrong on two counts: the body that tumbled into the water alongside me wasn't Alice, and I hadn't been totally responsible for the fall.

'Then I ran down the riverbank, tracked you both downstream to the tree. I could see you struggling in the water, him pushing you under over and over. Neil finally managed to get his light on you from the bridge, but he thought Ted was trying to save you. Still does. He was too far away to see the truth. To hear the threats.'

I shudder as my late husband's snarl echoes through my head. *I'll kill you both. I should have done it a long time ago.*

'You put up a good fight, Sadie.' Her dimples emerge as she gives a quick smile that doesn't reach her eyes. 'But Ted was strong. And when you went limp, I thought that was it. You were dead.'

My stomach churns at the memory. So did I.

'That's when he loosened his grip. Thought he'd won. He lost focus for a moment as Neil dropped the light so I kicked him in the head. Surprised him enough that I could finally drag you up onto the tree.' She sips at her tea and lowers her voice even though we're alone. 'We did the right thing, you know. Not saving him.'

My stomach twists. I don't know how I'll ever be OK with that decision. Sure, we didn't kill him. But our decision not to act caused his death. How can I live with that? I swallow and shift my frozen jaw from side to side.

She reaches forward and places a hand on my knee.

I flinch, and she notices. She looks me in the eye, her gaze steely. 'I was never here to steal your family, Sadie.'

After a couple of sips of tea, my muscles seem to loosen and I feel like I can talk without clenching my teeth. 'Then why did you come?' I ask, my voice hoarse. I clear my throat.

She leans back and stares into the fire, the flames illuminating her face. She's arrestingly beautiful, I notice again. I'd seen it when she first arrived at the house and knew – hoped, even – that Ted would notice the same thing. But now I can look at her without any agenda or intent, and I can see that she's beautiful in that way which causes problems for people: yes, I'm sure she's received a lot of attention throughout her life, but there's something about her self-contained nature which shows me that it's not always been good attention or welcomed attention.

There's a hard limit to the self-confidence you can receive from good looks, and after that there are detriments and disadvantages, too. I wonder, for example, how many people showed sympathy if she tried to confide she was in an abusive relationship. Because people tend to believe that beautiful people have charmed lives, and that nothing bad could ever happen to them.

She shifts, putting down her tea next to mine in front of the fire. 'Most of what I've told you was the truth. Ted's message – well, yours, really – did come at the perfect time. I was planning to leave Robin and I wanted to be out before Christmas. Before the over-drinking and the isolation of the holidays. But I didn't come here to win Ted back. When his message arrived and I clicked on his profile, I saw he had two little girls and a wife. And I remembered how he'd been with me. What he'd been like. Perfect at first, an amazing boyfriend. And then the digs started.'

A dark look crosses her face as she imitates his voice: '"Why are you wearing that short skirt? You flirted with that barman; do you take me for a fool?"' She shakes her head, as if shaking him away. 'And then the days of silent treatment, followed by the excessive love-bombing to make it up to me: flowers, chocolates, meals out...'

I nod and nod until my head aches. It's all so familiar.

I could never look directly at it. There was always a reason to deny the truth. It was never the right time, there was always a birthday, a holiday, something. And every time I thought about leaving, an image would appear in my mind's eye: Ted's face when I did something to anger him – the tense set of his jaw, the dilating of his pupils, the tightening of his fists. I'd convince myself I was imagining it, that he'd never raised a hand to me or the girls, not once in our entire marriage. Not even during the nastiest arguments.

But now I think about the friends I've lost – the ones who drifted away because Ted didn't like them, or the ones who stopped dropping around for coffee because he was so icy – and I wonder if he was the reason. And the stonewalling. The constant, unbearable silent treatment whenever I behaved in a way he didn't like.

Double standards: he could pick up my phone whenever he liked, but if I touched his he would accuse me of not trusting him. And then there were the accidents. Too many, always followed by profuse apologies. Scalding tea spilled on my lap the day I received an award at work. Stepping on my dress and tearing the hem after a friend's husband complimented me. Taking my keys and locking me in the house while he went to work on the day I was supposed to be flying to Barcelona with a friend...

And just while we've been here: refusing to top up our fuel tank on the journey here; ignoring my thoughts about the wine and then passing them off as his own; catching him almost kissing Alice; squeezing my hand too tight when I wasn't falling in line; an elbow to the face as I got into bed, easily excused behind too much alcohol.

I'm a good man, Sadie, he said to me, in the living room earlier tonight. But do the real 'good men' have to tell you that they're good? Don't you just... know?

Alice watches me closely, as if she can sense the pieces falling into place for me. 'I had to come. I'd seen it all with Robin: where it could lead. The violence. The danger. And then he'd started channelling some of it towards Natasha, too. I had to get out, and I had to come to you, to help you and your girls get away before it was too late. Before he hurt one of you.'

'What happened with Robin, Alice?' I ask, ready for any answer that she'll give. 'The police are looking for you.'

She closes her eyes and wraps her arms around her legs. 'There was a fight,' she says. 'A big one. The arguments had been getting worse and worse, and this one... well, it was the worst one yet. I knew I had to get Natasha away. When his anger was directed at me, I thought I could deal with it. But as soon as he turned on her...' She leans forward, her shoulders hunched up and her arms wrapped around herself like she's still freezing. 'He chased us down the stairs, as we were leaving. He fell.'

Tears gather in Alice's eyes. She turns her head, looking into the fire, which reflects the tears. In the fireplace, a log shifts, sending sparks up the chimney. Alice jolts as if shocked from a trance. 'Then we ran.'

I shudder in sympathy. 'If it was an accident... the police will understand.' I can imagine the fear of your child being hurt by the man you chose. The guilt. The terror for their safety. I feel sick just thinking about it. And lucky, too, that things never got that far with Ted, even though they might have done, eventually. 'Did Ted ever hurt you?'

She shakes her head. 'We didn't know much about coercive control and covert abuse back then, did we? It wasn't even legally considered a crime. But I knew something wasn't right. And we know now what those tendencies can become. When I got pregnant, I knew I couldn't stay. We were so close to the trip that I thought if I waited long enough and then dropped out, he'd go without me. And by the time he got back, I'd erased my social media, changed my number, and moved cities.'

'It's no wonder Ted couldn't find you.'

'But then you did. I guess I'd become a little more lax in my security attention by that point.'

'I'm so sorry I dragged you into all this. And Natasha.' I mean it, I realise as I swallow a lump in my throat. They're real people to me now, and Natasha especially deserves none of this mess. I shouldn't have used them like that.

She reaches out and takes my hands in hers, two sets of gloves pressed together. I can feel she's still shivering, just like me. 'Natasha needed to meet her half-sisters. Now that we've left Robin, she only had me. I couldn't bear her to be lonely.'

I close my eyes against the tears which threaten to spill down my cheeks. It's as if Alice has tapped into my thoughts over the past months: my desperation to avoid the isolation of my own childhood for my children, my feverish need to find Ted's other daughter so Tamara and Charley could have a relationship with her. Alice and I are more similar than I ever thought. Even down to our mistakes in choosing men.

I think maybe a part of me thought that if Tamara and Charley had another family member in Natasha, I would be free to leave Ted. That somehow the gain of a half-sister would cancel out the pain of separated parents.

I release Alice's hands and pick up my tea, taking another gulp. I feel the warmth slide down my chest and heat me from the inside. 'I think I had hoped when you came here... that you could help me leave Ted. I knew you'd done it once. Obviously, he could have been the perfect boyfriend to you... but I had a feeling...'

My voice trails away. Until the moment Alice rang the doorbell on Christmas Eve, I didn't know whether she'd come. Part of me really thought that she'd ignore the message, block Ted's account, and continue with her life. If she'd experienced a shred of Ted's bad side while they were together, surely she'd stay as far away as possible. But there was also no predicting how much I'd need her help, and in what ways. She saved my life.

She smirks, the smile not reaching her eyes. 'I knew that the moment I showed an interest in him, he'd be on me like a dog on a bone. And I hoped you'd see it. That you'd get the strength to leave.' She lowers her voice. 'People like Ted don't change. Not without extensive therapy, anyway. And Ted would never have accepted there was a problem. Introspection was not his strength.'

I flinch at her use of the past tense to describe him. He's really gone. A wave of relief washes over me once again. 'So yeah, it sounds like we had the same goal, in coming here. Half-siblings for our girls and freedom for ourselves.'

'Not exactly the same. But maybe our goals are aligning...' Alice's eyes twinkle in the firelight as she raises her mug in the air. 'A toast,' she says.

I tilt my head and raise my own mug, which shakes with the strain on my still-chilled muscles. 'To new beginnings?' I ask. 'And friendship?'

She shakes her head slowly, her eyes still twinkling. 'Ted is gone. But Robin is still alive. For now.' She clinks her mug against mine and a triumphant smile plays on her lips. 'To one down, and one to go. And next time, it's your turn.'

A LETTER FROM ROSIE WALKER

Dear reader,

I want to say a huge thank you for choosing to read *My Husband's Ex*. If you enjoyed it, and want to keep up to date with all my latest releases, just sign up at the following link. Your email address will never be shared and you can unsubscribe at any time.

www.bookouture.com/rosie-walker

This book had a very convoluted journey to get where it is today, beginning as a short story I wrote in 2011. A man bumps into his ex-girlfriend homeless in the street, and the story ends with him trying to choose between his wife and the one who got away.

When my dad read the story, he said, 'This felt more like the start of a novel than a short story.' His comment really stuck with me but it wasn't until years later – when my husband suggested exploring the wife's point of view – that suddenly I knew how this could be a thriller!

It's always so interesting how novels are formed, and *My Husband's Ex* has been on quite a journey to get where we are today, with massive thanks to Dad, Kevin, and loads of other people too, especially my agent and editor.

I love hearing readers' reactions to my stories. Is Red Hart Lodge the ideal holiday getaway for you, or does the remoteness give you the shivers? Did you feel sympathy for Sadie when Alice turned up, or should she have been more welcoming? Have you ever had an uninvited guest who outstayed their welcome? Did you see the twists coming, or were you surprised?

I hope you loved *My Husband's Ex*; if you did, I would be very grateful if you could write a review. I'd love to hear what you think, and your reviews make such a difference in helping new readers discover my books for the first time.

I love hearing from my readers – you can get in touch on my Facebook page, through X, Instagram or my website.

Thanks,

Rosie Walker

www.rosiejanewalker.com

 facebook.com/rosiewalkerauthor
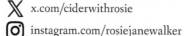 x.com/ciderwithrosie
instagram.com/rosiejanewalker

ACKNOWLEDGEMENTS

First thanks are to my dad, Alan, who over a decade ago read one of my short stories and told me he thought it should be a novel. *My Husband's Ex* is now completely unrecognisable from that original short story, but Dad's comment really stuck with me over the years and so this book wouldn't exist without him.

My Husband's Ex also owes its existence to my husband, Kevin, who gave me the vital puzzle piece that I needed to get started with this book: a new point of view. The secrets, lies and subterfuge of a thriller were much easier to plot as soon as I stepped away from Ted and into Sadie's head. As always, Kevin was a huge help throughout the writing process, too: talking through the plot during the planning stages, listening to me read it aloud when I was writing the first draft, and moral support when it felt like this book was never going to work.

While I was devising the initial plot, my literary agent, Charlotte Robertson, gave me the next vital step when she suggested really jazzing up the novel's setting. Instead of a normal house on a suburban Edinburgh street, why not take this family into the middle of nowhere, in a huge remote mansion? How much creepier would it be when Alice and Natasha turn up on the doorstep, if Sadie can't find a way to get them to leave? And Charlotte was so right: I love writing about big creepy houses, and the Highlands setting feels almost like a character in itself. I'm also so grateful to Charlotte for all of her support throughout my writing career so far: she really understands what makes me tick, and is always available with support to keep me going through both the tough times and the good ones.

I'm immensely grateful to my editor, Maisie Lawrence, who spent hours on Zoom with me to help unpick the plot and build it back together into something much more gripping, engaging and thrilling than what came before. That was a massive learning curve for me, and one which I know will make me a much better writer in the long run. I hope that *The Baby Monitor* and *My Husband's Ex* are just the start of my partnership with Maisie and Bookouture.

Thank you also to the rest of the team at Bookouture for their tireless work on *My Husband's Ex* and *The Baby Monitor*: Helen Jenner, Jessie Botterill, Jenny Geras, Ria Clare, Hannah Snetsinger, Mandy Kullar, Jen Shannon, Jane Eastgate, Liz Hatherell, Alex Crow, Ciara Rosney, Melanie Price, Occy Carr, Jess Readett, Kim Nash, Noelle Holten, Sarah Hardy, Marina Valles, Stephanie Straub, Mark Alder, Mohamed Bussuri, Lauren Morrissette, Hannah Richmond, Imogen Allport, Alba Proko, Sinead O'Connor, Melissa Tran, Peta Nightingale, Richard King, Saidah Graham. Thanks also to the excellent audiobook narrator Helen McAlpine, and the amazing book cover designer Lisa Horton.

This is my fourth published book, and not one of them would exist without my best friend, writing partner and first reader, Suzy Pope. She read and gave feedback on an embarrassingly early draft of *My Husband's Ex*, and did the same with a much tidier second draft too. She's always available for a plot chat, and her 'mad' ideas are always dark, often hilarious, and frequently genius. Writing is so much more fun with her around.

Big thanks to my sister Emily Walker for helping me pick character names, which was so much fun.

I owe so many thanks to fellow writers and readers for their support and insight, including Suzy Aspley, Katy Brent, Bethany Clift, Jacky Collins, Catherine Cooper, Madeline Dyer, Philippa East, Jen Faulkner, Dawn Geddes, Kelly Lacey, Katy Lane-Ryan, Lauren Kay, Gillian McAllister, Caron McKinlay, Stuart Neville, Christie Newport, Robert Rutherford, Holly Seddon, Tracy Sierra, Nikki Smith, BP Walter, Vic Watson, Daisy White, Trevor Wood, and Edith and Teacup of EZ Fiction.

The writing communities I belong to are invaluable, and no acknowledgements' section would be complete without a shout-out to the D20s, the Savvies, and those who share a drink with me at Harrogate, Bloody Scotland, Noir at the Bar, and many other writing events throughout the year. Thanks also to all my wonderful readers, whose support and recommendations are invaluable and so appreciated.

And finally, thank you to my fellow Bookouture authors who are so generous with their time and support. There are too many to name, but I am grateful to every one of you for sharing your experiences, offering advice and just generally being lovely people. I'm so lucky to be part of this community of amazing writers, and I hope I can offer just as much help and solidarity to you all in return.

PUBLISHING TEAM

Turning a manuscript into a book requires the efforts of many people. The publishing team at Bookouture would like to acknowledge everyone who contributed to this publication.

Audio
Alba Proko
Sinead O'Connor
Melissa Tran

Commercial
Lauren Morrissette
Hannah Richmond
Imogen Allport

Data and analysis
Mark Alder
Mohamed Bussuri

Editorial
Maisie Lawrence
Ria Clare

Copyeditor
Jane Eastgate

Proofreader
Liz Hatherell

Marketing
Alex Crow
Melanie Price
Occy Carr
Cíara Rosney

Operations and distribution
Marina Valles
Stephanie Straub

Production
Hannah Snetsinger
Mandy Kullar
Jen Shannon

Publicity
Kim Nash
Noelle Holten
Jess Readett
Sarah Hardy

Rights and contracts
Peta Nightingale
Richard King
Saidah Graham

Made in the USA
Columbia, SC
20 May 2024